The Sapphire Intrigue

A Crown Jewels Regency Mystery
Book 3

Lynn Morrison

Anne Radcliffe

Marketing Chair Press

This novel's story and characters are fictitious. Certain long-standing institutions, agencies, and public offices are mentioned, but the story are wholly imaginary. Some of the characters were inspired by actual historical figures, and abide by the generally known facts about these individuals and their relevant time periods. However, their actions and conversations are strictly fiction. All other characters and events are the product of our own imaginations.

Cover design by Melody Simmons

Published by

The Marketing Chair Press, Oxford, England

LynnMorrisonWriter.com

ISBN (paperback): 978-1-917361-00-2

Contents

1

Few men went without trepidation when summoned by the Breaker of Northumberland. After all, Gideon Percy had earned his nickname fairly. Roland, however, followed his grandfather's butler not with dread but with a curious sense of savage anticipation.

London might be far from Napoleon, but Mayfair was still its own kind of front. Unlike when Roland had first returned to England, this summons was to a battle for which he was happy to gird himself. The Breaker was wroth with him, and Roland knew this particular meeting with his grandfather would be a key fight in the war between them.

The Percy family's main London estate seemed the pinnacle of vanity, especially when it took several long minutes to make his way from the front doors to reach the right room. He tried to maintain a guise of patience, but in the last hallway, Roland outpaced his grandfather's elderly butler and pushed open the study doors.

"Roland," his grandfather growled, his eyes flicking to the butler in an unspoken demand that the servant get out. At once.

"Grandfather," Roland replied coolly, clasping his hands in front of himself as he stepped towards the duke.

The old man sat behind his massive wooden desk, positioned in the bright streams of sunlight coming through the windows. Gideon likely thought it would make him look intimidating and put Roland at a disadvantage, especially since the duke seemed to have instructed his servants to remove other seating. Roland was becoming rather familiar with these kinds of bon ton antics. He did not even drop the old man's gimlet stare to acknowledge the message that he wasn't welcome to sit.

He did not care. Passing strange how a few short months could remake one's entire world twice over, especially when one kept crossing paths with Queen Charlotte.

The duke scowled at Roland's serenity and launched his offensive. "I dragged myself all the way from the north for a wedding. Why am I somehow not surprised to find that it has been so precipitously called off before I even arrived?"

Pushing his dark hair back with studied nonchalance, Roland replied, "Lady Charity had her reasons."

"Oh, aye, I should imagine she did. For Queen Charlotte herself informed me she arranged a marriage for her own diamond to a man in his bedamned eighties!" the duke snarled, shoving the papers off the corner of his desk in his rage as he struggled to his feet.

Roland caught himself before he could wince. The last time he saw Charity, scarcely a week ago, she told him her purpose in visiting the queen: to break off their engagement. He had not wanted to speak of it, but there had been quiet speculation in his household that she likely sought the queen's help in securing another marriage in haste. He never imagined that it would be to a gentleman older than his own grandfather.

The duke's eyes narrowed as he considered his grandson, and Roland realised the duke took his silence for the ignorance it was. "Your only task," the man drawled, on firmer footing now that he held an advantage over Roland, "was to secure a suitable prospect capable of breeding the next heir by the time you left London. For the most eligible bachelor of the season, it should have been a simple matter. But not only did the prize cow determine you were unworthy, she decided she was better off marrying a man who would most probably die in her wedding sheets. And if that somehow was not an embarrassment enough—"

The duke stopped, his chest heaving in ire. Roland cocked his head, waiting to see if the man was about to suffer an apoplexy. He betrayed no further sign of the emotions running deep inside of him.

"If that was not embarrassing enough," Gideon repeated, gaining control of himself, "you have somehow failed to arrange another marriage. Any idiot should have been able to do so by waving his title in the air. I should know—that is how your father baited your mother to his hook."

The lid on Roland's temper—quick to rise at the best of times— threatened to crack open. Counting numbers in his head, he struggled for control, but he let the displeasure glitter in his eyes as they held Gideon's.

They had barely seen one another in the years since Roland had applied to his grandfather for assistance with purchasing a military commission. It seemed his grandfather still thought of him as the nigh-desperate seventeen-year-old lad who had begged him for help. How very wrong Gideon Percy was.

That commission secured Roland's relative freedom from his father Thaddius, and provided a much needed opportunity to mature away from the influence of his family. It also allowed Roland to provide for Thorne, the only man he trusted to guard his back. He had leveraged both his grandfather's ego and connections to secure a speedy enlistment and assignment of Thorne as his batman.

Thoughts of Thorne, the good-natured man who now served as his valet, quenched Roland's anger as swiftly as glowing iron plunged into a smithy's bucket. Thorne had ever the way of gentling 'Sir Barbarian.' And... he suspected one other person would soon have the trick of it as well.

Lady Grace. Whom he missed like the sun on a winter's day.

Grace, whose mama was determined to keep her cloistered until they departed for Brighton. He had spent—continued to spend—far too much time lingering near her house, hoping to glimpse her in the window. At least her maid Elsie consented to trade their hasty letters since they talked a week ago. If she hadn't, he would likely have gone mad with distraction.

"I am afraid you are misinformed, Grandfather," he murmured, regaining his aplomb. "There is a young lady in my life, and I expect her to agree to my suit when I visit her in Brighton in a few more days."

Duke Gideon Percy, preparing another verbal salvo, stopped short with a swift intake of breath and narrowed lids. "Is that so?"

Roland nodded. "So you see, you did not stir your old bones without purpose, Grandfather. You merely stopped here to do some brief business on your way to the seaside resort, where I am certain you will be happy to help with the arrangements."

His presumption caused the Breaker's brows to draw low, like clouds gathering before a storm, but he did not refuse out of hand. When he grunted and waved a rude dismissal of his grandson from the study, Roland knew the duke would follow him south—if only to assuage his curiosity about the woman he planned to marry.

It seemed they had established an armistice of sorts—at least, for now. But the war was not yet over.

2

Lady Grace Tilbury sat at her dressing table, taking great care to hold perfectly still while Elsie, her lady's maid, put the finishing touches on her coiffure. Elsie smoothed a wayward lock into place with a bit of pomade and then stepped back to give Lady Tilbury a look at her daughter.

The lace collar of the hastily altered gown tickled Grace's neck fiercely, but she resisted the urge to tug or scratch. Her mama was already in a mood, and Grace dared not do anything that might further raise her ire. Unfortunately, Grace's unruly chestnut locks seemed to have their own mind, for the wayward strands picked that moment to spring free.

"We have been in Brighton only a few short days and look at you! Your nose has twice as many freckles as before and those long walks in the sea air are causing your hair to curl in a most unfashionable manner." Lady Tilbury swayed on her feet in distress. She was also utterly scandalised by the unsightly, still-red scar Sir David had left upon the side of Grace's throat. She had paid the modiste a hefty sum to redo the neckline of Grace's summer wardrobe, and another sack of coins to remain quiet about the reason why.

Elsie proved her value by coming to the rescue with a jewelled clip. She pinned the loose strand back into place and set a matching clip on the other side. Bright blue sapphires winked in the flickering candlelight of Grace's bedchamber.

Grace reached out to capture her mother's hands in hers and gave them a squeeze. "You see, Mama, everything is under control. You are working yourself into a frenzy over nothing."

Lady Tilbury turned her head away and shut her eyes for a brief moment before again facing her daughter. "This is far from nothing, as you call it, Grace. And your carefree attitude is what has me most worried. Lord Percy is the heir to a dukedom. He was engaged to your dearest friend until a few weeks ago. Now, he is once again unentangled and seemingly enamoured with you. But why? Why, I ask?"

Her mother's worries were not exactly unreasonable, but Grace was unconcerned. For all the ups and downs of her season thus far, Roland's behaviour had been her one constant, even when they had been at odds with one another early on. Over and over again, he had shown his true self to her. He was a creature of duty who put other people's needs and wants before his own—both hers and Charity's. That was how he had ended up engaged to her friend.

But she could not tell her mama of this. So, she summed the situation into its simplest form.

"Because... he chose me."

Grace's words hung in the air until her mama pulled free and drew herself up.

"So you say. And so he has said to your father. I should be praising the heavens over such a high-placed match, but dear daughter of mine, I am nervous for you. Surely you understand the source of my concern. What is to prevent Lord Percy from waking up tomorrow and 'choosing' another debutante? One unmarked, unopinionated, compliant..."

"One like Lady Charity?" Grace hazarded. "Mama, you must trust me. Lord Percy and I had occasion to speak to one another this season, and we found much common ground. I have every faith he will stand by my side, no matter what troubles we face. Come, let us go now. Lord Percy will arrive at any moment, and we cannot leave him waiting."

Lady Tilbury did not let Grace go just yet. She did, however, step back to allow Grace to rise from her stool. Now eye to eye, she searched her daughter's face for any hint of doubt. Finding none, she released the breath she had been holding. "I know not what to make of this season, for it has had more rises and falls than the rolling countryside of our home. Charity shone from the start, and yet she has ended up in a rushed marriage to someone in Scotland. You spent most balls watching from the side, and are now the one betrothed to the man to whom she was engaged. I suppose you are right, and I, too, must have faith you have kept your head. That Lord Percy is as dedicated as you say. You have been many things, but lovesick is not one of them."

Grace was not sure about that last remark, for she had suffered much while watching Roland stand at Charity's side. It was a small comfort that he had scarcely done any better.

A polite rap on Grace's bedroom door put an end to the conversation. "Lord Percy awaits your pleasure on the front steps, my ladies," the Tilbury butler said with a small bow to them.

Grace surged forward with an eagerness that Lady Tilbury would no doubt call indecorous—if she hadn't moved with the same haste—and struggled to maintain a calm pace as she made her way down to the front door, nearly forgetting her light wrap in the process.

The man waiting outside was impeccably dressed and groomed, standing in a dark tailcoat and a shirt with a high, starched collar. Grace barely even had a chance to notice his clothes before her gaze was caught by his piercing, dark eyes. And she fell headlong into his smile.

"Roland," she said as calmly as she could manage, which was difficult when she was certain she was beaming back at him like a fool. "It is good to see you again."

Roland laughed shortly, a low sound that set the butterflies' wings in motion in her belly. "And you, Grace."

"Where is your carriage?" Lady Tilbury queried, looking about.

"Ah, well, Lady Tilbury," Roland said, turning to her mother and releasing her from the spell of his gaze. "I hoped you would not mind walking. I was rather selfish and left it at the house, desperate to come up with a ploy that would extend the too-short time I have this evening with your daughter. Fate conspired to grant my request for this passing fair weather."

Lady Tilbury, of course, cooed at these genteel words and beckoned for her husband to join them. Amused, Roland offered Grace his arm, a challenge sparking in his eyes. Before she could think too hard about it, she slipped her hand into the crook of his elbow, her hand trembling slightly as they began the short walk to the Royal Pavilion.

Despite her many assurances to her mother about her relationship with Roland, Grace did not have the same confidence about facing society. She had spent the remaining two weeks of the season confined to her bedchamber while the cut on her throat healed. To emerge now, in Brighton, on Roland's arm... she was sure to attract notice.

Roland looked down at her hand tucked in his right arm. "With everything that you and I have been through in these last few months, only now you're nervous?" he teased her softly.

Grace could not help but scowl at him, and just the very act of doing so settled her. "It is a very different thing to pretend to be courted by the most eligible man of the season than to actually do so."

"How odd," he murmured, bringing his left hand up to rest atop hers on his arm. With gentle pressure, he spaced her fingers apart, letting his own weave between hers. "I was thinking about how much it felt just the same. My enjoyment of it certainly was."

She could think of no immediate reply to that that wouldn't result in her Mama having a fit, so together they strolled in comfortable silence for a time, her mother and father trailing discreetly. There were a thousand things they should be asking one another. A hundred plans they should be making for the future. But these felt like mere details, and they had all the time in the world..

All too quickly, their steps brought them to the elegant neo-classical building that played summer home to the Prince Regent. The queen, of course, was not in attendance. She often spent her summers at the tranquil Windsor Castle. The seaside resort of Brighton and its pavilion were her son's holiday spot, and it was he who had issued the invitation to tonight's event, a musicale featuring a soprano from Italy.

Grace's visits to Buckingham House and St James's Palace in no way prepared her for the opulent decoration of the Marine Pavilion. She had read of King George's affection for the Far East, but did not truly understand what that meant until she glimpsed the hand-painted Chinese wallpaper lining the corridor. Heavy furniture finished in black lacquer contrasted with the porcelain vases painted with delicate traceries of floral blossoms. If not for Roland at her side, she might imagine herself on an adventure to a foreign land.

Perhaps the idea was not so far off. For whom might have imagined that Lady Grace Tilbury, third child of an earl, would find herself invited to an intimate evening with the prince regent?

"Are you ready?" Roland whispered. Grace nodded, for she had no other choice. The footman was already announcing their arrival. He reeled off Roland's name and title first, then her parents', and lastly hers.

Though she was the lowest of rank, she found herself the centre of all attention.

Roland's firm hold on her arm kept her moving forward, while her mind stuttered to catch up. Though the group was not large, she found not a single familiar face. She nearly sighed in relief when she spotted Prinny standing with his crowd of admirers. He cast a pleased nod in their direction and then returned to his conversation. The blister of curious gazes set her face aflame. She held her head high despite the whispers rippling around the room. Her mother had issued a myriad of instructions regarding how to behave during her first public outing on Roland's arm. Keep her gaze low, and a pleasant smile pasted on her face.

It took Grace all of a minute to realise that would not do. Not for her. And so she squared her shoulders, pulled free of Roland's arm and stood tall at his side. In a voice pitched to be heard by those nearest, she said, "Come, Lord Percy, we must pay our respects to our host. It was so thoughtful of him to extend a personal invitation."

Roland hesitated, but then he smiled, finally understanding what she was about. "I am your servant, Lady Grace. Lead on."

They barely had time to make their curtsies and bows to His Royal Highness before the musicians played the first strains of music. Roland accompanied Grace to one of the wooden chairs set aside for the women to use, and left her in the company of her mother.

Though she believed herself impervious to the judgments of

strangers, she could not help but note that several women in attendance made a point to avoid passing near Grace and Lady Tilbury. One odious woman even went so far as to scowl at Grace.

"That is Lady Waddington," Grace's mama supplied in a low whisper. "Ignore her. She debuted with Lady Fitzroy. It appears she has picked up the torch Lady Fitzroy left behind." And so it went, with her mother providing tidbits of information about each person in the room. With barely more than two dozen in total, it did not take long.

Grace finally did see someone she knew: Sir Julian Montgomery, who stood with Roland and another military man. Now that she knew better, she saw how Sir Julian's florid face gave evidence of his tendency to overindulge. She might have approached, but she caught sight of the other military man casting an angry glare his way.

If there was an argument afoot, best not, then. Grace allowed her gaze to move on. She focused instead on a young man dressed in an ostentatious waistcoat standing near Lady Waddington.

"That man is a rake," Lady Tilbury warned when she caught the direction of Grace's gaze. "I shall not even tell you his name, lest you speak it aloud. Simply standing near him would be enough to ruin a woman's reputation."

Grace made a note to ask Roland who he was later. As the soprano's voice filled the air with the soaring notes of one famous aria after another, Grace discretely continued studying the other guests. By the concert end, she had categorised all into either 'neutral' or 'foe.' The 'friend' category was still barren.

Before she could despair, a couple approached Grace and her mama with a single-minded determination. She judged the pair to be of a similar age to her own parents, so she took her cues from her mother's response to their arrival.

Lady Tilbury's smile was, thankfully, genuine. "Lord and Lady Barbour, I did not know you were coming."

"We were among the last to arrive," the lady explained. "We got caught up in a conversation with the most incredible painter this afternoon and time simply slipped away. We might have sent our apologies had we not received a note from Lord Percy telling us of his plans to attend."

"Oh?" Grace asked.

Lady Tilbury's expression further brightened at this news. "Please, allow me to introduce my daughter. Lord and Lady Barbour, this is Lady Grace."

Lord Barbour gave Grace the strangest smile, almost as though he had discovered a rare bloom hidden among a field of chaff. Lady Barbour offered Grace her hands and then leaned in to kiss her on either cheek.

"We have been most eager to gain a proper introduction," Lady Barbour said. "Lord Percy spoke most highly of you in his letter to us."

"And why should I not?" the man himself asked, coming up from behind. "Much like yourselves, she is not afraid to form her own opinions."

Grace raised her eyebrows at Roland's description of her, accurate though it was.

"Hopefully you have a more cultured opinion of poetry and literature than your husband-to-be," Lord Barbour gave her a gentle wink to show he was teasing. "We must have you over for dinner to discuss the arts sometime."

"Oh dear," laughed Grace as she looked at Roland, trying to imagine him discussing anything of the sort. "That will be an interesting evening."

"When I gate-crashed your wife's salon, I do believe you promised me a stimulating conversation on military strategy, Barbour," Roland said with an arched eyebrow.

"If not the arts, I have another proposition," Barbour stage-whispered to her. "We have known Percy since he was a small, savage child, barely out of leading strings. Those antics would be interesting to discuss too."

Roland mock scowled at them, but the Barbours grinned. Once they moved on their way, their warm welcome remained the bright spot of Grace's evening. Though the rest of society was slow to embrace her courtship with Roland, she was not entirely without allies, after all.

Lady Tilbury said as much when she came to wish Grace good night. Her mother perched on the side of Grace's bed, as she had done when Grace was a child. "You did well tonight, my dear. And I am happy to find my fears regarding Lord Percy to have been misguided. He made his intentions clear to all tonight, in a way he never did with Charity. I have no clue how you have accomplished it, but it seems you have found the rarest jewel of them all."

"A good man?" Grace asked with a devilish smile.

"A love match," her mama replied. "Do not worry about those who snubbed you tonight. They will come around in time. With any luck, they will find something else to discuss before we are forced to be in close company with them again." With that, Lady Tilbury took her leave, with absolutely no idea just how wrong and how right her statement would prove to be.

3

The next day dawned fair again, so Roland met Grace at the Royal Pavilion's stables for an early ride. What they did not expect to find, however, was a tremendous sense of tightly wound agitation among the stable staff.

"Is something amiss?" Roland queried the young man fumbling with the bridle of Grace's mount. The horse had picked up on the tension, flattening his ears, and Roland urged Grace to stand back with a cautious hand, lest the beast act on the emotions in the air by biting or lashing out. Fortunately, she didn't argue and seemed no more interested in approaching the nervous gelding than the horse was interested in being ridden.

"Something is wrong at the pavilion," the lad confessed. "I know not what, exactly. There has been a great deal of shouting and activity. A footman said that someone has died."

Roland looked at Grace, who appeared just as troubled by this information as he did. "A death?" she queried. "Did a servant pass from an ailment?"

"I—I do not think so, my lady," the stableman said after the briefest of hesitations, fretting.

The horse's eyes began rolling as it tried to pull loose, but the stableman held fast. Roland gently took the reins, soothing the animal with soft murmurs and a steady hand on its neck.

"You must get a hold of yourself, lad," Roland spoke in a low voice, hooking the reins upon a post. "Calm your emotions or find another stable hand to take over. Lady Grace, I think we should find other plans for our day."

"That does seem wisest," she conceded with a small smile. "I can take a walk in my riding habit instead."

This did not seem to discomfit her, so Roland offered her an arm and together they left the stable, walking towards the front of the pavilion. Before they got far, however, a footman rushed out to intercept them. "Lord Percy? Lady Grace? The Prince Regent heard you were nearby and sent me to fetch you."

He stopped, his mind whirling as he went through the possibilities of why they would be summoned. None of his conclusions were reassuring.

Grace clearly made some deductions of her own. "If we are being summoned," she stated to Roland, "then it would seem that the death in the pavilion was not due to natural causes."

The footman looked from Roland to Grace. "Will you please come at once?" he urged.

"Of course... We can hardly refuse," Roland answered for both of them, checking Grace's face to gauge how she took the change in plans. The last time they had done a favour for the royals, Grace had ended up with new necklines on her dresses. There was something calculating about the set of her eyes, but it wasn't fearful—or even cautious.

He sighed inwardly. The footman escorted the pair of them into the building, through the grand main room, and from there, into the lavishly decorated saloon. An impressive chandelier drew the eye upwards, illuminating the painted ceiling. But for once, the lavish decor failed to compete with the people occupying the space.

One could say that the saloon rather resembled opponents before a boxing match, for the four noble personages present had split into pairs, each eyeing the other warily. Three footmen and two guards lined the walls, anxious and stern by degrees. Glancing about, Roland casually noted the guardsmen were poised on either side of the entryway, as if to prevent them from leaving.

Grace studied the nobles in turn. She recognised the lady and the gentleman her mother refused to name. "The woman is Lady Waddington. My mama said she was a contemporary of Lady Fitzroy." As if to prove Grace's point, the woman wrinkled her nose at them and turned away.

Roland made a comprehensive grimace of understanding and pointed with his chin to the other group, where the pair of gentlemen waited, casting hostile looks at the guards. They were an unlikely pair, one white-haired and wrinkled, the other only a few years older than Roland. No doubt, it was only present circumstances that pushed them into such proximity. "Of all of them, I know only the older fellow, Baron Langley, who was introduced yesterday evening as a well-known scholar. We should begin with him."

With Grace at his side, Roland approached the men where they stood near a window. "Good morning, Baron. May I introduce Lady Grace Tilbury?"

"A morning it is, but I fear it is of bad omens instead of good ones. I mean no disrespect, but you should consider escorting your young Lady Grace somewhere else today."

"Would that I were able to," Roland replied, feigning ignorance. "The Prince Regent has requested our presence, though I am not certain as to why. It is obvious things are amiss. Might you be able to shed any light on the matter?"

"A guest was found murdered earlier, or so I am told." The Baron paused to look at his compatriot. "It was Lord Blackwood here who told me that they have determined it to be unnatural. Lord Blackwood, this is Lord Percy."

"I beg your pardon, but do you mean to say that someone has been murdered?" Grace asked, raising a hand to her mouth. "Here? In the royal abode?"

"So I have been told by a footman," Lord Blackwood replied. He leaned against the wall and crossed a foot over the other. "The guards barely allowed anyone time to dress before herding the lot of us in here. I am not sure whether they fear we shall fall victim next, or if we are being viewed as potential suspects."

Roland offered him a solemn nod. "Hopefully, it is simply an abundance of caution. But surely you are not the only guests staying here. Where are the others?"

"We have not yet seen them," Blackwood answered. He shrugged his shoulders. "At least one is murdered. The others have either made a run for it out of guilt, or are standing over the corpse. Neither of those options is particularly appealing."

Grace cast a look over her shoulder at Roland, conveying an unspoken message. They needed to split up.

"Gentleman, may I leave Lady Grace here in your company while I determine why Prinny asked for us? I do not want to be careless with her safety." After the two men reassured him on that score, Roland gave her arm a quick squeeze of reassurance and then left her there, making his way to the guardsmen standing at the entryway.

Grace faced the noblemen and gave them her undivided attention. Baron Langley had shifted his scrutiny to the gardens outside. The early sunlight softened his white hair and wrinkled skin, though proved no match for his furrowed brow. Was he wondering even now which of the visitors had been felled? She waited for him to offer some opinion, but Lord Blackwood spoke up first.

"This is not the first time you have been caught up in court intrigue, is it?" he inquired of Grace. "You assisted Lord Percy in his search for the queen's diamond. Am I correct?"

"You are. Lady Charity is a dear friend," Grace replied, almost by rote.

"A strange claim when here you stand, escorted by her former beau. And where is she now?" Lord Blackwood scratched at the narrow patch of hair on his chin. "Married to a doddering fool in Scotland. Yes, intriguing is indeed the correct word to describe your activities this season. Now Prinny has called you and Lord Percy to pit your wits against a new mystery. Tell me, Lady Grace, why does our valiant regent think you more capable than the constable?"

"I would not dare to speak on behalf of His Royal Highness," Grace declared. "And I certainly would not jump to conclusions. Perhaps he merely wishes to ask about something we saw yesterday evening."

"Perhaps," he granted, though his tone dripped with doubt. "Look around here, my lady, and tell me what you think."

Grace accepted the invitation, shifting until she saw Lady Waddington, who now sat alone on a settee in the centre of the room. The other man, the rake, was speaking softly with a guard.

The lady appeared placid at first glance, but closer inspection revealed her hands to be so tightly clasped that her arms nearly trembled. Worry lines bracketed her flattened lips. What did she have to fear? As if sensing Grace's gaze, she raised her eyes and glared at Grace.

"I would not take it as an affront," Lord Blackwood whispered, having moved closer while Grace was distracted.

"She abhors any woman who dares to marry above her station. If the guilty party is here, my money is on Lord Ravenscroft."

Grace followed the direction of his gaze until it landed on the notorious rake. "Surely you do not believe Prinny would extend his hospitality to a murderer."

"The odds would not be impossible. Ravenscroft trades in secrets," Blackwood explained. "Add in an English father and French mother, and you get someone who is welcome everywhere and beholden to no man. I have long suspected that we hear only the rumours he intends to reach our ear."

Grace peered at the rake's muscular form, showcased in tight breeches and a narrow coat. Even the guard standing at the door was not immune to his charms. Had another not arrived at that very moment, Grace wondered if Lord Ravenscroft would have talked his way out of their elegant holding place.

The newly arrived guard marched directly to Grace. "His Royal Highness requests you join him. If you shall follow me, I will escort you to where he is waiting."

Grace did not need to turn her gaze to know all eyes were on her as she left. Not a one was friendly.

Roland set aside any fears of leaving Grace behind. She would learn what she could, and this would spare her the sight of another corpse. The murder, it seemed, had happened in a guest's room on the first floor. The guard dispatched a servant to guide Roland to the correct spot, although Roland reckoned that he would have been able to find it easily enough. It was the only bedroom with another guard stationed beside it, and the sound of arguing from within carried into the hallway.

The stationed guard inclined his head respectfully to him, allowing him to pass, and Roland entered, interrupting the fight.

With the disorder in the guest room, all he could observe from the doorway were the legs of the victim. Whoever he had been, he was laid out in his own bed, still in his nightclothes, but Roland could make no identification of the body since two men and a guard were in the way. All turned to greet Roland with severe looks.

"Who is this? You should not be in here," a grey-haired gentleman told him, scowling.

"At ease, Danforth." The person beside Danforth was somewhat younger—likely in his mid forties—but he was dressed in his dark blue military uniform. "I am sure he is here with a purpose."

"Major General Sinclair," Roland greeted him respectfully. Roland had met with him, at least, at the musical event the evening before.

"Percy," the general replied. "I wish it were possible to say it is pleasant to cross paths again, but... given the circumstances, I cannot. Is there some way that Lord Danforth and I can assist you?"

"Given the Prince Regent's summons, I believe I am intended to assist you," Roland said candidly. "Those downstairs mentioned there had been a murder. I happened to be on the premises today, and have only just arrived."

Sinclair nodded with cool acknowledgement, but Danforth's brows drew down farther. "As you plainly see," Danforth muttered, stepping away from the bedside.

As Danforth moved, Roland realised with a shock that he knew this particular dead man. "Sir Julian Montgomery?" he breathed, looking down at the still body.

"You knew him?" The general asked. Roland bobbed his head in confirmation.

"He was... briefly a person of interest in an incident that happened at St James this summer."

Danforth, despite the fact that Roland had never met the gentleman, clearly knew who he was. "Lord Percy helped apprehend Sir David," he informed Sinclair.

"Yes," Roland confirmed shortly with a pang of guilt and sorrow. That particular day, without question, was the worst of his life—and for more reasons than because Sir David had injured Grace. The betrayal of his old commander still hurt, and when Sir David took his own life in the days following, he could not mourn that. He stared down at Sir Julian's lifeless features.

The military man's eyebrows lifted in surprise. "That would do much to explain why Prinny sent for you, then," Sinclair murmured kindly, as if sensitive to Roland's torn feelings about Sir David. "We have taken charge of things here, for Danforth has some experience in land dispute inquiries." Given Sir Julian's military career, Sinclair's own involvement needed little explanation. "Your assistance is welcome. Observe the bruising that has formed at Sir Julian's mouth. We have agreed that smothering is the cause of his death," the general continued.

"I would agree with your assessment," Roland murmured thoughtfully. "But a person being smothered should have woken up to fight his assailant. Sir Julian looks as though he did not stir."

"Yes, most likely a draught rendered him unconscious. Poison, perhaps, or laudanum."

Roland agreed. "Dosed, he would be quiet and easy to kill by nearly anyone. Do you have suspicions as to the identity of his murderer?"

Danforth had grown less irritated as Roland examined Sir Julian's body, and he tilted his chin in acquiescence. "I worry about whether we have too many cooks in the kitchen as it is, but it is possible your timing is fortuitous. On the suspect list, Sinclair and I are in disagreement. The pavilion, I'm sure you have noticed, is not so grand an edifice. Though Prinny dreams of expanding it, for now, it is unable to house legions of guests. Surely the villain entered the building from the grounds to do the foul deed."

Sinclair tucked his hands behind his back. "The logistics of committing the act within the pavilion would be difficult to navigate. For someone coming in from outside of the building... he or she would not only have to navigate those same challenges, they would also have to overcome the added issue of gaining entry and avoiding all the guards stationed there."

Danforth appeared as if he sucked upon a lemon. "More difficult, but surely not impossible. After all, Sir Julian is dead."

"Not impossible, no," Sinclair acknowledged calmly. "But certainly less likely."

"Do not take offence, Sinclair, but I do hope you're wrong," Danforth grumbled, pushing a hand through his trimmed hair restlessly. "Because if you are not, that means that you wish to hold everyone in the same house as a murderer. And if I am discomfited by that... well, I only imagine how Lady Waddington and the others shall feel."

"You want to keep Prinny's guests here, still?" Roland questioned the general. "Even if you are that uncertain as to who might have killed Sir Julian?"

"I am afraid we must implement those precautions, Lord Percy," General Sinclair said with a heavy sigh. "Because Sir Julian's death was not the most serious crime that occurred last night."

Before he could expound, a sound in the hall pulled all their attention to the bedroom's entryway. "The Prince Regent would like to speak with you—all of you—in the library downstairs immediately," the guard announced as he turned to them.

Straightening his waistcoat, Danforth left, answering Prinny's summons. As Sinclair moved to follow, Roland touched his arm to gain his attention. "You were saying that some other incident happened, General?"

Sinclair looked positively grim. "Given your years of military service, I trust this means more to you, I suppose, than it would to a civilian such as Lord Danforth. Sir Julian possessed a copy of a sixth coalition cipher book—and when I looked for it, I could not locate it anywhere."

4

R oland and Grace arrived in the library to find the head of the royal guard standing at attention. The Prince Regent had settled himself in one of the plush armchairs near the glass, his bearing very much that of a king upon a somewhat unconventional throne.

Danforth and Sinclair had arrived before them, for he had stopped to collect Grace from the saloon. Roland strode forward to join the group of men. Lord Danforth and General Sinclair nodded at him, but their expressions shifted when they caught sight of Grace lingering behind.

Roland turned back to check on her. The tall sash windows in the pavilion's library flooded the gracious room with natural light, brightening the mahogany of the bookshelves to a warmer shade and gleaming off the polished wooden floors. By contrast, Grace looked a shade pale, but resolute. Roland extended a hand, reminding her that she would not face the group alone. His offer was enough to urge her forward.

"Lord Percy," Prinny said, acknowledging his bow. "I am pleased that you and Lady Grace could join us."

Sinclair and Danforth now tilted their heads in Grace's

direction, finally deigning to notice her, but both gentlemen looked uncomfortable with her presence.

"Your Highness," Grace said clearly. "We are happy to serve."

Sinclair cleared his throat, preparing to object. "Your Highness, the subjects to be discussed might prove to be... too much for a delicate constitution. Perhaps it would be best if we reserved such matters for a more private setting, away from sensitive ears."

Prinny barked a laugh, startling the general. "I am certain she appreciates your concern, General Sinclair, but I believe Lady Grace has more fortitude than you would give her credit for. She was no shrinking violet when enlisted by my mother for her plotting in the early part of the season. Besides, she has likely already heard the worst of it by standing in the saloon. She has not fainted, has she?"

The Prince Regent turned his head in her direction. "Allow me to make introductions so that everyone's skills are clear. Lady Grace, this is Major General Sinclair, whose strategic acumen has been invaluable in the war with Napoleon, and Lord John Danforth, an adviser to the crown who has the most useful and prodigious experience with land law."

Offering both men a brief curtsey, Grace inclined her head. "It is a pleasure to make your acquaintances. You are correct, Your Highness, I am not faint, but I learned of the death before the saloon, if I am being honest. Even the men in the stables knew someone had been killed."

"Lady Grace also knew Sir Julian Montgomery," Roland said, squeezing her arm gently to flag the import of his statement.

Grace blinked slowly at that. "Sir Julian was the man who was murdered last night?"

Danforth gave her a frown that bordered on blatant

disrespect. "Yes, my lady. Did you want to examine the body as well?"

Prinny gave Danforth a decidedly jaundiced look, and the lord's posture straightened slightly in apology. "The crown appreciates the lady's wits, and willingness to persevere in unconventional situations. Since she has done my mother a great service, it would serve you well to remember your manners, Danforth. Forget your injured sense of propriety and explain what you found so that Lady Grace is properly informed."

"As you will, Your Highness. Those of us who viewed the body—" Danforth paused to emphasise the fact that Grace had not been one of those, "have concurred that Sir Julian's demise was a carefully planned act. His arms and fingers showed no signs of trauma that would indicate restraint or combat, so we believe he was most certainly dosed or poisoned in advance of the murder to render him unable to fight back. It would also keep the deed silent. His murderer would have only had to obstruct his mouth and nose. A pillow would have done the trick."

Sinclair took up the thread of it, "Sir Julian's room was searched and his body was quite cool when we found him this morning, meaning that the act had taken place many hours before. Given the events of last night, it was probably shortly after he went to bed, which was—according to the footman stationed at the bottom of the stairs—just after one in the morning. Any time between half-past one and five in the morning would have been an opportune time for the murderer to strike."

Prinny leaned forward. "If he was poisoned, then there may be a vial to be found that held the substance, which might expose the villain."

"Yes, Your Highness," Danforth agreed.

"I would recommend that you order a search of the guest rooms and grounds to find it—and any other clues, Your Highness," added the general. "But there is another item that we must scour the grounds for with all haste. As I informed Lord Percy just moments ago, the Sapphire cipher is missing."

The Prince Regent's jowls trembled with anger. "You suggest that Sir Julian was targeted for military secrets."

"Cipher?" Grace murmured, so low only Roland could hear her.

"The military encodes their sensitive communications so that an intercepted message cannot be read by the enemy," Roland told her. "A cipher book helps the officers to encode and decode these messages at either end of its route."

Grace's mouth made an O of understanding.

"Lord Percy is correct, Lady Grace," Sinclair said, having been standing to Roland's right, near enough to overhear his explanation. "It is something that we cannot risk having compromised, for an enemy with a cipher book would be able to interpret the communications."

"Which would be a tremendous advantage for them in war. I understand, I think," she replied. "But why is it called sapphire?"

"To put it as simply as I can without divulging military secrets, my lady, it is because there is more than one cipher in use. Names help distinguish them, their purpose, and their sender," he explained.

Prinny's face had grown black with anger. "You are suggesting this is more than a mere murder of Sir Julian. There is a traitor at work here."

"So it would seem, Your Highness," Danforth said, his face weary.

"Would it not be possible to just replace the books with a

new cipher?" Grace asked, and Roland squeezed her hand again to caution her.

Sinclair spread his hands, looking disturbed. "There are many countries that are part of the coalition, and their forces are ranged over a good portion of the continent. Until all the books could be replaced, communications using that cipher would either be impossible or vulnerable. In the end, that might be the only solution, but it would be a terrible one."

"I see," Grace said, her face growing more solemn. Roland wondered if she truly comprehended the size of such an undertaking it would be to replace a lost military codebook, but he reckoned that at least she had fathomed it would not be a simple matter.

"Your Highness," Sinclair continued. "I must strongly recommend that we put the guard to work conducting a thorough search of the entire Marine Pavilion and grounds at once. I am happy to put the members of my contingent to work for the cause and run the investigation."

Danforth nodded, crossing his arms. "That would cover the matter of searching for physical clues, Sinclair," he conceded, "and it is something that should be part of the course of the investigation. However, someone smart enough to conduct espionage underneath the crown's very nose would find it easy to hide such evidence. We must interrogate the staff, and I believe my experience stands me in good stead to assist there. It would be the next logical course of action, especially in determining whether the traitor broke into the Marine Pavilion to commit the act—or only escaped from it."

"I still believe that it is unlikely that someone from the outside committed the crime, Danforth." Sinclair shifted his weight onto the balls of his feet, thinking.

"I agree with Sinclair," Roland spoke up suddenly, interrupting Danforth. And just as well, because the man had opened his mouth to argue. "Reason dictates it would most probably be someone who was here. That is where we should seek our answers first, before casting a wider net. A servant may have been able to depart the grounds before the alarm was raised, and at that point, it would be easy to deduce the culprit if they have gone missing. And if it wasn't a servant..."

"Your Royal Highness, my lords, I beg your pardon, but I have some information that pertains directly to your discussion," the guardsman interjected. "Once Sir Julian's body was discovered, I secured the grounds at once and spoke with all the men standing guard last night. We had a full complement that evening, and I will stake my very post upon the surety that no one would have been able to enter the pavilion unnoticed."

"That is a considerable relief to know," Sinclair murmured. "It narrows the scope. What about people leaving?"

The guardsman shook his head. "The only people who had left the grounds were the housekeeper and a single footman. Both have been recalled for questioning, so everyone has been centralised. We have the murderer here."

"Well, my feelings are mixed about that," Danforth grumbled. "However, I understand Sinclair's concern. If the murderer and that missing... sapphire book," he said thoughtfully, stumbling over the words, "are here, then, of course, they cannot be allowed to leave."

"Do you disagree with the reasoning?" Roland asked him, but after a pause of consideration, Danforth finally shook his head.

"No, Percy, I cannot fault the logic of it at all. But penning the murderer is most certainly going to make him—or her— dangerous. Your Highness, we must ferret out the culprit before they will harm someone to escape. What will you have us do? How might you like me to proceed?"

Prinny paused, resting his hand against his chin in

deliberation. "I agree we must work with all haste, so I am afraid we cannot appoint just one to this task. Percy, as you are... somewhat experienced with both the nobility and the military, I would ask you to oversee the investigation. Sinclair and Danforth, I am grateful for your offers of assistance. I would ask you to cooperate with him to ferret whatever clues may be available, and Lady Grace can also help in questioning some of the guests."

Both Sinclair and Danforth looked disturbed by this revelation, but surprisingly, Sinclair seemed most offended by the idea. Grace suspected that, being the most senior in military experience, he felt he should have been the spearhead.

"Of course, Your Highness," Grace agreed immediately, forestalling any argument. "It seems it is vitally important."

"With respect—Your Highness, gentlemen—" Roland interrupted, leaning closer to her. "Grace... this will be a dangerous matter for you to get involved in." He hoped she understood what he couldn't say aloud in front of the others. That chasing down a traitor would be even more dangerous than what had happened with Sir David.

"Gentleman, might I have a word alone with Lord Percy and Lady Grace?" Prinny asked pointedly, glaring at Roland. Sinclair and Danforth exchanged looks, then bowed and backed out of the room.

"I would hope you are not planning to refuse my request, Percy." The Prince Regent's tone was icy.

Roland looked down briefly. "I would not, Your Highness. I do wonder if our skills are up to the task, particularly when you have other investigators. And I worry for Lady Grace. It was... too near a thing, when we crossed Sir David."

Prinny's glare softened, becoming more sympathetic. "Yes, I expect you would feel so. But Percy, if there is a traitor underneath my roof, there is not a single person here who can be held above suspicion. Not even Sinclair, Danforth, or the head of my guard. And that is why I need you. The entire sixth coalition might be at stake and there might be a dagger pointed at my own back. I find this utterly intolerable. If the lives of your countrymen are not sufficient motivation, I am prepared to give an additional incentive. I will owe you a very large boon of your choosing, if you can find the murderer and retrieve Sapphire by any means necessary."

He glanced at Grace, but Roland already knew what he would find writ upon her face. Bowing his head in acceptance, he murmured, "Of course, Your Highness. With your permission, we will begin with the Master of the Household."

5

Before leaving the library, Roland took a moment to pen a note to Thorne. He scribbled a few lines of instruction and then folded the note in half and then half again. He sealed it with a few drops of candle wax and wrote Thorne's name and address on the front. He handed it to a footman and asked that it be delivered forthwith.

With that task done, Roland and Grace found the Master of the Household easily enough, for he stood outside of the room, awaiting instruction from Prinny. In his perfectly pressed uniform, he stood as tall and straight as the military guards. Only his rotund stomach and thinning hair set him apart.

When Roland asked to speak with him, he widened his stance and crossed his arms behind his back. "Of course, my lord. I am here to serve."

Roland opened his mouth and then closed it again. Here in the corridor was hardly the right place to conduct an interview of any sorts, particularly one about a murder.

Grace caught onto the problem at once. "Might you have someplace we can speak privately?"

The house master glanced at Roland, looking for his

confirmation, and Grace fought a scowl. But Roland gave his nod of approval, supporting her query.

"I have an office." The man led them towards a plain wooden door with reluctance. "Although—I beg your pardon, my lord, but might you not be more comfortable in a sitting room?"

"We are fine to go below stairs," Roland assured him. "Privacy is of the utmost importance—not comfort."

Thus reassured, the older man opened the door and led them down a set of wooden stairs. Unlike on the main floor, there was no elaborate wallpaper or crown moulding. Only white paint and oak boards worn by decades of use. It was more than passing strange for Grace to venture into the servant's part of her own home, and even more to be in the bowels of a royal residence. The class lines never seemed so stark and so strange.

The man turned left at the bottom of the stairs and guided them along a corridor until they reached the door to his office. Inside, Grace took note of the battered old desk, the hand stitched cushion on the seat of the chair, and the giant ledger resting on the desk. High-set windows lined one wall, allowing in sunlight. Beneath them, whitewashed shelves played home to more books and ledgers, small keepsakes, wooden boxes, and various candlesticks in need of polishing.

This was the office of a working man, one who had little time for fripperies or lounging around with a book in one hand and a glass of Port in another.

The three of them shuffled awkwardly for a moment, and then the house master motioned for Roland to take his chair, but Roland seemed ill inclined to oust the man from his normal post. They needed the Master of the Household's full assistance, and to do whatever was required to make the man feel comfortable around them. With that in mind, Grace gently suggested appropriate seating arrangements.

"Lord Percy, shall you and I take these lovely wooden chairs? Mr—oh dear, we have not been properly introduced, sir. I am Lady Grace and this is Lord Percy. How should we address you?"

"Mr Walker, my lady," the older man said. "Please, call me Walker."

"Very well, Walker. If you will take your seat, we can explain why we are here." Grace sought for something else she might say to make the man feel at ease. "That is a lovely cushion. Did your wife or daughter make it for you?"

Walker lifted the item in question and held it up like a prize on display. "Princess Amelia, God rest her soul, presented it to me one summer. She knew I sometimes suffer from joint pain and wanted me to have a comfortable place to rest my back."

"What a thoughtful token," Grace said. She settled onto a wooden chair opposite the desk. "Please, do sit, sir. It is your insights into the household we seek. You might as well take advantage of the break from running around."

Roland sat beside Grace without any hesitation, and finally, Mr Walker unbent enough to sit in their presence. He kept his back straight and rested his arms on the armrests, ready to leap into action at their first request. Grace caught Roland's eye and gave a nod of encouragement for him to explain why they were there.

Roland adopted a relaxed position before explaining, "Walker, I am sure you are aware of Sir Julian's untimely demise. We suspect Sir Julian may have either been drugged, or he took a sleeping draught himself and was unable to fend off an attack. Do you know if he requested Laudanum or something else to that effect?"

"No, my lord. Sir Julian required only a spoon to take his dose of magnesia. I do not believe he took any sleep aids, for he often ventured out of his room for a walk to the library, should his stomach upset prevent him from resting. He claimed the movement helped."

"I see. And do you know if Sir Julian took leave of his room at any point last evening?"

"Not to my knowledge, my lord." Mr Walker rushed to add, "There was some movement on the part of the guests, with varying times for turning in, but Sir Julian was not listed among them. If only he had cried out, or given us some hint of his distress, I am certain a footman or guard would have come to his rescue."

As much as Grace wanted to agree, there remained a possibility that a footman or guard might have been the killer. At least here in Brighton, the household size was reasonably small. "Walker, please do not take offence, but we must ask you about the servants. Is there anyone new? Or has anyone been recently dismissed?"

Mr Walker shook his head before she finished speaking, his face growing severe. "No, my lady. We only hire the most qualified of individuals with impeccable credentials. In fact, most of us are from the Prince Regent's own household in London."

Grace had expected this was the case, but a lingering question remained. "Do you know if any of the servants previously worked in the household of one of the current guests?"

"I do not believe so, but I will check to be certain."

"Then let us move on to the guests," Roland said, taking control of the conversation. "I must confess that Lady Grace and I are in sore need of your insights into these individuals. Lady Grace only made her debut this season, and I was away on the front lines until this spring. Neither of us has had any real interaction with his highness's guests until we met them last night at the soiree. We will very much appreciate any forthrightness and unabridged observations of them as individuals."

Mr Walker shifted in his chair. A flush stained his neck and crept up his cheeks. They were at risk of losing him if Grace did not find a way to convince him to break the servant's code of silence. She glanced around the room, hoping for inspiration, before remembering the cross-stitched cushion at his back.

He was not just the Master of the Household. He was a trusted retainer, one whom the royal family valued enough to make the children want to see to his comfort. That spoke of a tight bond between master and servant.

Grace raised her fingers in a silent request for Roland to pause. "Dreadful as the situation is, we are very lucky that the Prince Regent was not the victim of this crime. We want to ensure that there is no chance the villain will target His Highness next."

The Master of the Household paled, as though this was the first time he had considered this possibility.

"You must not fret. His Highness has tasked myself and Lord Percy with making sure that does not happen, but we would do better at fulfilling our duty to the crown if his loyal people help us—people like you, Walker. The Prince Regent would never wish for you to betray his confidence, nor would we ask you to. But if someone among the guests or staff has betrayed him, surely we owe it to the royal family to uncover their identity."

Mr Walker pulled a handkerchief from his pocket and mopped his brow. "Of course, my lady. I understand the situation fully and will do all within my power to comply however you need."

"Excellent. I promise in turn, we will keep anything you tell us confidential, so long as it does not affect the Prince Regent or anyone else's safety." Grace turned to Roland. "Shall we return to the topic of the guests?"

"Yes," Roland replied. "Walker, could you take us through the list of houseguests who stayed overnight, and tell us about their connection with the Prince Regent? Any information such as how long they are expected to stay, whether they have visited before, and what the servants think of them will be useful."

Mr Walker shifted again in his chair, but this time to get more comfortable. He crossed his hands over his chest and began his response.

"Lord Danforth is the one we know best, for he has visited the last several years. I can check my records for the exact dates and length of stay. He is one of the close advisers to the Prince Regent, nearly a right hand man for lack of a better description, and the servants treat him with great respect. Baron Langley is an unusual choice of guest, though not unknown. He was a great support for the king, often spending hours discoursing on the latest scientific advancements. He came this week to oversee a donation of books to the local library."

Grace committed that to memory. "What of the others? Is it usual for the Prince Regent to have two military guests?"

"No, my lady. Not here at the seaside, at least. Given the fraught times on the continent, we have had more interaction with the military leaders. Sir Julian Montgomery attended many events at the palace over the years. I am less familiar with the Major General."

"Let us move along to the others," Roland said. "Can you tell us anything about Blackwood, Ravenscroft, and Lady Waddington?"

"They are members of the court, my lord. We tend to see a steady stream of court entourage over the summer. They come, stay for a week or two to take part in the entertainment, and then move along to their next destination. Nearly all have all visited at least once before."

"Was anyone here for the first time?" Roland asked.

"Only the Major General, my lord." The Master of the Household leaned forward and lowered his voice. "He is not a confidant of the Prince Regent, and he did not seem to be close with Sir Julian. I cannot say his visit is exactly unusual—there have been several new faces in the ranks the last year—but of the guests here, he is the only one who has not been here before."

Roland nodded his head in thanks. "Were there any fraught relations we should know about?"

"Besides that of Sir Julian and General Sinclair? No, I daresay the rest get on well enough. Lord Ravenscroft and Lady Waddington often walk around the grounds together, though that might simply be out of a shared interest in fresh air. Lord Blackwood prefers the game room and Baron Langley spends most of his time in the library."

Though interesting, little of this was useful in pointing them in a direction. Grace decided to cut to the heart of the matter. "Is there any of the group whom you might suspect of being capable of murder?"

Mr Walker blanched at Grace's bold words. "No, my lady. Not unless they acted on the continent. The court deals in societal cuts and wars of words, not in weapons."

Grace knew that all too well. His words served as a reminder of the risks she and Roland faced. If they alienated the wrong person, they might find their social standing even lower than now. They would have to tread very carefully, especially with all eyes on them from the start.

She needed to speak with Roland before they went any further.

"Walker, we do not wish to take up too much of your time

on what is proving to be a busy morning. Might it be possible for you to check your records and write up a short overview of each guest? When they arrived, how long they planned to stay, their habits, and anything else you feel would be useful. You may send it to the Percy residence."

"I will do it today, my lady. You may depend upon me for whatever you need." Walker rose from his chair and showed them out of his office. At Grace's request, he guided them to a rear door that opened onto the grounds, rather than the upper floor.

Outside and once again in the sunshine, Grace latched her arm through Roland's and urged him to walk with her. She moved away from the pavilion, venturing into the garden. After checking to make sure no one was within earshot, she stopped and faced Roland.

"This will not be an easy task. But I think we can help them, Roland."

"I know," he said softly, one corner of his mouth lifting in an expression that might be wry resignation, "but... this was not what I had envisioned for us, these weeks in Brighton. We were supposed to be talking of the wedding and our future."

"Surely we can do both. This may even give us more excuses to be together. My mama can hardly deny the Prince Regent's direct request of us."

"Your mama is more likely to put my head on a pole, and likely I would already decorate the lawn if she knew what part I played in the mark on your neck. Zounds, what are we going to tell our families? Prinny is not a discreet creature, and I doubt he will hesitate to tell people what we are doing. It will be a mess."

The memories of her family's reaction to her previous injury came to mind. Her mama had blistered her ears, but it was her father's tears of joy at seeing her return home that hit her the hardest. No, they would not thank the crown for putting her in danger, or Roland.

Still, she did not want him to refuse to let her help. To lighten the mood, she swatted his arm. "My mama knows the queen has called upon me in the past. Let her think that it is my fault we find ourselves with this assignment and you are there to keep me safe."

"I will always be there to keep you safe. At least, I will try—which brings me to my primary concern. I want you to promise me one thing above all else, Grace."

"What would you like me to promise?" she asked warily, refusing to agree outright without hearing the request.

Roland took her hands. "I am keenly aware I would have more success in asking you to transform yourself into a mermaid than insisting that you stay out of the matter. I know you well enough to understand that. But in return, I would ask—if things grow dangerous, you must retreat to safety. And please, do not under any circumstances venture off on your own as you did with Sir David. Wait for me, or at least take Thorne. I lost ten years of my life when I saw him holding the knife to your neck, and I do not think my heart could bear to see that happen again."

Thankfully, this was a promise Grace could make without worry or doubt. "I agree, if you will do the same. Now that we are able to be together, I do not want to let anything spoil our future, whatever we decide it should be."

6

Roland noted that Grace appeared somewhat weary as the noon hour approached. He wondered what troubled her more—the murder, or their necessary departure from the pavilion to meet their families for luncheon.

"We cannot avoid the subject forever," he said slowly, "but perhaps we should not mention Prinny's assignment today."

Grace looked up at him from beneath the edge of her bonnet. "There must be a reason, I imagine?"

Roland shifted uneasily. "I expect my grandfather will be difficult without added provocation. I had... a rather unpleasant meeting with him in London before convincing him of the need to come to Brighton. The news of the broken engagement only reached him there, and it caught him off guard."

She bit her lip slightly. "Yes, I can imagine that would be a surprise. I will be on my best behaviour with him."

Roland placed his hand over hers on his arm, squeezing gently. "Of course you will. On that score, I have no concern at all. Just... do not be surprised or disheartened if he also directs the anger he has with me at you as well."

Grace offered him a small smile, her eyes taking on a

familiar, determined glint. "Your grandfather is an old man. How much trouble could he possibly give us?"

Sighing, Roland ran his free hand through his hair. He had not told Grace of his grandfather's nickname, and perhaps she was unaware of it. "Hopefully, not as much as I fear he might."

"Stop fretting," she told him, swatting at his hand. "You're mussing yourself."

And with that comforting exchange, they made their way into the charming little seaside inn chosen to stage their first confrontation. Being near the beach, it enjoyed a lovely view and a stiff breeze redolent of salt and the earthy tang of the limestone cliffs nearby. Few people were seated on the veranda due to the force of the wind, but fortunately, they had reserved a private room with plenty of large windows that let in the light.

They arrived only a few moments after everyone else and found the Tilbury family still settling into their chairs at the sturdy wooden table. The smells of seafood and freshly baked bread promised an excellent meal.

Roland remained standing, briefly holding Grace beside him as he turned his eyes towards his grandfather, already seated at the head of the table. "Since we are all here, I shall take this moment to perform the introductions. Grandfather, may I present Lady Grace to you? Lady Grace, this is my grandfather, Gideon Percy, the Duke of Northumberland. Grandfather, I also wish to introduce you to her family. This is her father, Lord Byron Tilbury, her mother, Lady Lilian Tilbury, and her brother, Lord Felix."

Grace's father smiled somewhat thinly from the foot of the table, which he had commandeered as if it were his right. "It is a pleasure to meet the famous Breaker of Northumberland."

Roland darted his eyes towards his grandfather, but the old man seemed perfectly at ease with his moniker being well known. Young Felix, seated between his father and mother, gave his sister a comprehensive glance as Grace settled in the chair to the duke's left. Roland took the chair to Lord Tilbury's right, beside her.

"I always enjoy a good meal," the Breaker rumbled in response.

After the tension of the introductions passed without incident, Roland relaxed as the first course was served: a light and savoury dish of flaked salmon mixed with rice, hard-boiled eggs, and spices. For his grandfather's part, the man studiously applied himself to his food rather than talk.

"Do you visit the Assembly Rooms, Your Grace?" Lady Tilbury asked his grandfather, trying to stir him to conversation. "They had a rather famous pianist performing there a few days ago. I heard he was remarkable."

The duke grunted. "I do not usually stir myself to partake in entertainment outside of my home these days. Indeed, I only came as far south as London because I expected a wedding involving my grandson."

Lady Tilbury looked briefly confused before she realised the duke was referring to Roland's engagement to Lady Charity. Colour rose to her cheeks.

Roland lowered his fork and glared across the table at his grandfather. "Sir, given our conversation in London, I will not pretend that you were not made privy to the entire story when you conversed with the queen. Queen Charlotte would hardly enjoy her 'strokes of genius' without a few knowing how she puppets people behind the curtain."

The Breaker leaned forward, eyes narrowing. "That the engagement to Lady Charity was to protect her from scandal? She took pains to inform me, indeed. I rather wonder why you failed to inform me you had planned to marry a ruined woman."

Lady Tilbury gasped, bringing her hand to her mouth, and

beside him, Grace grew very straight in her chair. Lord Tilbury set both hands on the tabletop, thunderstruck.

The Breaker lifted one eyebrow, observing their reactions. "I suppose not everyone at the table here was aware of this, then. How many secrets are you hiding from the woman who is the object of your affections this month, Roland? How can there be talk of an engagement when so much has clearly been left unsaid?"

"Lord Percy has no secrets he has kept from me, Your Grace," Grace said as calmly as she could manage. "Mama—it is not what you think. I was helping search for Charity."

"If it is not what we think, what is it, Grace?" Lord Tilbury asked her, his voice sounding strangled.

Grace looked at Roland, but he bowed his head. He must leave it to her to explain, because the words would not hold the truth he needed them to, coming from his lips. This seemed hardly the time or place, but if they did not come out now, things would fester. He gave her a small nod. She could tell them, or not, as she pleased.

Splitting a look between the three adults, she took a breath, steeling her courage. "Roland's engagement to Lady Charity is —well, you might lay the blame at my own feet." Grace could no longer meet the eyes of her father or the duke, so she instead explained to her mama, her voice growing rougher with emotion, but she lowered her tone so that hopefully the words would not carry farther than they needed to.

"Mama, I begged him to help Charity because I love her too much to have let her be ruined. The story from the queen about her hiding away Lady Charity so that Lord Percy could enact a grand rescue is a lie. The truth is that she truly was kidnapped," she began, twisting her fingers together in her lap.

The silence at the table was deafening, and Grace refused to look away from her mama. But Roland was free to see how the others at the table were taking the news. Grace's brother seemed stunned as he looked from her to Roland, but Roland nodded his confirmation to the boy. These words, at least, were true. Lord Tilbury, however, seemed aghast.

It was in this uncomfortable silence that the second course was served, the entire table lost in their own thoughts while they waited for the waiter to depart. He could hardly imagine what gossip the waitstaff would take to the rest of the inn.

For her part, it seemed Lady Tilbury was nobody's fool. Although he was unaware of the others' knowledge about the entire matter, Roland knew that Grace had informed her mother about their search. So, while she was surprised and horrified, her expression quickly shifted as she added together the few bits and pieces she knew.

"Lady Fitzroy," her mother said. There was no question in her tone, but she still waited for her daughter to confirm it.

"Yes, Mama."

"How... how dare she?" Lady Tilbury breathed. "Why would she do that? Why did you not tell me this? My goodness..." She tapered off as she was struck by a thought, and she brought her hands to her lips. "Oh, poor Vanessa!"

Though it was abominable table manners, Grace reached across the table to take her mother's hand. "I will explain the how and why later. I promise, Mama. For the moment, all you need to know is... the Queen's tale and the engagement to Lord Percy, that was the favour she granted for our aid. It saved Charity's virtue."

"A waste of your time and effort then when she went and married that ancient Scottish codger." The duke made a rude sound, looking disagreeable. Though he had learned his lesson about making wagers, Roland was willing to bet the duke was dismayed that dropping the gossip regarding the engagement did not play out as he intended.

Grace, however, clearly thought about no such thing. She swallowed at the mention of the 'Scottish codger.' "I wanted her to be happy."

Before his grandfather could say something else boorish, Roland placed his hand on Grace's shoulder. "I am certain Lady Charity has no plans to sit quietly and be forgotten. She is... a thoughtful, clever sort."

"Yes, she is," Lady Tilbury said, sensing her daughter's need for reassurance too. "Vanessa and her daughter are the plotting sort, unlikely to forget or forgive such an insult. Marian would be best off keeping a low profile on the continent until her dying day."

Lady Fitzroy, however, was also the plotting sort. Roland knew how few people were aware of her activities with Sir David Green and the Swedish ambassador. He doubted her disappearance was anything less than an opening gambit in a new game that would play out at a later date. But he took a sip of his Madeira and kept this thought to himself.

"Nevermind Lady Charity and Lady Fitzroy," Lord Tilbury said, finally finding his tongue, but still sounding angry. "What I want to know now is whether you have any ulterior motives in your courtship of my daughter." He pinned Roland with a hard stare, as if considering the value of tossing all propriety out the window and choosing violence.

On this score, however, Roland had no difficulty reassuring her father. "Only if you consider it an ulterior motive that your daughter caught my heart—and rather unexpectedly," he added, taking her hand beneath the table and brushing his thumb over her knuckles. "I confess, I have spent my whole life believing duty must come first. I was sworn to my country, in the cavalry. When Grandfather wished me to marry quickly to secure our line, I went to London. Even when I realised my affections were being drawn to Grace, I agreed to set my own wants aside, unrequited, because Grace had won my loyalty. Your friend, Lady Charity, saw things more clearly than either of us, and she wanted you to be just as happy as you wanted happiness for her."

He said this last to Grace, and Grace's eyes got shiny with emotion at that. Not wishing her to be embarrassed at the table, he looked back at Lady Tilbury, who beamed at him, and then Grace's brother, who also looked pleased.

The duke narrowed his gaze, considering his grandson. "Well," the old man finally drawled. "It is good to know there is perhaps some purpose behind your... rather inappropriate behaviour, Roland. At least where your engagement is concerned. However, I have been made most painfully aware of how the rest of the ton feels about your... antics in finding another engagement so quickly. To the peers, you are a cad. Fickle. Wholly lacking in decorum. And those were not even the aspersions being cast last night."

Roland pressed his lips together, knowing exactly what people had been saying last night. All that, and worse.

"It is unfortunate you have been thinking with your breeches instead of your head," the duke continued, the razor edges of the Breaker's mask shining clearly through the pleasantries. "I insist you use this time to bring yourself back into order. Our line is too new to have you set it tumbling like a careless infant putting his hand through building blocks. There are people speculating about how fit this shrinking violet is to be a duchess."

As he was in the middle of another sip of Madeira, Roland nearly choked. Shrinking violet! Grace? Lady Tilbury didn't blush with shame this time at the Breaker's words. She glowered. But Roland caught her eye, hoping she would bide her peace. The duke was notorious for insisting on having the last word, but it was action that would win the day, not protestations or offended sensibilities.

"Of course, Grandfather," Roland murmured, not wishing to provoke further argument. Not now.

"Wonderful. Since we are all very good friends now and not keeping secrets—" the old man said, dark amusement in his voice, "perhaps you wish to recall your servants to avoid creating more gossip. For there are already whispers among my own staff about how you have decided to treat yours to a grand seaside holiday."

When all eyes fixed upon him again, Roland shifted, trying to maintain a casual pose. "Grandfather, I put my servants up elsewhere simply because our Brighton home is too small for everyone. They still have their work, even if they are briefly lessened. It is just the two of us and there is no need to double the efforts. I will ask Mr and Mrs Archer to coordinate to spell your own staff so everyone may enjoy some free time here. There is nothing untoward in giving an occasional reward for hard work and loyalty."

Grace shot him a curious glance, but she was determined to apply herself to her food instead of showing any signs of discord between them in front of his grandfather.

7

If the other events of the season had been trying, they seemed easy by comparison to the luncheon. It was with relief on both their parts that Grace and Roland took their leave.

"You said that your grandfather might be difficult. You were not jesting in that respect!" Grace laughed, hoping it did not sound as strained as it seemed.

"Things could have been rather worse," Roland told her. "They assuredly could have been better, but it was not as terrible as I feared it would be."

Grace sighed at that, putting one hand to her cheek in weariness as they stood in the dappled light beneath a tree planted close to the door. "Goodness. I suppose I must be glad I cannot imagine what you expected might have transpired. Shall we head back to the Royal Pavilion to speak with the guests?"

"It could wait until tomorrow if you are too weary," Roland said, being solicitous. "Or I can begin alone so you can return to your residence."

"No, I want to help," Grace said, frowning. "I just need a bit of quiet to collect myself."

Roland froze. "If you require a moment alone..."

"Do not be absurd," Grace said sharply, looking down at her feet. "You are not one to disconcert me, and I... enjoy your company. Immensely." A normal debutante should flutter her eyelashes at this, or some such, but Grace had always found pretending to be fawning a horrible practice. Compliments, she felt, should be honest.

There was a pause before Roland spoke. "You flatter me, but I am afraid you have just told a lie." His voice took on a teasing note. "I most definitely disconcerted you when I danced with you, and as a gentleman, I must forewarn you—I plan to do so wherever I can find a moment to waltz again. Prinny adores the waltz."

Grace lifted her chin and scowled at him. It was a hard face to maintain since he was smiling back at her, his grin wide. "I am terrible at dancing. I hate it!"

He grew sly. "Do you, truly?"

She sighed with enough false drama to be worthy of the theatre. "No. Not when it is with you."

"Well, dances with me are the only ones that count. You may hate them with impunity when they are taken with anyone else."

That made Grace laugh aloud, and she felt much better. "The more I get to know you, the more it is so clear why your valet calls you 'Sir Barbarian.' You must be very trying to him."

Roland's smile grew a little strange at that. "Trying to him! You say that as though you believe he is some sort of paragon of virtue. I assure you, he is not; he is just good at deception and acting the part where others are watching. You will see his true colours after we are married." He cupped her hand in his, running his thumb over her palm. "I wish I did not have to call our attention back to the business waiting for us, but... speaking of that paragon, he should be expecting us by the stables. I asked him to collect some information for us."

"Oh!" Grace said, tugging at her hand and marching in that direction. "Then we should not keep him waiting."

Indeed, Thorne stood awaiting the pair near the entrance to the inn's stables on the side of the building. "Lord Percy, Lady Grace. How did the luncheon with the Breaker go?"

Grace frowned at Thorne's careful, dignified tone. It was so different from when he had helped distract her while the doctor laid stitches in her neck or even the lighter formality he employed while he enjoyed a breakfast in her company.

"We are still upright and breathing, so it was fine," Grace said with just a touch of cheek, hoping he would bend a little. But she could not help bringing up the one thing the duke had mentioned that troubled her. "How are you enjoying your leisure time in Brighton?" She had never heard of anyone taking their servants on a holiday, and while Roland's servants were his own to deal with, she was uncertain she approved.

"I, err," Thorne stuttered, glancing at Roland.

"The duke had a few words to say about how I spoil you lazy layabouts while his servants are being worked to the bone."

"Ah," Thorne said. Somehow, the tone of that single syllable was comprehensive. "In Lord Percy's defence, it is not all play. We are spending much of the time working with the Sprouts. Albert and Mrs Archer are tutoring them in reading and writing, while I take them out for exercise and... other kinds of learning about the world."

Grace placed her hands on her hips, dividing her attention between the two men. "I hope you are not uneasy in my company just because Roland and I plan to marry, Mr Thorne. I rather enjoyed our meal together."

When Thorne stiffened and glanced at Roland, Grace thought she had hit the nail squarely. Roland, to be fair, had raised an eyebrow at his servant that was clear in conveying *I told you so.*

"Do not be too angry with him, Grace. He is being cautious. I have been the most lenient of employers, but you might imagine how another lady would view our informality."

"Or even the ton at large, considering that we stand in public," Thorne added with a look of censure aimed at Roland.

"I suppose I can," she replied with reluctance. "Please know, however, I do not wish to upset the household with rigidity. Roland considers you the nearest thing to a friend. You two have, perhaps, been a bad influence. Because of how the two of you are, I have rather come to enjoy a similar relationship with Elsie."

Thorne relaxed his shoulders a bit, but he frowned at Roland. "That is kind of you, Lady Grace."

"So. You were saying about the Sprouts? I do hope you are finding just a little time to spoil them."

"If food is involved, you may be certain," Thorne said dryly, but at least he lost some of his stiffness. "They are eating us into the poor house."

Grace well remembered how slender and hungry the waifs had been when they had first found them, and now did not mind at all that Roland was giving everyone a small taste of holiday. After all, the Sprouts might end up having to work hard for the rest of their lives. "Have they tried the taffy yet?"

Thorne rolled his blue eyes, and Grace stifled a giggle. "Neither one of them cares for it. But they do love the honey cakes. Mrs Archer will be stuck making them forevermore."

Roland had been carefully watching this exchange, and Grace laid a hand on his arm to reassure him she was not upset by this, strange as it was. She smiled first at him and then at Thorne. "I think it is a lovely idea that Roland is letting you enjoy some leisure, and I wonder why more do not offer their staff the same."

"Well," Roland said mildly, "since I was put so suddenly upon the spot, I offered you up to spell the Percy house staff so that they too could enjoy a holiday. I hope you do not mind working again from time to time if my grandfather shows a united front to the stuffy nobles in letting his staff also enjoy some free time."

Thorne didn't seem bothered. "Easily done."

Inspired by a thought, Grace tugged at Roland's arm again. "Elsie could help if you do! In fact, do you think Mrs Archer and the Sprouts might enjoy a visit from Elsie now? She is due a half day, but she has not yet made any plans. I might suggest she visit."

"They would certainly welcome her anytime she likes," Thorne replied. "I will stop by your lodging and give her our direction, so that she will know where to find us. Now, shall I update the pair of you on what I learned while you were otherwise occupied?"

"Yes, by all means," Roland said. "Come, let us take a walk along the beach toward the pavilion."

The unusual trio waited for a break in the line of carriages and men on horseback to cross the busy road to the waterfront. There, Roland offered Grace his arm as they made their way to the pebbled beach along the water's edge. They were far from alone, as many other summer residents had flocked out to enjoy the sun, but the lapping waves provided enough background noise to prevent them from being overheard.

"I focused my efforts on Major General Sinclair, as you asked," Thorne said, by way of beginning. "That his reputation precedes him made my task somewhat easier. The pavilion guards had plenty to say."

"And what reputation is that?" Roland asked.

"He is very capable and well-liked by those who have served under him. But, how should I put this?" Thorne paused for a moment. "Do you remember Captain Stansom?"

"I daresay the queen herself would recall the man if their paths ever crossed," Roland replied with a dark laugh. He looked over to explain to Grace. "The man fair assumed that the sun rose and set on his head. Yet, he was an excellent leader, and his men all looked up to him. I do not know if it is right to call him pompous, given he was eminently qualified, but I did not call him a friend."

"Why not?" Grace asked in return. Roland had so few friends to the best of her knowledge, so she was curious about why he picked those that he did.

"Stansom is a glory hound, and I cared little for glory, Grace. My reasoning in heading to the front was... complicated. But suffice it to say, a large part of that reason was to be out of my father's reach. I do not fault Captain Stansom for his actions, for he had not half the privilege of position I enjoy, and mayhap that was part of it. Had I sought a friendship, he would have turned it into a competition. It was far easier to cede the floor to him, and to keep my head down and focus on my task."

Grace considered his response and recognised the truth in his words. This was part of the reason her own friendship with Charity had lasted as long as it did. She had been content to be overshadowed and allow Charity to shine. And for her part, Charity had not viewed Grace as any sort of competition. Not even when it came to the matter of marriage...

If her latest missive was any indication, Charity had borrowed Grace's original plan to find herself a near-corpse to marry. However distasteful she found it, it would grant her immunity from certain future risks from Lady Fitzroy. Not all, but many. Grace hoped her friend did not regret this path, but

Roland was right. Charity was not the sort to do things without a purpose.

Roland pulled her tight against him when her kidskin boots slipped on a patch of wet pebbles and took his time relinquishing his hold. "We are nearly to the pavilion, where we must get to work interviewing our suspects." He glanced at Thorne. "Was there any more to Sinclair? What about his relationship with Sir Julian?"

"Sinclair does not seem to count himself among Sir Julian's admirers," Thorne said. "And that sentiment was mutual. Sir Julian made that clear, time and time again, over his last few days."

Grace leaned forward to look past Roland. She asked Thorne, "What did he do that was so egregious? I imagine it must have been serious if you heard about it from the lower ranks."

"The Major General arrived at Brighton first, and set to work reviewing the plans of the guards and the local regiments. He called for inspections, asked about assignment rotations, and the like."

That did not sound too bad to Grace, but the expression on Roland's face made her think otherwise. "Was that usual?"

"Not at all," Roland answered. "The royal guard does not fall under the purview of the army. In truth, Sinclair did not have any right to make demands. However, I assume he must have outranked everyone here and took advantage of that fact."

"That is it exactly," Thorne confirmed. "He explained he wanted to ensure security was sufficient given the nearness to France's coast. He was worried about spies sneaking around, or so he said. Prinny is always eager for a show of strength, and having a senior military man fawn over his safety fed into his ego."

"He was fretting specifically about spies?" Grace asked, glancing at Roland again.

Roland shrugged. "French espionage is always a concern wherever the royal family is. Brighton would be an opportune target, both with Prinny's presence and being so near France. So that is not an unusual fear."

"All right. So then Sir Julian arrived." Grace could well imagine his reaction to the situation. "What did he do?"

"He plucked Sinclair from the heights of his ambition and put him straight back into his box of a junior officer, at least with respect to him. He called him out for overstepping and made him apologise to the head of the royal guard. They had a terrible row, witnessed by multiple guard members."

"Public humiliation would not be the strangest motivation for a murder," Grace murmured. And in that case, perhaps Sapphire had been mislaid by Sinclair in order to make Sir Julian look incompetent and careless.

"You have given us a solid foundation to begin with our questions," Roland said. "When you add this to Sinclair's insistence on being involved in the search for the guilty, it raises eyebrows. Was he acting out of concern for Sir Julian, or to cover up his own actions?"

"I suppose we will not know until we pose the questions," Grace answered.

The trio arrived at the path leading to the entrance of the royal pavilion grounds, still somewhat out of sight. "Thank you, Thorne," Roland said, clasping his valet's arm. "For being so quick with this." Grace noted that Thorne barely allowed the gesture before pulling free, as if worried they would be seen. With that, Thorne took his leave.

Grace frowned after his departure. "Is he upset we are getting married?"

"Indirectly, perhaps," Roland admitted. "My grandfather's

presence is also not helping matters. I would like to explain more, but now is not the time or place. Suffice it to say, one of the things he worries about is whether you will keep him in the house once we are married. I wouldn't take it personally; he was just as uneasy when I was engaged to Lady Charity."

"I cannot imagine having the gall to dismiss any of your servants! He has nothing to fear. But you are right; sorting our household is not urgent at the moment... a killer in the pavilion is." She sighed, then gave him a cheeky wink. "Our life would seem so peculiar to someone else, Roland. But I am enjoying the adventure."

8

The guards on duty stopped Roland and Grace as soon as they got within earshot of the pavilion grounds. The burlier of the pair stepped forward, one hand out to stop them and the other on the gun tucked into his belt. "Ho there, the pavilion is closed to visitors."

Roland raised both his hands to show he was unarmed. "I am Lord Percy, and this is Lady Grace Tilbury. We are expected."

The guard glanced over his shoulder at his colleague, who stepped into a small hut set aside for their use and returned a moment later. "They are cleared to enter."

Only then did the burly guard drop his aggressive stance and wave the pair forward. Roland thought it best to offer an explanation, especially given how often they would come and go. Learning that two members of the ton, one of whom was a lady, were investigating a murder did little to ease the man's confusion. Yet, he accepted the matter without argument and stepped aside.

Roland and Grace proceeded apace, striding up the drive to

the main entrance. A footman had the door open by the time they reached it.

"Good afternoon, Lord Percy and Lady Grace. The Prince Regent has made available a small parlour for your use. If you will follow me." He guided them along the corridors to a small but elegantly furnished room containing a settee and a pair of wingback chairs. Soft light filtered through the large window. "Would you like me to send for someone?"

"Yes, please," Roland answered. "Could you ask Major General Sinclair if he is available to speak with us?"

The footman nodded and then did an about-face to head off on his assignment.

Eyeing the seating arrangements, Grace asked Roland how he wished to handle the discussion.

Roland rubbed the back of his neck. "The man already has his back up with me. I fear if I take the lead, he will shut down. He will find it much harder to be rude to you. Do you mind terribly taking control of the questioning?"

Grace beamed at him. "I do not, and I must say, I appreciate your willingness to trust me."

"It is the first rule of any military engagement. Use whatever advantages you are able. In this case, the rules of polite society work in our favour."

The one thing they did not account for in their planning was the absence of the man in question. The footman returned with a grim expression.

"The Major General was not in his room," he said, taking a deep breath. "I found broken glass and blood on the floor."

"What?" Roland leapt from his seat, with Grace hot on his heels. "Take us there immediately."

Grace had to practically run to keep up with the footman and Roland as they dashed along the corridor and up the stairs to the guest rooms.

The footman led them to a room halfway down the corridor and opened the door. He stepped inside and immediately moved out of the way, clearing space for Roland and Grace to follow. He pointed toward the armoire.

"There, you can see the glass shards on the floor."

Roland beckoned Grace to stay close. He sank down to his haunches and eyed the shards of glass, resisting the urge to touch their sharp edges. Grace glanced around the room and spotted a letter opener on the writing desk. She hurried over to get it and then passed it to Roland. "Can you tell what sort of item broke?"

"Something round. Maybe a glass? There are drops of blood speckled around. Hold on, let me see if there are any larger pieces under this." Roland took care not to put his hand in the glass as he dropped to his hands and knees to peer under the heavy oak wardrobe. "Bring a light over."

Grace motioned for the footman to light a candle inside the nearest lamp and pass it to her. She set it on the floor and angled it so the light shone into the shadows underneath the furniture. "Do you see something?"

Roland slid the letter opener into the gap and nudged something. With a delicate clank, a glass vial rolled out.

Roland lifted it up so Grace and the footman could get a better view. Fine traces of white powder dusted the inside of the vial. After showing it to them, he pulled the cork from the top and lifted the vial to his nose.

"What are you doing?" Grace gasped. "It could be poison!"

Roland grimaced. "I doubt it—it smells and looks like opium. It might be added to a drink, but it would need to be mixed with something to disguise the bitterness. If this is what rendered Sir Julian insensible to an attack, he would have been unconscious within an hour or so of consumption."

Before Grace could respond, a deep male voice boomed from the doorway. "Why are you in my room?"

Grace whipped her head around to see Major General Sinclair striding into the room. His face was red with fury, but the white bandage wrapped around his left hand caught her attention.

Without hesitation, Roland shot back, "The better question is: why was an empty vial of opium powder in your room?" He waved the vial in the air. "It might also be wise to tell us where you have been."

Sinclair lurched sideways at the sight of the vial and rushed to defend himself. "I have never seen that before in my life. It was not here when I left an hour ago."

Grace raised her eyebrows.

"I speak the truth!" he insisted.

Grace glanced at Roland, who seemed to be biting his tongue. The vial was small enough to be kept concealed in a pocket. It could have been planted to incriminate Sinclair, but it seemed just as possible that the man had concealed it on his person during the search and then stuffed it beneath the bed.

First, she needed to lower the tension in the room. Roland was counting on her to calm the military man.

"We asked the footman to invite you to speak with us. When he found the broken glass and blood drops on the floor, we feared something had happened to you. Now you are here, in one piece, and some of our concerns can be laid to rest. Might I suggest we return to the parlour the Prince Regent made available to us, so we may talk?"

Sinclair narrowed his gaze and looked ready to argue, but Grace forced an apologetic smile onto her face. It was enough to buy his compliance, although he wasn't happy about it. He shook out his hands. "Lead the way, my lady."

Roland chose to follow last, placing their suspect between

them. The back of Grace's neck itched all the way down the stairs and along the corridor, and for once, it was not due to the lace collar of her gown. She glanced back once, and though he was quick to fix his expression, she caught Sinclair glaring at her.

So be it. Some might have found the man fearsome, but not Grace. After speaking her mind in front of the queen herself, no military man was going to cause her to tremble. She dug deep and found the courage to face the man head-on.

Back in the parlour, Grace marched over to the wingback chair and claimed it for herself. She pointed to the settee and said, "Please, Major General, have a seat and let us talk."

The man sat, but not comfortably. The sunlight brought out the grey in his hair, reminding Grace of the differences in their ages. He would treat her as a child if she were not careful. She imagined herself as her mother and called upon all the gravitas of her position in society. She was not merely Grace, but Lady Grace, daughter of an earl and promised to a future duke.

"General, please, do not take our questions as a personal insult. Prinny asked us to investigate."

"What I would rather like to know, Lady Grace," the man said in a low voice just short of a growl, "is whether I am now on your suspect list because of the vial, or because the Prince Regent has decided I cannot be trusted?"

Roland inhaled sharply. "Mind your tone when speaking to the lady, General Sinclair."

Grace gave Roland a brief look over her shoulder to let him see she was all right. "You are not being treated differently than any other, General. His Highness told us we cannot leave anyone who was in the pavilion off the list. It is simply the way things must be until the guilty is identified. So, let us begin with the vial. You said you were out of your room for an hour. Where did you go, and who was aware of your plans to leave the room?"

Sinclair held Grace's gaze. "As you saw, I dropped a glass in my room. Foolishly, I attempted to tidy it and cut myself. It was rather deep, and I visited the doctor to have it stitched. A guard accompanied me there and back. As to who knew I was gone? Well, it could have been any of the guests. I did not keep my departure a secret. My room door was open when I asked the guard to come along."

His answer raised more questions than it answered. Had he cut his hand on purpose so he could leave the premises? To pass the code book along to someone outside? Or, if it was truly an accident, then who had snuck into his room to plant the vial?

Whether or not Sapphire was still present, Grace was uncertain. The only thing she was certain of was that the individual responsible for Sir Julian's death must still be at the pavilion. That realisation, however, brought little consolation; they must tell Prinny at once—for his own safety.

She turned to Roland, but he had the same thought. He refused to leave her alone in the room with Sinclair, but he opened the door enough to speak with the guard outside in such a soft voice that it did not carry.

"If I may," Sinclair interrupted before Grace could ask another question, "it would be more useful to you both to speak with me about the security of the pavilion and the risks from overseas. I must say, I identified some weaknesses in the security when I arrived, where someone could sneak in or escape. Had Sir Julian not countermanded my suggestions, he might still be alive."

"Perhaps," Grace demurred. "You and Lord Percy can speak about that later. While I am here, I would like to discuss your relationship with Sir Julian. It is interesting you mention him countermanding you. I have heard there was no love lost on either side. Is that why he stepped in to stop you?"

"I am certain it is," Sinclair admitted. "Did you know Sir Julian?"

"We met at the Swedish ambassador's state dinner," Grace replied evasively.

"Then you saw him. He was a man not in control of his own excess, and yet the royal family trusted him to advise them on military matters. Expert in strategy he might have been, but Sir Julian had only minimal time on the front lines. He was an academic. That is why he failed to appreciate the risks of our position. He was careless with the Sapphire codebook, he prevented additional security measures, and look where it got us." He waved his hands to encompass Grace and Roland's presence in the room.

"He is now also gone, forever out of your way," Grace pointed out.

Sinclair sat up straighter and glowered at Grace. "Just what are you implying, young woman?"

"I imply nothing, sir. I am merely stating a fact. Sir Julian had both the Prince Regent's ear and respect. Now, he is not here, and you are."

Grace waited, watching him gape like a fish before she continued. "It would be a simple matter for an experienced military man such as yourself to incapacitate the man, especially if you dosed his drink with opium. And if it was not you, that is certainly the conclusion the real villain hopes we draw."

At her deductions, Major General Sinclair leapt to his feet and turned his anger upon Roland. "That," he spat, "was not left there by me. You spent ten years in service, and I would expect you to understand the honour of being in the military. I would never stoop so low, and certainly I would not be thinking of it as a way to progress in rank. What you suggest is treason."

"Then provide us with your alibi," Grace said, drawing the man's ire her way.

Sinclair sniffed in disdain. "Other than a brief conversation that included Lord Percy as well, I did not speak with Sir Julian yesterday evening. I avoided the man outside of official meetings. I certainly did not have any opportunity to put something in his drink. And if I had truly been the one who had stolen Sapphire, I never would have pointed out its absence. I daresay no one else here would have known he even possessed it."

"If it was not you who had dosed Sir Julian, who would do such a thing?" Grace asked. "The most suspect behaviour we have seen so far is yours. It does seem strange that you would act well beyond your remit with regard to the royal security forces. Did you receive some word of a specific threat that prompted you?"

The military man closed his hands into fists, but he did not raise them. He clenched his jaw as he wrestled with himself.

Grace prodded him. "Shall I ask the Prince Regent to pose this question to you instead?"

Sinclair huffed in frustration, but his hand and jaw unclenched. "I tell you this only because the Prince Regent has instructed us to cooperate with you. I am not aware who might have dosed Sir Julian... but... I do know that there is more to Ravenscroft than meets the eye. Prinny says the man is on our side, but I do not share his convictions."

Grace bit back a laugh of disbelief. "Ravenscroft? The rake? I would think the only risk he poses is to innocent young women."

"You, of all people, should not underestimate someone. The man has recently returned from France. His mother is from France. And I heard him boasting of a lover he left behind. Perhaps someone has wooed him into helping the opposition."

With that, Sinclair marched out of the room, never once looking back.

9

"Grace." Roland's voice was serious. "I think you should not be a part of the discussion with Ravenscroft. Confirm Sinclair's story, and then perhaps you should move on to speaking with Baron Langley. But do not go alone. Take one of the guards with you."

Grace peered at him. "You do not want me in the room with Lord Ravenscroft. Why?"

"Must I spell it out? The man is a known libertine. This next interview might be rather ungentlemanly," he confessed. "I would prefer it if you were not in the room."

"Are you worried that he will scald my ears with talk about his romantic conquests? I would think that you know me well enough by now. I will not swoon."

He gave her a brief look of admonition. "I am worried that if you are there, he will either say things just to shock and provoke you, or he will be a perfect gentleman and refuse to speak of what we need to know."

Grace sighed. "I suppose that is a fair point. Fine. Given the discovery of the vial, there is little time to waste. I will verify Sinclair's story with the guard and then return here, where I will make myself useful by speaking with the baron. But you must promise to tell me everything Ravenscroft says. Even if it is scandalous."

Roland would promise her no such thing, not without hearing what came out of the rake's mouth first. Fortunately, Grace flounced out of the room without waiting for him to promise.

He had not lied to Grace, but there was another reason he did not want her present. He himself might be required to be rather... ungentlemanly. He knew very little of Lord Ravenscroft besides his reputation and his heritage. The man was a dissolute socialite. Inconstant, forever flirtatious with the women, chummy with the men. Despite his debauchery, however, Ravenscroft was charming. So much so that he seldom suffered consequences more serious than the dour looks of prudish matrons and mamas protecting their impressionable young charges.

Ravenscroft might only be a shallow puddle of a man, but like a reflection on the water's surface, it could be a pretence that hid an unexpected depth. Roland did not care for this feeling of walking into a chat with Ravenscroft completely ignorant of what he might be dealing with, but they did not have the time to dally for days while collecting information.

Wanting to leave the parlour for Grace, he sent a guard to collect Ravenscroft and bring him to the library. Roland arrived first and took advantage of the lull to look through the window at the back gardens.

"Lord Percy. I suppose it is my turn to be interrogated, is it?"

Roland turned and met Lord Ravenscroft's gentian blue eyes. "You do not seem upset by the need."

Ravenscroft gave Roland a jaunty smile, showing even white teeth. "I am not worried about you finding that I was responsible for the murder of Sir Julian, so I see no reason to be upset about any questions to that effect."

Roland narrowed his gaze as he studied the slightly older man. Ravenscroft, he judged, was in his prime. Late thirties, well polished, and still blessed with a full head of glossy hair. "Tell me what happened in the evening following the musicale."

The man shrugged his shoulders. "There is not much to tell. Some of the others who attended the musicale stayed on for a while—we gossiped in the saloon, and some of the men spent time in the library. As the evening wore on, those who were not guests here at the pavilion left. We went about our ways and retired to our bedrooms."

"Did you see anyone acting in a way that might be unusual?"

"I most certainly did! Lady Waddington absolutely refused to spend the evening in my bed. I say, it was rather devastating."

"You say that as though you have not been on the receiving end of a rejection before."

"Well, you did ask about unusual behaviour, Lord Percy. Given my reputation for generosity, few of the objects of my interest turn me down."

Roland's eye twitched, and he could feel his temper rising. Ravenscroft was baiting him by being outrageous and rather smug about it. He refused to rise to it. "I would hazard then that she was put off by your demeanour."

"She was certainly put off by something, but I am rather certain you are barking up the wrong tree, young Percy. She was as nervous as a woman with her affair hiding in the closet from a husband come home early."

He was happy Grace had not argued about not attending this interview. "If I were to clear around the hedge thorn of your commentary, what you are implying is that Lady Waddington was far too nervous to put up with your escapades."

"As you say, Lord Percy."

"Was there any other suspicious activity transpiring?"

"You mean beyond Sinclair and Sir Julian acting fit to kill one another, and the baron skulking about the hallways in the dead of night? No, nothing comes to mind."

"Skulking?"

Ravenscroft shrugged. "He had that look about him."

"And what did you personally get up to, Ravenscroft?" Roland asked.

He ran a hand through his wavy dark gold hair, mussing it. Rather than dishevel himself, he only looked charmingly rumpled. "I spent some time with the gentlemen and Prinny, then made something of an early night of it and retired to bed. Alone too, since Lady Waddington was so unaccommodating."

"What time did you retire?"

"I cannot be certain. Sometime between midnight and one, I believe."

"I assume, then, someone can vouch for all your activities yesterday, and the time you went to bed," Roland commented in a droll tone.

"Of course. I am certain Lady Waddington will be happy to tell you she rebuffed me, and any of the royal guards can confirm I was playing Whist with the Prince Regent. I also chatted with the footman on the way to my room, if you wanted to check below stairs."

There were many perfectly legitimate reasons to speak with a footman... but something about Ravenscroft's phrasing raised his suspicions.

"I see." Roland put a hold on that line of thought for the moment, since Ravenscroft was clearly prepared to answer these questions. It was time to ruffle the unflappable lord. "Tell me about your mother."

Ravenscroft's jaw tightened for only the smallest instant. "I cannot begin to imagine what she has to do with any of this, and so I will not answer."

"I understand she is the reason you have spent so much time in the French countryside, yes?"

"Ah," Ravenscroft said, settling himself. "I follow you now. You think, somehow, I may be a spy for France. A viper at Prinny's bosom, who gladly killed one of his military advisers for the glory of Napoleon. You would not be the first person to make such poor assumptions, Percy, but your only proof is that my French mother married my English father."

"If I were to ask the others who are here, would they give that as your motivation for murdering Sir Julian?"

As intended, that caught Ravenscroft by surprise. "I do beg your pardon, but are you mad?"

"I am impatient with your games and busy trying to find a killer, Lord Ravenscroft. 'Mad' is a word that has never been assigned to me. Answer my question."

Ravenscroft's eyes were as wide as saucers. "I—I do not know what the others would give as my motivation, because such a baseless accusation is completely laughable. Indeed, I barely knew the man."

"I would not think you have to be well acquainted with Sir Julian to put a knife in his belly."

"That is not how—" Ravenscroft stopped abruptly, his eyelids flickering as he realised his tactical error, and Roland made a discreet gesture to a guard with his hand as he stepped closer to the blond lord. As both he and Sinclair suspected, the beautiful, dissolute Ravenscroft was not as much of a simple fop as he might pretend.

"'That is not how Sir Julian died,' I think, is what you were trying to tell me. Which rather makes me wonder how it is you know for certain."

Lord Ravenscroft looked distinctly distressed now as the

guard stepped up behind him, but he fixed Roland with a hard glare. "Just because I know Sir Julian had been smothered instead of stabbed does not mean I had anything to do with his death, Percy."

"It does not absolve you of it, either. In fact, I am certain that you will agree it makes you look only more suspicious."

"Well, I hate to disappoint you, because the manner of his death was a poorly kept secret," Ravenscroft said irritably. "Prinny's maids gossip like birds, and it would only take one of them to have overheard the truth before it was blathered to everyone below stairs."

"You are a curious man, Ravenscroft. First the footman, then a maid? How much do you dally with the staff—and for what purpose?" Roland loomed closer. "I think it best we should have you returned to your room."

"You are imprisoning me? You have no right!"

"I do not, it is true. I would ask you to remain available, however, while I investigate further."

Ravenscroft relaxed somewhat, adopting a hostile pose. "As you will, if that is what you feel you must do. But I think you have no idea who has done this deed, Percy. You are either looking for a scapegoat, or you are like—like a child shaking a tree, hoping for fruit to fall out. Best take care it does not land squarely on your head."

The guard took Ravenscroft back to his room, and Roland took a calming breath, thinking very hard. After talking with the man, he was uneasy. Ravenscroft was most certainly more clever and deceitful than most people assumed, and Roland was certain the man was hiding something. That said, however, his gut insisted that Ravenscroft was not the one to smother Sir Julian in his sleep.

He had been wrong before, but even if he was not wrong,

Ravenscroft was not necessarily absolved. Roland stalked off in search of whichever footman had spoken with the rake.

By happy circumstance, the Master of the House let him know that the servant had been positioned in a hall nearby Prinny's study, close to the contingent of armed guards blocking the regent's door. Roland guessed that the Prince Regent was not feeling secure in his own palace at the moment, but Prinny did not wish to advertise that to the rest of Brighton by residing elsewhere. In more ways than one, he was very much like Queen Charlotte.

"I would speak with you a moment," Roland said, guiding the man a short distance away from the guards.

"Certainly, my lord." The man looked nervous, but he met Roland's gaze well enough. "How may I be of assistance?"

"I wish to ask if you were indeed the footman who saw Lord Ravenscroft on his way to bed last night."

"Aye, my lord. Er, although I can't say if I was the only one. Lord Ravenscroft is a rather chatty fellow."

Frowning, Roland considered that. "What did you speak of with him?"

"He... he asked my opinion on some of the guests, my lord. Then he inquired as to who had already gone to bed."

"What did you answer?"

"It was rather early in the night yet, so only Sir Julian had retired. Then he asked me if I'd seen Lord Blackwood pass by recently, but I hadn't. I asked if he would like me to seek out Lord Blackwood for him, but he said no. His business could wait until the morning."

"And then he went to his room?" Roland asked.

"Yes, Lord Percy. But he came out straight away. He had a letter he wanted added to the mail collection."

"I assume you took it for him, then?"

"Only downstairs to one of the stable lads, so it could make it to the receiving house in time for the morning dispatch. I was gone perhaps... five minutes?"

Roland did not bother asking, then, whether Lord Ravenscroft had returned to his room. Even if he had, it would have been easy to slip back out again once the footman had departed. Speaking with a footman was a clever move, because the footman would remember the action. But it was also an opportunity to establish an alibi where there was none to be had.

"I appreciate your time," Roland told the footman, and the servant's demeanour noticeably eased. "You may resume your post for now, but I may think of something more to ask later."

"Of course, Lord Percy."

Roland's temples ached, and the urge to find Grace and ensure she was safe was overwhelming, but he was right at the Prince Regent's doorstep, and only Prinny might have the answers he needed. He was escorted through the contingent with alacrity into Prinny's drawing room when he inquired if he might have a moment of His Highness' time.

"Your Highness," Roland said, bowing. "I appreciate the chance to pose another question or two to you."

"I have little else to do, Percy," Prinny grumbled. "I am nigh a prisoner in my own home here. Ask your questions."

"I wished to let you know that I would like to have Lord Ravenscroft confined on suspicion. I also wanted to know in what capacity he serves you," Roland asked, "and whether you trust the man."

"Do I trust the man?" Prinny laughed aloud. "Roland, I am a heartbeat from the throne and someone here murdered my strategic adviser for a cipher. I do not trust anyone."

"Relatively speaking, Your Highness."

Prinny pursed his lips. "I trust Lord Ravenscroft to bring me useful information. He is rather like a magpie, you see, bringing me secrets in exchange for a coin. And he is rather deft at extracting them from others' lips in the guise of careless gossip and pillow talk."

Roland rocked back on his heels, considering. "He is not just an adviser. He is a whisperer, if not an outright spy."

Nodding his head, Prinny set his chin upon his fist, leaning on the arm of his chair. "I will not have him confined if you have no firm proof—but I will have him watched more closely. If you have flushed him as the pheasant, and if he has hidden Sapphire, perhaps he will seek it out, and we will catch him red-handed."

"If you think that best, Your Highness. But if he is a spy—"

Prinny waved his hand in irritation. "It is not enough. Do not let yourself believe for a moment that he is the only member of the Bon Ton who collects other people's secrets, Roland. In politics, one is either an utter fool, an informant, or an informed party. All of those noble personages here would step over their own mamas to bring me a shred of gossip that might win my favour. Lord Ravenscroft just happens to be rather better at collecting secrets than most."

10

Grace found the footman waiting in the corridor and asked him how far away the nearest doctor's surgery was.

"The nearest is a five-minute walk from the front gate, my lady. I presume you are asking with regard to Major General Sinclair?"

Grace was caught off guard until she remembered the footman had been in the room upstairs when Sinclair arrived and offered his explanation. "Yes, I need to verify his story. Can you find out which guard accompanied him?"

"I took the liberty of finding out. Sergeant Briggs is waiting outside." The footman led Grace back through the pavilion and out another door, this one opening to the rear near the stables. "He's the bald man over there."

Indeed, Sergeant Briggs's bald head shone in the sunlight, as his hat was tucked under his arm. When he spotted Grace coming his way, he quickly put it back into place with a sheepish grin. "Apologies, my lady, but we've had so many cloudy days of late, I couldn't resist a moment to bask in the sunlight."

Grace could not help but agree. Without her mama around to chastise her about her freckles, she took advantage of a nearby pair of wooden benches for their discussion. "Let us both bask a little longer, Sergeant. Follow me."

Though the guard was initially hesitant to sit in her presence, Grace eventually won the day. "What can you tell me of Major General Sinclair's injury and trip to the doctor?" she asked.

"The general was bleeding something fierce when he came outside looking for help. I thought of running for the doctor and bringing him here, seeing as how we're not supposed to let anyone leave the grounds. Then he showed me how deep the cut was, and I opted to escort him straight for help. I hope I did the right thing." The sergeant glanced over at Grace, worry lines creasing his forehead.

"You made a decision under pressure, as you are trained to do. In your place, I likely would have done the same."

"Thank you, miss." Briggs's cheeks reddened. "If it had been anyone else, I might have acted differently."

Grace sat up straighter. "Tell me, Sergeant, what is your opinion of Major General Sinclair?"

"If you're asking me whether I think he killed Sir Julian, the answer to that's a no."

"But what of the row they had? I caught wind of Sir Julian dressing him down in front of a crowd." Grace lowered her voice and leaned forward, inviting the guard to share his secrets. "That must have been uncomfortable for everyone involved."

The sergeant wiped his hand over his face and blushed again. "I'm sure the general's heart was in the right place, but Sir Julian had a point. Our unit head was none too pleased to have the general run rampant over all his preparations, especially given he was unfamiliar with the layout of the grounds. From what I heard, the general made the head guardsman show him every entrance, exit, and break in the walls. Didn't do us no good in the end, since the killer seems to reside within."

Grace had to agree. Despite the sergeant's vote of confidence in Sinclair, she was not ready to strike him off the list. Sinclair could have had the vial of opium in his pocket when his room was searched, and then cut himself and placed the vial there to find while he was out. Or—it was also possible the man was innocent of everything except poor luck. Until Grace could prove things one way or the other, she would continue to scrutinise his actions.

"Thank you, Sergeant Briggs. One last question before I let you return to your duties. When you and the Major General arrived at the doctor's surgery, did you stay by his side the whole time?"

"Yes, my lady. I posted myself at the door to the treatment room and made sure no one else went in or out. There were two assistants monitoring other patients, and a woman working in reception, but none of them ventured our way."

"What about inside the room?"

"Inside the room?" Sergeant Briggs scrunched his brow. "There was the doctor and the general, miss. I didn't pay too close attention to what the doctor was doing. When they get out the needle and thread, I prefer to focus elsewhere."

Without thinking about it, Grace raised a hand to the scar on her neck. Though it no longer pained her, she still recalled the way her stomach had roiled when the needle and thread were meant for her. In the sergeant's shoes, she would have also looked elsewhere. Unfortunately, that left open the possibility that Major General Sinclair had taken advantage of his accident to pass the codebook to someone else. If that were the case... Grace shut down that line of thought. It was defeatist at best. Even if the codebook was gone, they still had to prove Sinclair was responsible.

Sergeant Briggs stood and bade her farewell. Grace lingered for a moment longer, wanting to gather her thoughts before she spoke with the baron.

The master of the household had explained that the baron was there to oversee a donation to the local library. His name was vaguely familiar to Grace, but his field of expertise remained out of reach. From that, she could only surmise that he must be someone her brother Felix had studied, but he was not an expert in a field that held her interest.

Of course, none of that helped her with her preparation for speaking with him now. If Roland were there, he would accuse her of dragging her heels—and rightfully so. Grace forced herself to get up from the wooden bench and wound her way around the pavilion entrance. Once again, the footman stood ready to do her bidding.

"I'll need Baron Langley, if you please. I can find my way to the parlour. Oh, and might you send in a tea tray after you fetch the baron?" she added.

The footman executed a bow of understanding and strode off.

Thus, Grace found herself standing alone in the corridor of the royal pavilion. As she glanced around at the priceless antiques, pale silken wallpaper, and thick carpet runner on the wooden floor, she suddenly felt out of her depth. Yet, the sense of being overwhelmed subsided just as quickly, replaced by a rising feeling of adventure. She was in the royal pavilion on her own.

Before wiser judgement set in, she tiptoed along the hallway to the nearest room, intending to peek inside. She took only a few steps before she drew up short. Was this how the murderer did it? Had he slunk along this same hallway until he reached Sir Julian's bedchamber?

The thought was enough to put a permanent damper on

Grace's enthusiasm. She picked up her pace and hurried along to the small parlour before anyone caught her wandering around.

A guard stepped into the room and took up a silent watch against the wall next to the door. A maid bearing the promised tea tray arrived at the same time as the baron. Grace took on the role of mother, pouring a cup of tea for both herself and the baron, and then offered the old man his choice from a plate of sugared biscuits. The baron's white hair and wrinkles reminded Grace of Roland's grandfather. Though the two men moved with a deliberate slowness, she would be a fool to underestimate them.

After a round of pleasantries and a biscuit each, Baron Langley skipped to the point. "I have no intention of discounting your intellect, Lady Grace, nor of questioning your fitness for this task."

Grace was so off guard, she choked on a bite of biscuit and had to cough several times to dislodge it. She waved the guard back into his place and took a gulp of tea to set herself back to rights. "I feel I must say thank you for your confidence, but can I ask why you have so much faith in me? We are barely acquaintances."

"That is true, but I know Queen Charlotte well. Prinny says she thinks highly of you, and that is sufficient for me. I am no expert on military matters, and had little contact with Sir Julian, other than across a dinner table. I had no reason to want the man dead, but I suppose the others will say the same. For this reason, I do not envy you this task."

"It is certainly far from simple or straightforward," Grace admitted. Saying the words aloud put her task in perspective. It was highly unlikely that a single conversation would produce the answer to this riddle. She had to puzzle it out, piece by piece, and now she sat with someone who appreciated the difficulty she faced. For no other reason, Grace found herself liking the baron. He showed none of the ill intent of Lady Waddington, the dismissiveness of Sinclair, or the cattiness of Lord Blackwood.

And so Grace allowed herself to relax her guard, just a little. "Baron Langley, if you do not mind, will you indulge my curiosity and tell me about yourself?"

"I have little else to occupy me, given we are not allowed to set foot outside the pavilion grounds," the man replied. "Where would you like me to begin?"

"I've been informed of your reputation as a distinguished scholar, but I haven't been told your specific field of study."

"Ahh." The man leaned back to recline against the back of his chair. He crossed his hands over his stomach and got comfortable. "I share the king's love of astronomy. In our younger days, we would peer at the sky through his telescope to track the movement of the heavens. I still recall hearing the news that the scientists had discovered a seventh planet. Magnificent!"

The man's passion shone through in his every word, enough that even Earth-minded Grace experienced a certain sense of intrigue. But looking at the stars would not bring her any closer to identifying a murderer on the ground beside them. Eventually, Grace intervened to bring the discussion back to the present.

"The Master of the House said you are here to oversee a donation to the local library. Is that correct?"

"Yes, I brought along a chest full of books from my own collection. I felt they would be put to better use here than in London."

"Why is that?" Grace asked as she topped up their teacups.

"They are on the topic of celestial navigation and usage of

the chronometer. They will be of great interest to any aspiring sailors."

At that, Grace perked up. "Sailing? Do you know many sailors? I imagine you must have consulted a fair few to develop your texts."

"I prefer to stay on land, my lady. I did not need to set out on a long sea journey in order to gather information. The stars are the same all over. It is merely our position with reference to them that changes."

"Still, I am surprised King George did not invite you to speak with members of the Royal Navy."

"He did, years ago, when I was a much younger lad. There have been few advancements in technology since then. To reliably calculate one's position when at sea, you need a very specific, and very precise timepiece called a chronometer. They are, unfortunately, also extremely expensive and thus available sparingly, at best."

Grace did not know enough about the topic to judge whether he was telling the full truth. However, she believed it was significant enough to later share with Roland. If the baron had access to one of the chronometers, might that be reason enough for a sailing captain to do him the favour of transporting a valuable, stolen codebook? It was a stretch, but not impossible.

For that reason, Grace chose to turn the conversation toward the most important question. "I apologise, but I must ask about your movements yesterday evening."

Baron Langley's face shifted into a bemused expression. "Rather boring, I am afraid. I stayed up late discoursing with Lord Blackwood. He has invested in a trading company and wanted my opinion as to the possibility of making the sea voyages less dangerous. We had a lengthy discussion of the chronometer, weather patterns, military protection... Well, several things, as you can see. He proved to be a surprisingly good student and time got away from us. I went straight to bed when I noticed how late it was, and did not rise again until roused this morning by the guards."

"Shortly thereafter, we encountered one another in the saloon," Grace added. She cast her mind back to the morning, remembering again how the guests had split into different parts of the spacious room. "Is that why you and Lord Blackwood were standing together this morning?"

"Yes. He wished to return to our discussions, but I was tired and out of sorts."

"That is understandable. I do not suppose you noted anything about the others' reactions to being roused from bed?"

"Blackwood, I have told you about. Lord Ravenscroft seemed wide awake, enough so that I wondered whether he had gone to bed at all."

Grace filed that away and then asked about the last guest who had been in the saloon. "Lady Waddington was certainly out of sorts when I made my appearance. How had she been prior to my arrival?"

Baron Langley tilted his head to the side and rubbed his chin. He stared off into the distance, seeing into the past rather than the artwork hanging on the wall. "She was very fidgety, I would say. She fluttered from one part of the room to another, tossing glances at the guarded doorway. Lord Ravenscroft eventually invited her to sit on the divan in order to make her settle."

"Do you have any guess why she acted so strangely?"

"I may be an expert in some fields, but the ways of women is not one of them. Mayhap she was simply nervous about the identity of the victim. Or, she might have seen something but did not dare speak up." The baron shook his white-haired head. "You will have to ask her yourself. Is there anything else you need from me?"

Grace had run out of questions, at least those for the baron to answer. She bid him good day and sat back in her chair. She expected Roland to be along soon enough, and in the meantime, she put her thoughts in order. But before she could get too far with that plan, the footman returned with an invitation to join Lord Percy and the Prince Regent for a discussion.

11

Grace seemed hale and even-tempered when she was escorted into the room by the guard. Roland met her eyes briefly to confirm that she was all right, but only briefly, so as not to be rude to the Prince Regent.

"Lady Grace," the Prince Regent greeted her. "Roland was telling me how he believes my little songbird, Lord Ravenscroft, is the guilty party."

Grace turned his way, and Roland explained, "He is an informant at the very least, and a spy at the worst. General Sinclair does not trust him."

"I should think Major General Sinclair's word would not have much sway," Grace said to both men. "Did Roland yet tell you of what we found in the General's room?"

Prinny frowned at her. "No, he did not. To be fair to Lord Percy, however, he arrived only a few moments ago."

"In Sinclair's room, we found a vial that had been used to store powdered opium," Roland told Prinny. "You may remember that we suspected Sir Julian had been dosed. Opium would have worked much the same as laudanum. Perhaps it would have worked better, for it would take longer to take effect, making it harder to trace the source. At least the good news is that we believe the proverbial fox has been ensnared in our trap. Whoever the murderer is, he or she is most likely still inside the pavilion."

"I am finding it difficult to believe there is a silver lining in that deduction, but I assume you mean to explain."

"While it is uncomfortable to think the murder might be here, the odds are good that if we have trapped the murderer before he could slip away, Sapphire is also still here on the premises."

"I take your meaning, then. Are you certain?"

Grace extended her hand slightly to catch Roland's attention before he could continue. "The murderer is here, but I must confess that there is a small chance Sapphire is not. I confirmed that General Sinclair has left the premises today. General Sinclair cut his hand sufficiently to warrant immediate attention. Before I spoke with Baron Langley, I conversed with the guard who escorted General Sinclair to the surgery, and he confirmed the story."

Roland shook his head, rubbing his temple slightly. "Then if Sinclair was guilty, he could have smuggled Sapphire out and then returned. Perhaps he cut his hand on purpose."

"Let me be certain I understand. General Sinclair not only left the pavilion when everyone was under orders to remain here, but you also found the nearest thing to a murder weapon in his room? Yet you thought Lord Ravenscroft the more likely villain?" Prinny scowled at Roland.

Pausing to collect his thoughts, Roland considered the gut instinct about Sinclair. "To be certain," he began, "Sinclair had the better motivation to act against Sir Julian. However, I do not sense that he possesses a strong motivation to act against his country. I may be wrong, but I feel like the true crime was intended to be the theft of Sapphire. In that case, Sir Julian's death would be best served as a distraction. Lord Ravenscroft has business and familial ties to France, and if the theft of Sapphire was to serve Napoleon, I would look to him first."

Prinny settled back into his chair, looking most displeased. "And who do you think is the guilty party, Lady Grace? For as I understand it, you were the one who pointed her finger at Lady Fitzroy from the beginning, during the ambassador's debacle."

She glanced at Roland and then back at the Prince Regent. "I confess, Your Highness, I was not present for Lord Ravenscroft's questioning, but I am not convinced that General Sinclair is not the guilty party. He could have left the vial in his own room to be discovered on purpose so that we might assume someone else left it there, and then returned to the pavilion to help with the impression of his trustworthiness. Lord Percy does, however, have a point in that we do not know what would motivate him against England. There might still be more to be found."

"Who else did you speak with today?" Prinny asked. "You made mention of Baron Langley. Is he a suspect, too?"

"I find it unlikely, Your Highness," Grace conceded. "Although if Lord Percy is correct, we cannot fully discount the man. He has connections to sailors who may be able to smuggle Sapphire to France, but that is the only real evidence against him."

The slap of the Prince Regent's hand on the wooden surface of his desk made Grace jump, even though she had been looking his way. To her credit, she did not cower, but her skirts trembled ever so slightly. Roland edged closer to her to show Prinny that, even if they disagreed, they were not at odds with one another.

There was a long silence while the angry Prince Regent turned his face away from them and considered the window. His face was ruddy with displeasure, so both Roland and Grace scarcely breathed. Finally, Prinny shouted loud enough for the footman outside the door to hear him. "Bring me more wine! And send for the steward!"

Prinny took several large breaths in an attempt to bring his emotions back into order. "This..." the Prince Regent said, gesturing about him, "is intolerable. A whole day gone, and we have not even interviewed all the guests. I cannot hold everyone here forever, and I have already cancelled one event. The gentle lords and ladies are already quietly speculating. By tomorrow, if I cannot release my guests and return to normalcy, there will be a froth of gossip that makes your engagement pleasant by comparison."

A knock at the door sounded, and the guard opened it to admit the steward with the wine. "You sent for me, Your Highness?"

"I know the hour is running late, but have dinner prepared for our unexpected guests and arrange for more entertainment," Prinny ground out. "They will all be staying another evening. You may pour, and leave the bottle, then summon the head of the guard for us. That will be all."

The steward bowed and hastily left, while Prinny lifted his glass and took two long swallows, waiting for the head of the guard to arrive.

Since the Prince Regent was ignoring them but had not dismissed them, Roland chanced a look at Grace, who had stopped trembling but now simply looked troubled. Glad that she was recovering her composure, Roland wondered how long they were destined to always be at the whims of capricious royalty—and his grandfather.

Prinny left them standing until he had conveyed directions to the head of the guard for managing one more day of detaining the guests, and then he finally turned his attention back to the pair of them.

"I expect far more significant progress to be made before the end of tomorrow. You are dismissed," he said coldly.

"Your Highness," both murmured, issuing their appropriate obeisance and backing towards the door.

In the hall, Roland finally took Grace's arm, just savouring a moment of stillness before he began leading her towards the room set aside for them. "Come, we must put our heads together and determine a course of action."

"Yes," she agreed. "I wish to learn the rest of what happened in your interview with Lord Ravenscroft."

Roland did not answer her until they closed the door behind themselves. "He was quite uncouth, leaving me with few regrets about excluding you from the experience. Among other things, he badgered me with a tale about how he had to spend the evening alone because Lady Waddington was too nervous to succumb to his charms."

Grace turned sharply to Roland at that. "He said Lady Waddington was nervous? For Baron Langley also commented on the same thing."

"Well, we need to finish our inquiry with the others at any rate. We can begin with her and conduct one final questioning before people head to dinner. Perhaps we will strike a lucky break."

She nodded her head, and Roland headed for the door to ask a footman to send for Lady Waddington. Quickly, he returned and cupped the side of her face, stroking her cheek lightly with his thumb. "How are you faring? Are you all right, and able for another trying interview? I saw you shaking when Prinny got angry, and I cannot imagine Lady Waddington will be more pleasant to talk with."

She relaxed into his touch with a gentle smile. "I am fine. His temper is very similar to his mother's. He only startled me with his display—that is something I cannot see the queen doing. Lady Waddington can hardly be more frightening than the royal family."

"It has been a rather trying day between Prinny and my grandfather," Roland admitted. "I dislike the idea of someone else imposing more unpleasant behaviour on you today, so I will do what I can to take the brunt of it. At least, with Lady Waddington questioned, tomorrow's load will be lighter. Let us hope we solve the case quickly so that we are not caught in a war on two fronts, between Prinny and the duke. I would like to enjoy our leisure time in Brighton some."

If Grace was about to respond, her words were cut off by the knock at the door heralding the footman's return. Roland took his hand away from Grace's cheek, grazing it softly with his fingertips before dropping his hand entirely. "Come in," he called out, raising his voice slightly.

But when the footman opened the door, he stood alone. "Unfortunately, Lady Waddington is suffering from a case of the vapours. She retired to her room immediately after tea."

"I see," Roland acknowledged slowly. "Then we have no choice but to wait until tomorrow. We will adjourn for the evening, and if anything significant occurs, you can send for me."

Grace followed as they were escorted to the front door. On the path, she settled her hand upon his arm again as they walked back through the contingent of guards.

"Perhaps Lady Waddington having the vapours was for the best," Roland reassured her, for she looked a little drawn and pale.

Grace shook her head. "I would have sooner had it done with. The longer we take to find the trail, the better the chances for the murderer's escape."

12

In her bedroom at the Tilbury's summer residence, Grace and Elsie eyed the contents of her wardrobe with matching expressions of dismay. Despite the wide array of new summer walking dresses, Grace found nothing she deemed appropriate to wear to question a lady of the court. It was not for lack of expense, for her mama had spared none once she learned of Roland's interest in her daughter.

"You say this woman is a friend of Lady Fitzroy?" Elsie asked.

"I am not sure I would go so far as to pronounce them friends. I doubt Lady Fitzroy trusts anyone enough to let them truly grow close. Mama said, however, they are cut from the same cloth, and that does seem to be true enough. Lady Waddington thus far has treated me with cold shoulders and sneers of derision."

Elsie shivered at Grace's description. "She sounds terrible, miss. Perhaps you should allow Lord Percy to be the one to speak with her."

"If I thought he would get any farther with the woman, I

would. However, he would have to tread gently, lest he risk her claiming the vapours or collapsing into a puddle of tears. He could not force her to speak without being called ungentlemanly." Grace crossed her arms over her chest. "No, it must be me. I will do my best impersonation of Queen Charlotte, and hopefully just like with the queen, Lady Waddington is afraid to raise my ire."

Elsie looked askance. "The queen? Can I make a suggestion?" She waited until Grace nodded permission. "Might it be easier to act like Lady Charity instead? You do a remarkable impersonation of her. When you showed me how she faced down Lady Fitzroy on the night of her rescue, I could have sworn you were Lady Charity herself. And if she said and did all you showed, then she is a strong character, indeed."

Grace had to concede that Elsie's suggestion was a good one. It would take little effort for Grace to don Charity's persona, and it certainly gave her a fresh idea of how to carry herself. She stepped forward and rifled through the gowns hanging in her wardrobe. A lawn green gown of light muslin caught her eye. The hand-stitched embroidery spoke to the cost of the garment, and it was at the height of fashion.

She pulled it free and moved so she saw her reflection in the mirror. The colour brought out the golden strands in her hair and green flecks in her hazel eyes. It lacked the high lace collar of her other gowns. She pondered for a moment and then asked, "Did you pack my emerald velvet ribbon?"

Elsie met her gaze in the mirror. "I did, along with your spencer in the same shade. It's not too warm today. If you keep it on, none will be the wiser about your scar." Without waiting for a reply, Elsie set to work retrieving the various items. Once Grace was dressed, she turned her attention to Grace's hair. "If it's not too forward of me, can I ask if you've had any word from Lady Charity? She was always so kind to me."

"Of course you may ask!" Grace replied, glancing at her maid over her shoulder. She considered Roland's relationship with Thorne and followed his example. "Elsie, you are more to me than my lady's maid. You alone will come with me when I marry. I already depend on you for so much, and I cannot imagine that will change with time. If we cannot speak openly with one another, it would be a great shame and do us both a disservice. Please, do not hold your tongue around me."

Elsie flushed with pleasure and blinked a few times until she got hold of her emotions. "Thank you, miss. I cannot tell you how much it means to me that you hold me in such high regard. It is somewhat daunting to think of moving into a new household."

Grace turned around on her stool to look Elsie in the eye. "Most of Lord Percy's staff is rather new in their service as well. I think they will welcome you with open arms. In fact, Mr Thorne said you are welcome to visit them while we are here. He and the rest of Lord Percy's household are staying in a cottage. They brought the Sprouts along and are attempting to fill the gaps in the children's education."

Elsie beamed and said she would go at the first opportunity. With that agreed, Grace returned to Elsie's original question. "But back to your question... Charity sent me a letter last week. She is now the Duchess of Strathclyde. We shall both have to call her 'Your Grace' from now on."

"I cannot imagine the missus making you stand on such ceremony."

"Me either, and that is why it will be so much fun to do so." Grace smiled mischievously as she shifted back into position so that Elsie could finish her hair. "She said the wedding was small, with only immediate family, but her new husband is kind to her. He has only one heir, a young son whose mother did not survive the birth, so she has her hands full getting acquainted with him before he goes off to school. Her only discordant note was a mention of Lord Fitzroy."

Elsie nearly dropped the hairbrush at the mention of the family name. "Lord Fitzroy?"

"It seems he sent her a letter."

"And? What did it say?"

Grace pursed her lips and shook her head. "She did not say. I do not know if she even opened it or if she burned it unread. I suppose there is the possibility he is not as bad as his mother. But still, I do not entirely trust him."

Elsie voiced her agreement and then pronounced Grace ready for the day.

One notable advantage to being in Brighton was that Grace's mother had relented enough to allow Grace to ride alone in the family carriage. With such short distances to cover between their home and the royal pavilion, there was little chance of Grace's reputation getting damaged. After Grantham helped Grace into the family carriage, he climbed into the driver's seat and picked up the reins.

The brief ride barely gave Grace time to adopt the persona she needed to face Lady Waddington. She started from the moment she descended from the carriage, by squaring her shoulders, lifting her chin, and striding forward with a determined expression on her face. The guards recognised her from the day before and waved her past without stopping. She found the footman standing ready to assist her once again.

"I would like to see Lady Waddington," she pronounced in her most serene tone.

"Her ladyship has yet to make an appearance. I can inquire how long she will need to dress and ready herself, if you would like."

Grace considered his offer and then brushed it aside. "Take me to her room."

The footman raised his eyebrows but did not question her unorthodox choice to call upon someone in their bedchamber. These were far from normal times. He smoothed his surprise into a smile of obeisance and led Grace to the upper floor guest chambers. "This is her room."

Grace glanced along the corridor, noting the rooms lining either side of the hall. This was the first time she had passed through this area, and she realised she did not know whose room was which, nor even which room had belonged to Sir Julian. "How are the rooms assigned?"

"Lords Ravenscroft and Blackwood are at the end of the hallway. Lady Waddington is next to Lord Blackwood, with Major General Sinclair across from her. Finally, a little further up ahead, we have Baron Langley's room, and the room Sir Julian was using." The footman added, "There aren't near as many guest rooms here as in the palace. This is in part why the Prince Regent is intent on expanding the house."

"Thank you. I will announce myself, but would you please remain here outside the door? Lord Percy does not want me questioning anyone without a guard of some sort present."

The footman took up his post beside the door, standing perfectly straight and staring at a blank space on the opposite wall. He was the perfect servant, available at a moment's notice but invisible until she had need.

Grace took a deep breath, rapped once on the door, and then brazened her way into the room.

Lady Waddington sat, fully dressed, on an elegantly carved chair next to the window. She jerked back in shock at Grace's sudden appearance and lifted a hand to her chest. "I beg your pardon!"

"Please, Lady Waddington, we are both aware this is not a social call. I thought to do you a favour by conducting my questioning in the privacy of your room. If you would prefer we move to the saloon—"

The lady narrowed her gaze and waved Grace forward. "There is little point in going anywhere else, for it only drives home the fact that we are imprisoned. Why Prinny has turned this into a game with you and Lord Percy as hunters is beyond me."

Grace did not let the woman's pointed words get to her. Instead, she replied as she believed Charity would have done. "Most people would cherish the opportunity to remain in close company with the Prince Regent. I find it odd that you do not. Is that because you harbour some guilt?"

Lady Waddington huffed in annoyance, but Grace did not miss the way her face had paled at the word "guilt." She had scored a hit, even if she did not yet know the woman's crime.

Again, without asking permission, Grace entered deeper into the room after taking care to leave the door ajar. She chose the chair opposite Lady Waddington and perched on it, keeping her spine stiff. She would not relax an inch.

"Please detail your movements on the night of Sir Julian's death."

Lady Waddington's nostrils flared, but she did as ordered. "I turned in immediately after the other guests departed. My lady's maid can verify this."

Grace was all too aware of how far a lady's maid would go to cover for her employer. "Did she remain in your room all night? If so, I will need to verify this with her roommate. Give me her name so I might send for her."

Lady Waddington stilled. "She did not sleep here. There is no space for her, and I had no need of her until morning."

Grace arched one eyebrow. "I suppose you will claim you never left your room."

"Of course I did not leave my room! Where would I go in the middle of the night?"

Grace let her question hang in the air until Lady Waddington shifted uncomfortably in her chair.

Sensing she had the advantage, Grace leaned forward and met the woman's gaze head on. "Several people have commented on your strange behaviour on the morning of Sir Julian's demise. Words like 'nervous' and 'guilty' were used more than once. The Prince Regent has been informed."

Lady Waddington swayed in her seat, and Grace feared she might swoon. But she got hold of herself by gripping onto the armrests for dear life. She took a minute to gain control over her emotions and then struck out like a wounded animal trapped in a corner.

"How dare you! Inform the Prince Regent that I am a lone woman here, dependent on his goodwill and protection. I have been a guest in many fine households without a hint of trouble. The identity of this murderer will be found elsewhere. Lord Danforth has been particularly on edge recently. Perhaps he is hiding something. Or Baron Langley—the man bored us all to tears over tea, prattling on about ships and long voyages. He could be planning his escape, even now, while you waste time questioning me."

Grace lowered her voice and hardened her tone. "That is where you are mistaken, for no one is leaving here until this mystery is solved."

With that, Grace rose from her chair and swept from the room. She marched to the far end of the corridor, to where a picture window allowed in sunlight. She grabbed onto the window ledge with her shaking hands and dragged air into her lungs. She had never thought herself afraid, and it was not fear that caused her to tremble. Instead, her stomach roiled with the thought that the woman hated her, simply because she had caught the eye of a future duke.

Charity could have high society and all of its power games. As soon as she and Roland were free from this burden, Grace promised herself they would leave London behind for a long time.

13

A polite cough from the footman recalled Grace to the present. She turned around and checked the time on a nearby clock. Roland was due to arrive at any moment. Before he did, she wanted to bring the question of Lady Waddington's strange behaviour to a close.

The footman still stood at his post. Grace approached him. "I presume you are familiar with Lady Waddington's maid?"

"I am," he confirmed.

"Could you please question her about Lady Waddington's activities on the night of the murder—what time she returned to her room, how long the maid remained, and that sort of thing? Once that is done, please double-check the timings with whichever servant is sharing quarters with the maid."

"Consider it done. I will provide a full update on what I learn. Where would my lady like to go in the meantime?"

"If the parlour is still available, I will go there to wait until Lord Percy arrives."

The footman escorted Grace to the aforementioned room and left her to her bidding. She barely had time to get comfortable before Roland joined her. She rose from her seat and offered him her hand. He bent over and brushed a kiss against her knuckles, and she smiled at him.

"Was your morning productive?" he asked after he took a seat on the settee beside her.

"Unfortunately not. I have no grounds to assume the woman was implicated in the murder or the theft, as I could not identify any motive. But she is hiding something. I would like to unmask her secrets, if for no other reason than to buy us protection from her poisoned tongue."

"Then we should continue with our final two suspects. I asked a guard to send a request to Lord Danforth." Roland stopped at the sound of a knock on the door.

Lord Danforth pushed the partially closed door open and came inside, his face wary. "It appears to be my turn to stand before the great inquisitors."

"Please, my lord, take a seat," Grace answered, waving him forward. She had not crossed paths with him since the first morning in the library, when he argued to Prinny that he should be the one to lead the search for the murderer and the missing codebook. Then, he had been quite dismissive of Grace and Roland both. Today, he seemed slightly more willing to cooperate. She hoped his open attitude continued.

Lord Danforth availed himself of a wingback chair and settled onto its cushioned seat. "Let us dispense with the necessities so that I might see how I can better be of use to you. On the night of Sir Julian's death, I stayed up late reviewing tax and tariff proposals in the Prince's study."

"Was the Prince Regent with you?"

"Prinny?" Lord Danforth chuckled as though Grace had told a joke. "I would say not. The Prince Regent has many fine qualities, but when it comes to dense legal documents, he defers to my expertise."

Grace chanced a look in Roland's direction, but his expression remained unchanged.

"How long were you occupied with your task?" Roland asked. "Do you often peruse important papers so late at night, particularly after attending an event?"

"Yes. I am a night owl. What can I say?" Lord Danforth cracked a small smile, but Grace could not help but note the way his left leg jiggled up and down. Before she could do more than glance at his leg, the man crossed it over his knee and relaxed deeper into his chair.

"And someone can vouch for your presence there?" Roland pressed again.

Danforth nodded. "Not in the room with me, of course, but there were footmen out in the halls. I told them I knew where to find them if I needed their assistance, and I called upon one of them once for some refreshment. Paperwork, I know, is not the most exciting way to spend the evening, but it has its... rewards."

She could well imagine.

"Now that we have dispensed with the necessity of checking my alibi, perhaps we can discuss how I can best be of assistance to you. Do you have any questions for our guests you would like to pose? Information to verify?"

Grace sensed Roland's shift beside her. Unlike Danforth, Roland sat up taller. "Thank you, but we are fine on our own."

Lord Danforth's smile grew slightly strained and wheedling. "Are you quite sure? While I do not want to impose myself where I am not wanted... well, I shall come out and say it. We are all being driven lunatic, cooped up like this. Personally, I would welcome any busywork to keep me occupied. And if you are concerned Sinclair will find out, you have nothing to fear from his swagger."

"I am afraid I do not understand what you mean," Roland

replied in a serious tone. "Has Sinclair made some threat towards me? Or Lady Grace?"

"Not to me—though the man does have a reputation for making threats. You must have heard of his rather awkward encounter with Sir Julian."

Grace considered this. "We heard that Sir Julian chastised him for acting outside his purview, but there was no mention of a threat."

"I happened to be standing in the stables when Sinclair came out. He must not have seen me there, for he muttered black words while he saddled his horse. I only caught some of them, but his fury was evident. I am certain he said something about showing the man. It has occurred to me... perhaps Sinclair could have invented a tale of the missing codebook in order to divert suspicion from a more mundane motive for murder. Or perhaps something more sinister."

Grace rocked back, and even Roland seemed surprised. He recovered first. "You do not believe that the codebook is genuinely missing? Why did you not say this in front of the Prince Regent yesterday morning?"

Danforth shrugged his shoulders. "I am saying that there is a slim chance there was never a codebook in Sir Julian's possession at all. I have had a night to ponder the unpleasant fact that the only proof we have that a codebook was stolen is Sinclair telling us it was gone."

Roland exchanged a furrowed look with Grace. "Knowing what I do of communications, there was an excellent chance such an object would have been entrusted to Sir Julian."

"It does seem logical—and even plausible," Danforth admitted. "That is why everyone is on the hunt for it. I only point out that it is suspicious that no one else in this building would know for certain it was here. Certainly the regent would not have known for sure if he brought it with him. I am quite fond of the prince, but such details are beneath him. Mind you, perhaps Sinclair is right; there is a book here. What if his only motivation for informing everyone is so that we can locate it for him?"

"That is some interesting fodder for thought," Roland sighed heavily. "While it is not ideal by any means, if it is true, at least prized military intelligence would not currently be at risk of falling into enemy hands. But another possible theory is all that it is. We have no more proof that you are correct in your guesses than we have in Sinclair's word."

Danforth looked like he was trying to bite his tongue. "I am aware I am a stranger to you—but Prinny trusts me implicitly to guide him on matters of the court. You barely know these people, but I have spent years with them. You are wasting time, Lord Percy. We are prisoners here, gilded cage or no. Do you think we are enjoying ourselves, treading on eggshells around Sinclair, who is prone to fits of rage and may have murdered one of our number?"

Grace did not like Lord Danforth's change in tone. She shifted, and Roland touched her gently with his hand, staying her objections.

"Lord Danforth, I do not doubt that the Prince Regent values your advice, and the truth is that we may yet come to find your assistance invaluable as well, but we have to do what we must to eliminate certain avenues of investigation first. I am sorry. Hopefully we are able to let you resume your normal duties soon."

With a stiff nod, Danforth relented, but he looked unhappy.

"Can you recall which footman served you? Perhaps a description so that we can more easily find him?"

"He looked like a servant. He wore a servant's uniform.

Beyond that, I have no earthly idea. I had no reason to take too close a look at him," Danforth said crossly, waving his hand in frustration. He uncrossed his legs and stood abruptly. "If there is nothing more, I wish to go to my room where I might be safe." Lord Danforth paused, waiting. When they did not stop him, he did an about-face and marched out of the room, with his hands balled into fists at his sides.

"That... did not go any better than our other interviews," Roland muttered, coaxing a groan of agreement from Grace. "I cannot blame the man for being frustrated at this confinement, but I get the oddest sense he is angrier because Prinny assigned you and me, of all people, to lead this task."

Grace thought for a moment before replying. "Fear that we might usurp his position of favour?"

"Potentially. At least we have something to verify. Remind me to speak to the footman about Danforth's late night."

"We can also ask Prinny if he had asked Lord Danforth to look into any documents, or was expecting an update on anything. As for Danforth's comment about the Major General, that was hardly anything new."

"True, but the idea that we are being sent, in all ignorance, to hunt for something is a bloody good one. Let us see what Lord Blackwood has to say on matters. After that, we can determine what we will say to Prinny about our progress." Roland threaded his fingers together and stretched his arms in front of himself, gearing up for the next round. "Pray it is progress we will have to report, and not another day of vague suppositions and little hard evidence."

Grace called for the guard standing watch outside their parlour to send for Lord Blackwood. The courtier must have been expecting their request to speak with him, for he arrived in record time. He swanned into the room and fawned over Grace before nodding a greeting at Roland.

When Lord Blackwood eventually flopped down in a chair, Roland found himself in poor humour. He supposed he should be pleased that anyone in court was treating Grace well. But there was something about the man's manner that made Roland suspect it was all a pretence. Or perhaps calling it playacting would be more accurate. It was as though Blackwood had adopted a persona on his first day in court, and it was now such a part of him that even he did not know where it ended.

As much as this annoyed Roland, it also made Blackwood a formidable opponent. Roland would have to keep a watchful eye on the man if he wanted to catch any hints of what he truly felt and thought. For that reason, Roland gave Grace a gentle nudge with his elbow to encourage her to start the discussions.

"Thank you for speaking with us," Grace said in opening.

"I am flattered that you saved me for last." Blackwood winked at Grace. "I assume this means I am at the bottom of your list. Since you spoke with Baron Langley, you must be aware that I was with him until late in the evening."

"Yes, Baron Langley indicated you spoke at length. For the life of me, I can no longer recall the topic. What was it again?"

"Sea travel, I am afraid. Dreadfully boring to anyone not actively engaged on the subject." Blackwood shrugged in apology.

"And yet, the baron said you spoke at length. He was quite complimentary toward you. Said you made for a good student."

Blackwood shifted forward in his chair and lowered his voice into a husky tone. He stared at Grace through a lidded gaze. "With proper motivation, I can excel in anything."

Grace blushed furiously, just as the man had intended. Roland tamped down on his desire to box the other man's ears, no matter how much he deserved it. Instead, he took the reins of the conversation.

Roland rocked forward, blocking Blackwood's view of Grace. "What motivation do you have to learn about sea travel? Are you planning a trip soon? Perhaps one to the continent?"

Blackwood's smile dipped. "Why would I want to sail into the arms of our enemies?"

"Uncertain times can make strange bedfellows," Roland retorted. He sharpened his gaze until Blackwood flinched.

"Not that it is relevant or any of your business, but I am interested in the Far East. There are still many fortunes to be made in those lands—but only if one can bring their goods safely into an English port. I have invested in a new venture and am keen to see it be profitable. I am hoping Prinny will see fit to offer a military escort to ensure the start of said journeys is safe."

"Do you have any proof of this investment? The name and contact of your business manager or banker?" Roland flashed a toothy smile that dripped with more bite than welcome. "We must verify everything. I am sure you understand."

"I will provide his details this afternoon. Was there anything else you required?"

"One last thing," Grace said. She laid her gloved hand on Roland's arm to coax him back. "After the talk with Baron Langley, where did you go?"

Blackwood's expression twisted into something, but he gained control over it before Roland could identify the emotion. "I returned to my quarters and did not come out again until morning. Now, I should see about getting that information for you. If you will excuse me."

Roland waved him on, happy enough to see the man's back departing the room. Between Ravenscroft's crude talk and Blackwood's innuendos, he was desperate for a walk in the fresh sea air.

Before they could consider stepping outside, however, there remained the matter of speaking with the Prince Regent. As if materialised from thin air, the guard stepped into the parlour and cleared his throat.

"His Highness would like to see you both now. Follow me, please."

14

When the guards admitted them to the Prince Regent's plush sitting room, Roland and Grace abruptly halted inside the entryway.

It was expected to pause just inside a doorway to acknowledge Prinny. But neither had expected Gideon Percy, Roland's grandfather, to be seated in an armchair to one side of Prinny's rather grand sofa.

"Approach," Prinny said gruffly, waving one ring-bejewelled hand impatiently.

Stiffly, Roland and Grace did so, making their greetings to both Prinny and then the Duke of Northumberland as they stood in front of His Highness. There was no extra seating, and at any rate, neither of their betters looked inclined to invite them to get comfortable.

Prinny did not speak immediately, looking even more displeased than when they had seen him last. Roland waited with his hands loosely at his sides, fighting the urge to clench his fists.

"Have you identified the guilty party?" the Prince Regent

finally asked them by way of greeting. There was no give in his tone whatsoever.

Grace and Roland exchanged a glance and then looked at the Breaker, who betrayed no surprise at Prinny's statement. Whatever the reason for his presence, it seemed that somehow he had been made aware of their investigation.

"We only just finished speaking with the last two lords," Roland ventured, uncertain whether their future king would welcome Roland discussing names and crimes in front of the duke.

The prince looked down his nose. "Then you have questioned everyone. Form an opinion, Lord Percy. Since I can see you hesitating to ask, you may speak freely in front of your grandfather—on the subject of the murder." But not about the missing codebook was implicit and unsaid.

Roland spread his hands in apology and confessed they were not prepared to point a finger at the killer. "Though we have spoken with everyone, I must remind you, Your Highness, that we have not yet had the time to corroborate all of their alibis. Several were acting suspiciously, and no guest was able to conclusively prove their innocence."

"I did not ask who is innocent, but who you suspect the most."

"Then, at the moment, it would be Lord Ravenscroft and the Major General," Roland told him.

"Why is my magpie still sitting on your list?"

"Lord Ravenscroft's heritage cannot be overlooked, and he knew the details of Sir Julian's death."

"And Sinclair?"

"Major General Sinclair is due to motive and... possession of the likely weapon wielded against Sir Julian."

"Do you mean to say that after spending hours looking into this matter, you are no closer than you were when I tasked you with it?" Prinny asked crossly, though clearly he did not expect a reply. The silence in the room was like the quiet after a deafening crack of thunder.

The Breaker lifted his cane and then hammered it down with a bang loud enough to make them all flinch. "I came here expecting an explanation, and instead you called the two of them here. Why? To show me that the rumour is true, and not only that, but they have failed you?"

"Grandfather—" Roland said, but he got no further than that.

The Prince Regent held up a hand to stay Roland, his face a study in complicated fury. "Your grandfather is here because he received a note this morning from someone in the pavilion. A note couched as a choice bit of gossip that you and Lady Grace have been dirtying your hands working like common constables in the investigation of a murder."

Roland sucked in a breath. Suddenly, he understood why Prinny was so properly vexed. At his side, Grace stiffened.

Prinny continued, "As troubling as it was to have an accusation of improper behaviour be sent directly to the duke, there is a more sinister implication. Despite my command to lock down the pavilion, information is being passed to the outside."

He turned to his grandfather. "Did you bring the letter?"

"I burned it upon reading it, lest it be seen by anyone else," the old man growled. He glared fiercely at both the king's heir and his own. He clearly disagreed about which issue was more important, and he opened his mouth to say so.

However, the Prince Regent cut him off. "At minimum, one unsigned note left this house. But if one has passed, it is not unreasonable to assume there might be other attempts at getting information out of the pavilion."

"Do we know how the letter managed to leave the premises undetected?" Roland asked.

"It was added to my pile of correspondence and delivered this morning. The address on the front was similar enough to my handwriting that the footman did not note the lack of the royal seal upon the back."

"Only a letter?" Roland was uncertain how to phrase the real question he wanted to ask with his grandfather there. But Prinny understood the direction of Roland's thoughts.

"Yes. I wrote three letters comprising a single page each yesterday, and there was only one letter—a fourth—that had been added. Anything more substantial would have been enough to stand out and warrant a closer inspection by the guards or servants. And now no further mail will go out without inspection for my own personal seal," the Prince Regent said with a small snarl.

Roland had seen a cipher book before; the codes were complicated enough that it would not consist of a single page. So, they were lucky. Lucky that Sapphire had not been torn into several smaller sections and mailed out. Then again, such a thing likely would have attracted notice and they would have stood a decent chance of intercepting all or even part of it, rendering the theft of the book useless.

The duke, like so many of the more dangerous members of the ton, was not about to let anyone forget his presence—or that he was far from addled. He narrowed his eyes as Roland and the Prince Regent exchanged this short but cryptic conversation. "What are you about, Your Highness? If I were as likely to place a wager as Roland here, I would bet that someone has snatched something right out from under your very nose. Something which you do not want known."

Prinny flickered a glance at the duke but would neither

confirm nor deny it. The duke barked another laugh, and then fixed the Prince Regent with as hard a look as he could without abandoning all civility. "I do not give a fig for stolen baubles, Your Highness. I care for the already vastly damaged reputation of the Percy line. It is bad enough that you try to press my new heir into service like a labourer. Why would you allow this... woman to investigate a crime like a common Bow Street runner?"

"Make no mistake, Your Grace. Despite my father's high opinion of you, I am not in the mood to entertain your questioning past a certain point," Prinny boomed. "All you need to know is that this situation requires both trust and rank to be able to pose questions to gentlemen and gentle ladies. Both have shown themselves capable."

The Breaker backed down, but not with his tail between his legs. "Of course. I apologise for this upset, Your Highness, but given what my family has suffered, surely you see my concern. My son Thaddius's death has already put the line in a precarious position, and my grandson has brought enough tarnish upon his head this year. I am quite unable to understand why you must have both him and his betrothed performing work below their station. Worse! Performing work that poses the risk of danger! If they lack the sense or the backbone to tell you this, then it falls to me to say the words. Lord Percy and Lady Grace are finished working."

"You are overwrought without cause, Northumberland," Prinny said dismissively. "Putting a few questions to a gentleman or lady qualifies as neither work nor a dangerous pursuit."

"Tell that to Sir Julian Montgomery. Instead of gadding about, questioning suspects, Roland should be learning to manage our estate instead of being an embarrassment to me. As for the lady, her only work of import is to spread her legs and continue the family line. That is how a woman serves this nation!"

"Your Grace!" Roland barked as Grace drew herself up beside him, grabbing his arm tightly.

"You have been most... expressive about your fears, but you cannot speak for me, Your Grace," Grace said in a cool voice that belied the whiteness of her knuckles. "I am a loyal subject to the crown, and stand ready to do whatever the prince or the queen asks of me."

"And I, the same," growled Roland.

The Prince Regent nearly gloated at their recognition of his superiority and the duke's eyes narrowed poisonously at the three of them. But then with a dangerous cunning, he charged like a wild boar in a new direction, seeking blood.

"I hear your concerns, Your Highness, so I have a proposition. If you require aid from my family, what if I will offer you another? You may take Thaddius's bastard. He is here, and familiar enough with everyone involved. You have kept him apprised, have you not?' the old man asked Roland. "Not to mention, Mr Thorne is readily available, since you have relieved him of his current duties as your valet and let him enjoy a holiday, Roland."

Roland heard Grace's shocked intake of breath despite the ringing in his ears. He shook his head at his grandfather, desperately wishing he had some way to silence him. The old man smiled again, his face wreathed with an amused malice that said he knew exactly what he was about.

The Duke of Northumberland would not be humiliated by any man or woman. He knew full well that Grace had not known the truth, and had played this card deliberately, in revenge, to sow discord between them.

His voice took on a more respectful tone now that he had neatly set Roland on his back foot. "Thorne would be a far better candidate for muddying his hands with a risky venture. He has no place in society to claim or besmirch, and it would be the highest honour for a man of his status to give his life to safeguard the rightful heir."

Roland's jaw was clenched so tight it hurt, but worse was the unfathomable look that Grace gave him before turning her attention back to regent and the Breaker. "He safeguarded my life for these last ten years, Your Grace," he gritted out."He has earned his honour already."

"You see?" the duke said, raising an eyebrow at the regent. "My grandson's inexplicable softness proves these two are not yet prepared to be ruthless, and that will be a great weakness in a future duke and duchess—let alone in a manhunt for a murderer, Your Highness. Let these two learn to respect the ducal line and gird themselves for the great responsibility of it. You know how sometimes sacrifices must be made."

The regent's eyes shifted, watching the drama playing out around him. "You have made your point clear, Your Grace, but I stand by my choices. Even if Thaddius's illegitimate son—this Thorne—is a most capable man, an unacknowledged bastard does not have sufficient authority to pose questions to the lords of the land."

The Prince Regent straightened in his seat. "Ask more questions. Verify all alibis. Leave no stone unturned. No guest may leave or have any contact with the outside. I will instruct the army to bivouac on the lawns, if I must. Until then, I require your line of descendants to work on my behalf. Include whomever you like. You will do whatever I require until we have a confession. You are all dismissed."

15

Grace immediately sketched a haphazard curtsey and backed out of the room. Roland followed as quickly as he might without being rude to the prince, but even so, he was forced to lengthen his stride to just short of a run.

"Grace. Grace!" he hissed, still reaching for her arm to halt her headlong progress. She did not turn or slow, but at least she was not heading for the front walk; she was headed in the direction of the room that they provided for them to use during their investigation.

Her face flamed when she finally turned to him in privacy. "Were you ever going to tell me the truth about Mr Thorne? That he is your brother?"

"I had planned to," Roland said. "I hoped that Thorne and I might tell you together. But..." he waved his hand, indicating the pavilion. The investigation. "There are reasons I stayed my tongue, I promise. Are you angry with me?"

Grace pressed her fingertips to her temples. "Angry, yes. I am a little angry that you left me ignorant so long that the duke was able to use this knowledge as a weapon against us. I am a little hurt, as well, that both of you seemed to be afraid to trust me with it sooner. But mostly I am angry with myself for being so... so blind that I overlooked all the things that seemed odd and inconsistent and thought nothing more of it." She studied Roland's face, as if internally cataloguing the features they shared. "Is he the older or the younger of the two of you?"

"Younger. By five months," he admitted. "I am so sorry, but it... would have been wrong to tell you his story without his permission. It was most certainly not my grandfather's place to do so. No slight was meant to you, I swear it."

"Not by you, perhaps. Your grandfather seeks to impress his reputation as a frightful old man upon me," she said in a muted voice, looking at her feet, and then she glanced up again. "My temper will pass. I hope you can understand, however, why I wish you had found a moment to tell me sooner."

Weeks had passed since Roland had wanted to pull his hair in frustration, but the urge rose again. "Can you forgive me? I promise I will see you get the full story but—"

"But not without Thorne present. Of course." She gave him a wan smile. "If you will excuse me for a bit, Roland, I—I need to take a short walk to clear my head. We have a murderer yet to catch, no matter what other distractions are there to trip us up. I must return home for luncheon. We can meet again this afternoon to verify the alibis and explore other possibilities."

She left the pavilion without saying a word to anyone else. She did not cross paths with the Breaker, thank goodness. He was sure to make her suffer for her decision to stand up to him, suffer more than by simply airing his family's dirty linen in front of the crown. He would oppose their marriage, or cut Roland's funds if they went ahead without his blessing.

One concern tumbled into the next as Grace left the pavilion grounds and ventured along the pavement. She did not note the faces of anyone she passed, nor even the direction of her steps.

Instead, Grace's mind was travelling farther and farther back in time. She remembered every encounter she had with Thorne, every word that passed through her lips. She could not recall any times in which she had spoken down to him, and yet, she could not help but worry that, through her lack of understanding, she may have mistreated him.

A rush of anger washed over her fears. Even if she had made a mistake, was she truly to blame? She had not known Thorne was Roland's brother. She had not realised it—despite the similarities in their build and hair, their casual manner with one another, that lord and supposed servant shared the dinner table. Once again, she felt the fool for not having seen what was as plain as the nose on her face.

Occupied with recriminations, she did not notice she had walked toward the seashore rather than her home until the damp sea breeze ruffle her hair. She spun around to correct her mistake and stepped into the road. A hoarse shout pulled her attention, but too late. Just in time, she cast a fleeting glance to the side and witnessed a pair of chestnut horses pulling a heavy wooden cart coming towards her. The driver waved for her to move, but her feet refused to obey.

A muscular arm latched around her waist and jerked her back to safety mere seconds before the horses and cart clattered past. A man whispered her name, asking if she was okay. She twisted around, expecting to find Roland's dark eyes, but a pair of bright blue eyes stared back.

"Thorne?" she gasped, unsure whether it was truly him, and if so, if she had somehow conjured him with her thoughts.

"Yes, Lady Grace. Are you unharmed?" He studied her face and must not have liked what he saw, for he guided her to a nearby bench and urged her to take a seat. He sat beside her, taking care to keep an appropriate distance, and murmured for her to take deep, slow breaths.

"I am all right, thanks to your quick thinking. I was so surprised I could not make myself move." Grace, otherwise, did not need to calm her racing heart, for it was not fear she felt, but curiosity. She latched onto his gaze and stared deep into his eyes. Her eyes traced a path from his forehead downward, taking note of every similarity and difference she encountered. Of course, this man was Roland's brother. He shared the same dark hair, although Roland's had a tendency to curl, and was nearly the same in height, though slightly leaner in build. How had she missed seeing this for herself?

For his part, Thorne remained still, his brow creased with confusion. The man was both innocent and not, for he, too, had kept her in the dark, but how could he have done otherwise? She blurted the words out.

"I know."

Thorne's face did not betray any understanding. "You know... who the killer is?"

Grace shook her head. "About you and Roland. The Breaker, he was at the Pavilion, demanding an explanation for why Roland and I are involved in the situation. He offered you up to Prinny in our place, and in doing so, outed your connection to the family."

His complexion grew a shade pale as he made several swift deductions. "You were told I am Thaddius's bastard son," he breathed. "I—I am so sorry, my lady. Let me swear now that I have no intention of making demands of the family. I never have, and never planned to."

She studied him, his honesty naked upon his face. "I believe you, but..."

"But you wonder how an unacknowledged by-blow became the leash used to bring your betrothed to heel. Like a dog," he said, a ghost of his usual humour coming to the forefront, though it was thin.

Grace set his words against what she had been told so obliquely in the past. "You mean to say that somehow the duke threatened Roland through you. Roland spoke of his need to provide for others, and about this being why he was in urgent need of a bride."

Thorne's gaze slid away.

"Somehow, it does not surprise me at all. Not that the duke would do such a thing to his own blood, nor that Roland would feel obligated to make up for his father and grandfather's faults."

"Aye. Our Roland does seem to be a rather singular creature of duty," he agreed dryly. "Thaddius had no use for me, but the Breaker saw me as a tool."

"You feel guilty," Grace observed. "You have been by Roland's side for many years, and even now, it is obvious to all that Roland depends on you greatly. He never explained things, and now I am left with even more questions." Grace threaded her fingers together to give herself strength. "He said this is your story to tell, and not his. So... I would ask you, if you would share it.."

Thorne nodded. "It is both a long story and, in some ways, a very short one. You may know that Thaddius married his own brother's betrothed for money, once the duke's original heir died. He did his duty in getting his wife with child and then returned to his debaucherous ways when she closed her door to him. He forced himself on several servant women, my own mother included. And when I was born, and they saw how I had dark hair so much like my father's and the lady's newly born legitimate son, we were sent away. More than a decade passed before I found out the truth. Eventually, my mother sickened and she was unable to carry on working. And I, with all the unwarranted and foolish, righteous anger of a young man, returned to Northumberland to demand he support her. Us."

He paused, then, to gauge her reaction. To see if she would storm off in disgust like another gently bred lady forced to consider the idea of a man spreading his affections.

Grace, however, did not shift her gaze or flinch. "I assume he refused. But why? And how did Roland come to be involved?"

He fidgeted, which surprised her. In all the brief meetings they had shared, he did not come across as the type. "It went about as poorly as you imagine. I do not know all of Thaddius's reasoning in refusing to support my mother, but some men simply assume it is their right to use their servants as they want, including taking what does not belong to them. At any rate... There was... a bit of a row. And I ended up bleeding and on the floor while Thaddius stood above me, shouting imprecations and threatening to call the magistrate to have me shipped to the colony—if not to swing.

"He planned, you see, to tell them I was there to rob him. You know how the magistrates are likely to punish a thief—even young ones. Roland could hear what his father threatened to do and threw open the door. Although he was the same age as I, he was much more..." Thorne stopped, searching for the words. "More at home in his body than I, I suppose. For even then, he was much like he is now, though I had yet to grow into myself.

"He stood between me and Thaddius, and he told his father we were leaving. We did. That very day. He took me with him and had me wait outside while he spoke with his grandfather to arrange a commission. And... then we joined the military. The rest... you know."

"But you were strangers? Why did you go along with him? What about your mother?"

"For Roland, the decision was simple. I was Thaddius's get, and he should have taken responsibility for my mother and me. Since he refused to... Roland decided that the responsibility fell to him. So, he did what he could. When he left home, he insisted the Breaker give him enough so that he was able to hire me on as his batman. He paid me a small stipend and covered expenses, so I was able to send every penny of wages home to my mother. How could I not take such an offer? But it came at a cost for him," Thorne whispered. "For I became the noose around his neck."

"You mean when Thaddius died, and the Breaker called Roland home? That is why Roland was so intent on marrying someone his grandfather approved of."

"I found out after he was engaged to Lady Charity, but aye. The duke had put codicils into his will to divert Roland's funds away if... if he didn't manage to marry before the duke died. And he also threatened to cut his purse strings entirely, if I were acknowledged. Thaddius had very little of his own, and Roland would have inherited practically nothing—or maybe just his debts. I..." he stopped, as if debating whether to tell her this next part. "I should have left Roland's service once I found out the truth so that I could not be used as a lever this way. But he did not want me to. When he threw open that door and we found one another for that first time, we found... family. True family. I was his brother, even if society would not see it that way. He believed it, and so did I, even though I have no right to claim it."

Grace dared to breach all rules of etiquette. She reached out and took his hands in hers, not caring who might see them. "Thorne, is this why you have been acting strangely in my presence? If so, let me be clear. I would never ask you to leave or ever want it at all. Even if you were not Roland's brother, you are an important person in his life. Many times, you have shown your willingness to risk yourself to help me and those important to me. I am afraid we are all tied together now. As a family, just as you said."

16

With Grace gone off to cool her temper, Roland left the pavilion for a brief stretch himself. High emotions were enervating, and as Grace said—there was still a murderer to catch. He needed to get himself in order, and perhaps something stimulating to drink to give him the energy to finish this tiresome day. Then he would be prepared to go through the methodical task of checking alibis.

"If anyone requires the knowledge of where to find me, I am going to The Castle Tavern," he told Prinny's servants, and then made his way to Castle Square, just a short distance away.

The open square took him less than five minutes to reach by walking, and at this time of the afternoon, it was fairly bustling with people visiting the shops. He had passed through the square several times already since his arrival in Brighton, so he was familiar with its layout, even if some of the street hawkers and vendors moved their carts about.

The Castle Tavern, advertised with a simply painted wooden plaque, had a decent reputation among the bon ton and was well kept. More importantly, it served coffee—an unusual, strong beverage he discovered since he returned from the front. He had tried it only twice before, and while he was still uncertain how he felt about it, that had given him enough familiarity to say that coffee certainly had a bracing effect he needed. The serving maid fluttered a little over serving him, but she did bring him a light luncheon and the promise of as much coffee as he wanted to drink.

Roland had planned to put his thoughts towards reviewing what they discovered about the suspects, but that was not where they wished to stay. Again and again, they were drawn to Grace, and how she had pulled from him in the audience with the Prince Regent.

She was angry. She had every right to be. But surely, he resolved, he could make her understand. He had acted with honourable intentions, and Grace would come to see it once her temper cooled. After all, she approved of what he had done for the Sprouts. How could she approve any less of him taking care of his brother?

Perhaps he had been somewhat selfish, keeping Thorne nearby for all this time. But it had been important to keep him out of the reach of Thaddius. And he had not saved up nearly enough money to set Thorne up with a business or some other means of income. Not yet.

He would explain to Grace and she would understand, eventually. She was the only woman of her station who might.

"Lord Percy?"

Roland looked up from the paper he had been staring at without reading, and suddenly his full attention was snared. For it was Prinny's Master of the House who was standing there, seeking him out. The man looked decidedly worried.

"Walker?" Roland asked, setting his cup down. It was so unlikely that the man would be sent to retrieve him like a common page that Roland realised something very serious had occurred. "What has happened?"

Walker darted his eyes around to ensure that no one was overly close and leaned closer, turning his head slightly to the wall so that no one watching could guess at his whispered words. "Lord Danforth was attacked. Will you please come immediately?"

"Needless to say." Roland glanced around, saying nothing further. The maid was not in sight, so he left three shillings on the table—certainly a generous enough sum to cover the cost of his food. As they made their way towards the front door of the establishment, Roland spotted one of the tavern's errand boys. "Lad, I need you to find a Lady Grace straightaway for me." He gave the boy her address, and enough coins that made the boy pay attention. "Tell her I would urgently like to meet with her. I will be at the pavilion."

"Yes, sir. Of course, sir. I will deliver this right away!" the boy darted off at full pelt, dodging several irate adults who nearly tripped over him.

Once they got out of the tavern and it was less easy to overhear, they quickened their pace. "Is he...?"

"Alive, your lordship," Walker confirmed shortly. "Yes, although he is dazed and rather bloodied. We have sent for the physician."

In a trice, they were back within the pavilion. It did not matter that Grace would be some time yet in arriving. It would not be appropriate to bring Grace to a gentleman's bedroom anyway, so he made his way directly to Danforth's room, where the lord was being examined.

Lord Danforth was seated on the settee near his bed, looking most furious and uncomfortable while the physician prodded his skull. "Lord Percy. How much longer is Prinny likely to keep us here in this... this... house of horrors of his?" The physician touched something tender, and the lord gasped, batting at him.

Roland drew himself up, running his eyes over the lord. There were dark spots that darkened his silvering hair and dripped onto his white linen shirt, but the man seemed likely to recover. That was a blessing.

Before Roland could reply, the physician issued his pronouncement. "I can find no skull fracture, and the cut to your scalp is small enough not to need the attention of a surgeon. Cuts on the head do tend to bleed more freely. You have a sizable lump though, to be sure, and I expect you will enjoy a rather fierce headache. Normally I would recommend a bloodletting to reduce inflammation to the brain—"

"You may keep your leeches to yourself, you quack!"

"—but since the patient has refused preventative treatment for apoplexy," the old physician said to Roland and Walker, looking unperturbed by Danforth's ranting, "I suggest instead that he be given some laudanum to facilitate rest and quiet for healing of the wound. Instruct your staff to check on him every hour or so. Send for me immediately if he vomits, his headache worsens, or he loses consciousness and cannot be roused."

Both nodded, and the physician packed his bag and left. Danforth peevishly turned his attention to both of them. "How dare you send such a charlatan to me? He wanted to apply leeches to my skull. As if I have not lost enough. I have bled through two handkerchiefs already."

"Doctor Smith is the regent's own physician, Lord Danforth. He is very highly regarded," Mr Walker told him.

"Not by me, he is not." Danforth muttered. "I should demand you take me to the surgeon at once so he can stitch me."

Roland stepped closer to the cranky older lord, pressing a hand discreetly down upon his shoulder to keep Danforth in place while he checked the man's scalp himself. "I cannot speculate much on the man's other qualifications, Danforth, but he was correct about the cut requiring no stitching. Already the bleeding has slowed. Do not disturb it or your hair, and it should cease shortly."

Danforth grumbled something mostly unintelligible, but Roland caught a few words about unqualified doctors and incompetent investigators.

"Yes," Roland agreed, "I have been remiss in posing questions to you right away, I suppose. The first would be about why you were not, after all, locked in your room if you felt so unsafe."

Heaving a sigh, the man pointed at the small table where a tray of half-eaten food lingered. "Laugh, if you must, but I forgot to relock the door after it was delivered."

"And where is the weapon that struck you?"

A pointed finger led Roland's gaze to where a pewter candlestick lay on the floor, and he picked it up. It was a hefty thing. Freed from Roland's grasp, Lord Danforth lurched to his feet somewhat unsteadily, and Walker moved closer to catch him if he fell.

"Lord Danforth, you should take to your bed," Walker told him sternly.

"I will not! I wish to be allowed to leave at once before the murderer realises he has not succeeded in killing me and returns to finish the job." Danforth pushed his way through them and into the hall, where a feminine gasp indicated that Lady Grace had arrived and had been standing there, listening.

Roland exited Danforth's room to find the man leaning against the wall. "Oh, I am dizzy," he moaned, bringing his hand back to the lump. "Do not let them make me stay in my room, Lady Grace," he turned a pleading look upon her. "I will rest— but at least let it be somewhere public."

Grace pointed to the drawing room behind her. "I do not believe you will be at risk while Lord Percy and I are in the room to question you about what transpired, Lord Danforth," she said evenly. Then she turned a look upon Roland that he could not quite decipher. At least she did not seem wroth with him any longer.

All three filed into the room, with Walker taking his leave after promising to bring them tea. Roland still held the candlestick, and in the better light of the drawing room, he stepped closer to the window to inspect it. The base had an edge that was darkened with a spot of blood, showing where it struck him. Danforth was quite lucky that the heavy object had not cracked his skull wide open.

"Did you see who attacked you, Lord Danforth?" Roland asked.

The man went to shake his head and then moaned in pain. "No," he finally said. "The coward struck me from behind. Just as I would have turned to face him, too, for I heard the door open and someone approaching me."

"What happened after you were struck? Do you remember seeing anything or hearing anything that would help you identify your attacker?"

"No... I fell to the floor, insensible. That must be why he let me be and did not hit me again—surely the villain thought I would bleed out or die there. I am not sure how long I was out, only that the footman I asked to locate Lady Waddington discovered me there."

"Why do you suppose he or she attacked you? Why now?" Grace said, a furrow forming above her eyes.

"I—I must confess something. Two things. For you see, I was angry with you and the regent for not allowing me to help. I have been quite useful in past investigations! It was... a blow to my pride, to be forced aside. So I have been conducting my own investigations still."

"You continued to investigate for that reason alone?" Roland asked, sceptical, even though he understood ego could be quite the motivator for members of the upper class.

"The other part of that is the second thing I had to explain, and I did not want to, because it would arouse suspicion towards me." The man said stiffly. "For I lied to you when you spoke with me earlier."

"Which part did you lie about?" Grace asked, the frown on her face deepening as she recalled their interview.

"That I did not leave the room. I actually left the Prince's study at one point," the man mumbled. "But it was just to stretch my legs. They have been troubling me with stiffness as of late when I sit too long."

"Forgive me, Lord Danforth. I sympathise with your pains, but I do not understand how that plays in your motivations to continue your own investigation," Grace said gently, drawing the man out.

"While I was in the hallway... I saw something. Someone else was moving about that late. Of course, there were several people who might be abroad quite legitimately at that hour, so I thought nothing else of it until the next day, when we found Sir Julian dead. But what if it was the shadow of the killer? What if... what if he saw me, and this attack was intended to silence me for that reason? Danforth turned to Grace, giving her a clear glimpse into the depth of his unease regarding the prospect.

Grace tried to give him a comforting smile. "He or she failed, Lord Danforth. They will surely be cautious before trying again."

"You said you asked a footman to find Lady Waddington?" Roland inquired. "Why?"

Danforth grimaced in confirmation. "Yes, and worse, I made the mistake of asking the one near my door to do so. You can be certain I will not do such a foolish thing again, for that is when the murderer found his opportunity to strike. I was looking for Lady Waddington because I wanted to press her about her nerves. I do not believe she is the killer... but I am given to believe her vapours lately might be because she has an idea of who it might be."

17

Lord Danforth moaned and pressed a hand to the bandage on the back of his head. "I really must lie down now. Is there anything else you need from me?"

"Not at this moment," Roland replied. "I will arrange for a guard to sit in your room."

Danforth flashed Roland a grateful smile. "I will take all the protection I can get, for I am starting to worry now that I have made myself a target. My valet will sit by my bed and see to my needs. I will be more at ease knowing that there is a guard outside the door."

With that, Danforth struggled to rise from his seat, causing Roland to hurry over to assist the man. Grace winced on Danforth's behalf, her sympathies rising at the sight of the man's suffering. Despite what the doctor said, the blow had obviously been hard enough to seriously rattle the injured lord.

As Grace watched them leave, she could not help but feel the burden of solving this mystery grow heavier upon her shoulders. Though she and Roland could hardly be accused of working at a snail's pace, the attack on Lord Danforth served as a reminder of what was at stake. Someone inside the Royal

Pavilion was a killer, and they were clearly getting more desperate.

The question was why the killer had struck again. And why against Lord Danforth? Had he truly seen something on the night Sir Julian Montgomery had been killed? More importantly, how did Lady Waddington fit into the situation? Lord Danforth had made an excellent point about her strange behaviour.

When Roland returned a few minutes later, Grace was pacing back and forth along the length of the room. "We must speak with Lady Waddington," she announced.

"I agree, but I must say that I am struggling to see her as our killer." He sat on the sofa and patted the seat beside him. "Come, let us talk through what we have learned thus far."

Though Grace itched to launch into action, she forced her feet to take her to where Roland sat. "I have been mulling over everything. Lady Waddington is most certainly keeping something from us. I also suspect her of sending the note to your grandfather. She could very well be in league with the killer."

Roland grimaced at that thought. "Getting her to admit such a thing will be difficult. We cannot and must not depend on her being honest with us. From where I sit, I can see only one way forward. We must split up once again and pursue this from two angles. How would you feel about questioning Lady Waddington again?"

"I relish the opportunity," Grace said, and meant it. "Women such as her and Lady Fitzroy have far too much power thanks to their willingness to ruin others. It is time to turn the tables."

"Excellent. You will take a guard with you. I do not want either of us venturing anywhere unescorted." Roland made to rise, but Grace held out a hand to stop him.

"Where will you be while I am pitting my wits against Lady Waddington?"

"I am going to question the two most dangerous men sitting atop our suspect list—Major General Sinclair and Lord Ravenscroft. Of the two, the latter has the connections required to get the Sapphire codes from England to France, so I will begin with him."

Grace could not fault his logic. "Excellent. But what of Baron Langley and Lord Blackwood?"

"Speak first with the lady and then see if you can learn anything about the whereabouts of the two men when Lord Danforth was attacked. I must ask that you wait for me before speaking with either of them. I am taking no chances with your safety."

Grace gave his arm a squeeze of agreement. "We have a future to share, my lord, and I do not wish to do anything that might put that at risk. I will find you when I finish with Lady Waddington."

With that, Grace stood to find someone to accompany her. She had her mind set on Sergeant Briggs, the guard who had spoken so honestly with her in the garden. A quick request in the ear of a footman accomplished the task.

The sergeant arrived a few minutes later, requesting permission to enter before coming into the room where she and Roland still sat. Grace remained quiet while Roland studied the guard, more interested in seeing her betrothed fully embody his role as a former military commander. Roland scrutinised the man through slitted eyes, scanning him from head to toe. For his part, Sergeant Briggs did not betray even a hint of worry or fear.

Finally, Roland rose from his seat and approached the guard. "You are aware of Lord Danforth's recent injury?"

"I am," the sergeant replied.

"There is no life more precious to me than that of Lady

Grace—not even my own. She will not come to any harm. Do you understand?"

Sergeant Briggs stood even straighter and raised his hand for a salute. "I will not let anything happen to the young lady, no matter the cost. I promise you that, my lord."

Roland gave Grace one last glance to ensure she was satisfied before taking his leave to see to his own assignment.

With Roland gone, Grace took a moment to explain where they were going and what she intended to do. "We must get a full confession from Lady Waddington about whatever it is she is hiding. I might be required to lie or cross beyond the lines of polite society to achieve this goal. All I ask is that you go along with whatever I say. Can you do that?"

Sergeant Briggs stood tall and gave a single nod of agreement. "I'll keep you safe and do me best to help in any way I can."

Grace steeled herself for the next course of action and then led the way to Lady Waddington's room. When they reached the wooden door, Grace stepped aside to allow Sergeant Briggs to knock and request entry. His masculine voice echoed along the corridor. Rustling noises from inside the room preceded footsteps. It was not Lady Waddington who answered, but her lady's maid.

The woman was middle-aged, with greying hair and fine lines bracketing her squinting eyes and pursed lips. She conveyed her disdain for the guard by shifting her mouth into a disapproving frown. "My lady is already suffering from nerves. I will thank you for keeping your voice down."

"Nerves or not, His Royal Highness has dictated that all guests must make themselves immediately available for questioning. If you'll step aside, Lady Grace will speak with Lady Waddington here. Unless, that is, you would prefer she do it in a public place."

The maid sniffed but shifted over to allow them in. The guard took up a watchful stance beside the door while Grace moved deeper into the room. Lady Waddington remained seated near the window. She did not instruct her maid to bring over another chair so that Grace could join her. Grace did not mind this in the least. In fact, she preferred to view it as an invitation to tower over the woman rather than as an imposition.

With her back straight and arms hanging at her side, Grace stared down at Prinny's only female guest. Threats would get her nowhere. That is why she skipped straight to the consequences.

"Lady Waddington, I am here to inform you that the Prince Regent is drawing up orders for your arrest, for both the murder of Sir Julian Montgomery and the attack on Lord Danforth." Grace glanced over her shoulder at the guard. "Given her tendency to attack, I suggest you bind her hands before she leaves the room."

"What?" Lady Waddington screeched. She shrank in her chair, almost curling over to protect herself from Grace's words. Across the room, her maid was frozen in place, her face ashen with terror.

"Lord Danforth has told us all, my lady. He saw you wandering around on the night of Sir Julian's death, and when he sent for you this afternoon, you attacked him from behind to keep him quiet. Fortunately for him, you did not hit him hard enough to incapacitate him."

Grace motioned for the guard to approach. As soon as he set in motion, Lady Waddington burst into sobs and buried her face in her hands. Had it been anyone else, Grace would have rushed to comfort them. But today, she wore the hat of an executioner. The only way Lady Waddington would reveal her real secrets was to save herself from a worse fate.

Grace was not, however, cruel. She did not stop the lady's

maid when she hurried over to her lady's side. Instead, she spread her fingers wide, issuing a silent, subtle command for Sergeant Briggs to stand down.

It was the maid who broke first. With her arms wrapped around Lady Waddington's sobbing form, she glared daggers at Grace. "You are wrong about all of this. My lady has had no part in any of that."

"So you say, but her behaviour is suspicious and it has been noticed by a good number of the guests here—on that they all agree. She is keeping secrets. Mayhap dangerous ones. If she is not the one who wielded the weapon herself, I am certain she is involved. Nothing will save her now short of unequivocal proof of her innocence."

At that, Lady Waddington lifted her tear-stained face from her hands. She glanced in Grace's direction, though she did not see her. Her eyes shifted wildly from side to side as she weighed the consequences of holding her tongue. When she reached a decision, she took a deep breath and held it for several seconds before loosing it all at once.

"I will speak with Prinny."

"You will speak with me," Grace countered. "The Prince Regent has more important matters to occupy his time than listening to the pleadings of a guilty woman."

Lady Waddington glanced away and clenched her jaw, biting back an angry retort. The maid laid a hand on her shoulder, offering her moral support.

"It is now or never," Grace added when the silence stretched overlong.

"Fine. But mark my words, if you gossip a word of this to anyone, I will come for you when you least expect it."

"Angry threats are not in your best interest, Lady Waddington, and do little to make you look less guilty. Speak."

"I was with Lord Blackwood."

Grace forced her face to remain expressionless. "When?"

"On the night of Sir Julian's murder. He and I have... well, an understanding, you might say."

"They are in love," the maid added, jumping to her mistress's defence. "They intend to wed as soon as he has the funds to support her."

Grace filed this new information with what she had already learned. Lord Blackwood had been speaking with Baron Langley about trade routes and safe travels. It was possible Lady Waddington spoke the truth. But Grace would not take her word for it alone.

"If Lord Blackwood offers the same alibi for himself, I will ask the Prince Regent to stay his hand." Grace spun around and swept from the room, with Sergeant Briggs following behind.

In the corridor, she found a footman waiting for her. The man bobbed his head in greeting and then explained he had a message. "Baron Langley has just returned to his room, if you would like to speak with him."

"Do you know where he was before now?" Grace asked.

"I believe he was in the library, but I cannot say for how long. I can ask the footman there."

Grace raised a hand to stay the young uniformed man. "I will ask him myself. Please, lead the way."

And so they went, with the footman showing the way, Grace following behind, and Sergeant Briggs guarding her back. For a moment, she wondered if this was what it was like to be queen. Queen Charlotte never went anywhere without a coterie of guards, aides, and ladies-in-waiting. Although it gave Grace the feeling of being important, she realised it would soon grow tiresome. The only person she truly wanted at her side was Roland.

The other royal footman was still in the library, busy putting a stack of books away. He paused his task when Grace entered the room.

At Grace's question, he answered, "Baron Langley came here this morning and did not leave until a few minutes ago. I brought in lunch on a tray and he asked me to remain. He said he needed help to fetch the books from the top shelves."

If Lady Waddington was to be believed, and Grace was certain she had told the truth of her affair, then three suspects were gone from the list. Lady Waddington and Lord Blackwood would account for one another, and Baron Langley could not have struck Lord Danforth.

That left Lord Ravenscroft and Major General Sinclair. To learn which one was the traitor, she would have to rejoin Roland.

18

It took rather longer to locate Ravenscroft than he expected. He pressed every guard and footman he spotted along the way, and no one knew where Ravenscroft had gone until the man was spotted returning to his room some quarter of an hour after he left Grace.

The hall's guard had secured him in his room when the man refused to be escorted to another questioning. Then he had sent for Roland, who let himself in with only the briefest knock of warning.

"Lord Percy," Ravenscroft greeted him, his tone one of studied boredom. "I would say it is a pleasure to see you, but given how you all but accused me of treason for being the product of my mother's birth... well."

Roland shut the door behind him, glancing about Lord Ravenscroft's bedroom with some discomfort. He suspected that Ravenscroft's choice of location was intended to disconcert him. He wanted Roland unbalanced and off guard. So Roland put aside his feelings of intrusion so that he might guess at the reasons Ravenscroft would do such a thing. The only conclusion he came to was that he very much had something he wished to hide.

Or protect—if it was being concealed within the bedroom.

"Lord Ravenscroft," Roland drawled in return, considering the dandy as he slouched indolently on the foot of his bed. "Can you truly blame me for asking the questions?"

There was a pause as Ravenscroft raked his gaze down Roland's body. "No, Lord Percy, I suppose I cannot blame you for asking if I am a viper. Or for attempting to imprison me in my room."

Curiously, Ravenscroft had barely left his room since the last time they had spoken. But fortunately—or perhaps unfortunately, for him—he had been abroad when Danforth was attacked.

"Would that I did imprison you, for there has been another attempt on a guest's life."

Ravenscroft's eyes flickered, but there was no other sign of distress on the man's face. Just grim resignation. "Too bad you did not, Percy. If you had, you would not be here, preparing to ask me if I were the guilty party."

Roland's gaze narrowed, studying the man. "Are you saying that you are?"

At that, Ravenscroft laughed bitterly. "Of course, I am saying no such thing. I am as innocent of... whatever attack you are here to accuse me of, as I am innocent of the murder of Sir Julian."

"If suspicion fell upon your head, it is because you made yourself privy to information that we had not disclosed."

"And by my heritage. One can hardly forget. I think if you asked, Lord Percy, my only mistake was accidentally disclosing that which most would have known—if not that very second, then most certainly within the day. I can guarantee that Lady Waddington was in possession of the same information that morning from a similar source. The other gentlemen might not have, but that is because they are fools for not having loyal people to use to the best effect."

Roland crossed his arms. "You did imply that the maids were... 'twittering' I think was the word you used."

"Of course they were. One of them had discovered the body. No matter what their class is, you know how women are when confronted with a body. Especially when one finds said body lying with its head squarely beneath a pillow."

"Who brought you that information?" Roland asked him. "You have a servant here with you, do you not? Was it he who brought you that below-stairs tidbit?"

Ravenscroft tensed. The movement was nearly imperceptible, but Roland caught it. "I do have a valet, yes, but no, it was not he who caught the gossip. It is perfectly possible for a man to do his own eavesdropping."

That was true. However, Roland was also near certain that Ravenscroft had told him a lie. On the heels of the statement about using one's loyal people to achieve results, why would Ravenscroft deny the involvement of his valet on the day that Sir Julian was found dead?

"You are right. There is nothing stopping a man from eavesdropping. And I can see how you might have extra motivation to do so. Prinny suggested you were something of a whisperer for him."

Ravenscroft's faint smile was the only agreement he got.

"He also told me you prefer extracting information from people while they are in your bed," Roland said casually, hoping to catch the man flatfooted. His query, however, had the opposite effect.

"Ah, yes. You have me. I confess, I am worse than a libertine, for I always have an ulterior motive. I bed widows, spinsters, and courtesans to, er, ply my trade," Ravenscroft said, a smirk growing as Roland's face pinkened. "Congratulations, Lord Percy. You have unearthed my dastardly plans."

Roland's lip curled. "If that was the case, that would suggest Lady Waddington was less of a diversion and more of a target."

Ravenscroft shrugged again. "Why not both? One may love their... work. So to speak."

He was about to retort to that, but the satisfied set of Ravenscroft's face caused him to pause and rethink what he was about to say. "I confess, Ravenscroft, I suspect you are actively hiding something from me you do not wish me to discover," Roland said instead. "The more I think of Lady Waddington and the boasting of your conquests, the more I have the sensation I am playing into your hands. Tell me truly: was it your intention to bed the lady after all?"

"It was." Ravenscroft's piercing gaze was steady, and Roland could detect no telltale sign of a lie.

"What secrets were you hoping to unearth?"

"I will tell you, Lord Percy, and happily. I daresay this will either tighten my noose or release it, depending on His Highness' willingness to vouch for it. He insisted on my absolute discretion. However, if you—as one of their creatures—are not an exception in this particular aspect, then I will bow to the inevitable swing. At least my part in the rest will end." Roland made a gesture for the man to continue, and after a moment's pause, he did. "Prinny suggested I might be able to build a rapport with the old maid and attempt to discover if she had been in contact with a certain... mutually known traitor."

"Which traitor might that be?" Roland asked, wondering how much the man really knew and not wishing to give the answer to him.

"Lady Fitzroy, of course."

Roland grunted noncommittally, and Ravenscroft smiled, but it did not reach his eyes. "Quite. I daresay neither the queen nor the regent are all that happy about you letting her get away. Well, the queen certainly is not. Prinny rather believes he can extend his net wide enough to catch her, regardless."

He would never regret his choice—only that he hadn't seen Sir David's duplicity sooner. "Since it would have been impossible for me to have been in two places at one time, I can see how facts and reason might make them unhappy."

Ravenscroft said nothing more on the subject, and Roland considered things. Regarding Ravenscroft's plans for Lady Waddington... it seemed a possibility. After all, Prinny had rather vouched for the man, and again, Ravenscroft had spoken the truth, as far as Roland could detect. He rubbed his forehead, feeling that there was something important he was missing.

"Well then, if you are such a close ally to the crown, perhaps you might provide an alibi by telling me what business you were about while today's attack occurred?"

"No. I will not." Ravenscroft shrugged and looked away.

"And? Why ever not?"

Another one-shouldered hitch. Ravenscroft was being beastly rude, shrugging so much in response to Roland's queries. And for a man who might end up facing the gallows, no less. He seemed not to care.

"Did you attack Danforth?" pressed Roland, looking for spoken answers that might betray more telltales.

The man was being as careful as possible to guard his body language, but Ravenscroft's eyes widened fractionally at that. "I did not," he said after a moment. "Not all of my business involves you or even the crown, Lord Percy."

Roland rubbed his thumb over his lips as he stared down at the man. Something was off, and he could not quite put his finger on it. Like Ravenscroft, the man had two parts of him that were mismatched. There was a tightness to his bearing and the skin around his eyes, and the slightest disorder of his hair that belied his impeccable dress and the flush of his skin—

His hair...

Steeling himself to look at Ravenscroft with fresh eyes, Roland forced himself to study the other gentleman far more closely than had ever been his wont. As he made a new tally, he noted Ravenscroft doing some calculations of his own.

"I say, Ravenscroft," Roland said softly. "Were you busy having your ashes hauled?"

Roland knew he scored a hit when the man paled, but Ravenscroft continued to deny it. "I have no idea what you are talking about."

"Your hair is mussed, and your mouth is puffy. How very odd. But Lady Waddington refused you, and there are no other women who are guesting at the pavilion. So, either you are sporting with one of the female staff—an act which surely would upset the prince—or..."

"Stop." The man's voice was so low it was barely more than a breathy hiss, and his face had turned grey.

Roland sat beside the distraught lord and folded his hands. "Which is it, Lord Ravenscroft?"

"You can bloody well guess. And that is as much as I will say, because whether I tell the truth about my whereabouts or let you implicate me for Sir Julian, I will hang for it. If Sir Julian's death warrants my own... Well, then I should allow it and protect the others." Ravenscroft brought his hands up to cover his face in despair.

He understood the lord's dilemma. The prince might overlook Ravenscroft's proclivities, but only so long as he was not confronted with direct evidence of it. However, if it came to light, the prince would most likely be forced to uphold the law. And the penalty for its violation was harsh.

"And your... assignations with the other ladies? They have been mere ruses?"

The lord's expression was droll. "Must desire always be so simple?"

"I suppose not, and in the end, it also matters not. It does not trouble me with whom you spend your private time, Lord Ravenscroft. It is not my business. Not so long as you are not abetting a traitor in the process."

Ravenscroft's brows furrowed, but he pressed his lips together and did not answer right away. Belatedly, Roland realised that Ravenscroft clearly knew nothing of the stolen codebook.

"I am not," the lord finally said with a small sniff, his shoulders drooping even lower. "We had nothing to do with Sir Julian or Lord Danforth. I swear to you."

Roland paused. "Then you met with someone after all, after you were seen going to bed the night of Sir Julian's death."

"Yes," Lord Ravenscroft agreed. "But I did not sneak out. He... he snuck into my room after I sent the footman on an errand."

"And you had another liaison with the same person just now? You must tell me whom you met, Ravenscroft; it is your alibi. If you trust me with your secret, I shall keep it as long as he will confirm to me you were with him. I do not care what you were about, because I promise, there are higher stakes than a man's reputation."

Ravenscroft closed his eyes briefly and then turned to give Roland a hard look. "If you are wrong, and we both swing, I will find a way to haunt you."

"You may trust me," Roland said simply. Readily.

Ashamed, Lord Ravenscroft looked away. "My valet. I adore him. And we would never be allowed together, even if... one of us had been born something different."

19

Grace studied the book-lined shelves of the library and contemplated what to do next. The logical choice was to return to the small parlour to await Roland, taking Sergeant Briggs along to protect her. Yet, the thought of sitting idle while the end was so near in sight chafed at her.

There had been no word from Roland, so she determined he must still be interrogating Lord Ravenscroft. She did not envy him the task, for the man was more inclined to say something vexing than be of assistance. But perhaps, like Lady Waddington, given the right incentive, Lord Ravenscroft might finally come clean about what he had or had not done.

Grace was certainly keen to find out. She asked the footman to accompany them upstairs, thinking he might prove useful again, especially if they needed someone to run a message. Her little group made it halfway up the staircase before they heard a loud crash of breaking porcelain and a woman's scream rip through the air.

The echoing screams reverberated through the hall, piercing and frantic, each cry escalating in intensity, as if she were pleading for help. The distinct desperation in her tone sent chills down Grace's spine. Hurried footsteps accompanied the screams. Every creak of the floorboards heightened Grace's sense of urgency and danger.

The footman she was following ducked his head, already moving to hide from whatever danger lurked ahead. Grace shoved past him, her feet moving as quickly as the long skirt of her gown would allow. Sergeant Briggs bellowed for her to wait, but his pleas fell on deaf ears.

All Grace thought was that it might be Roland. He had demanded she keep a guard at her side, but what about him? What if Lord Ravenscroft struck out at him? Or worse?

Terrible images flooded her mind and sent her heart beating faster than ever. All common sense fled as her desire to reach Roland took control of her mind.

She did not see the thick red carpet runner or the silk wallpaper. From their portraits hanging in the stairwell, the former kings and queens of England witnessed her frantic dash to find the sources of the screams.

The screams did not stop. Whoever the woman was, her voice rose higher and higher as she shouted unintelligible words. Only when Grace reached the top of the stairs did she see the shaking form of an upper floor maid. The woman cowered in the corridor, across from an open doorway, surrounded by the detritus of a dropped tea tray.

"Lord Percy?" Grace blurted.

The maid lifted a shaking hand and indicated the room across from her.

Grace picked up speed, throwing all decorum aside, and ran as she had not done since she was a small child. The soft soles of her slippers caused her feet to slip. She spun her arms like a windmill to keep from falling, somehow managed the turn into the room in question, and stumbled straight into Roland's open arms.

"Shhh," he whispered, "I have got you. I am safe."

Grace pulled back, and Roland brushed her cheeks with his thumbs, drying tears she had not noticed before then. She fought to gain control over her racing heart, taking comfort in Roland's obvious good health.

It was not him.

Roland positioned himself between her and the view of the room. When she tried to lean to the side to discover what had occurred, he took a firm hold of her and held her head in place between his two hands.

"Do not look," he cautioned. "It is Sinclair, and the scene is rather gruesome."

"Murdered?" Grace asked in a croaky voice.

"It would seem not," another man replied. It was Lord Ravenscroft. He came up behind Roland so that Grace could see him. With her view into the room now completely blocked, Roland loosened his hold on her and helped her to straighten up. Grace smoothed her gown and brushed a stray strand of hair back into place.

Ravenscroft continued, "He left a note—a confession, that is." He held up a sheet of paper flecked with blood. He read the words out loud. "I cannot live with myself with my betrayal of all I hold dear. They forced my hand, and once the codes were gone, there was nothing I could do. God have mercy upon my wretched soul."

Roland took the note from Ravenscroft's hand to read it with his own eyes. Grace shifted so she might do the same. It was not the penmanship, however, that gave her pause.

"Roland, look at the blood."

He moved the note further away. "Do not focus on that."

"No, Roland, I am not horrified. Well, I am, but that is not my point. The ink is written on top of the bloodstains."

Roland and Ravenscroft both reacted to her words. The

men leaned closer to one another, and Ravenscroft grabbed Roland's arm to drag the note more into view where they could see how the line of the quill had pulled through a small droplet of blood, causing a run of black and red.

"Egads," Ravenscroft groaned. "She is right."

Roland spun around to stare anew at the dreadful scene, too caught up in the possible significance of this discovery to remember he was hiding it from Grace. Thus, Grace finally caught sight of Sinclair's body. The man sat in the chair at the writing desk with his back to the room. Though Grace could not see his face, the growing bloodstains on the carpet beneath him told the story. She dragged her gaze upward and landed on the handle of the knife sticking from his neck.

The scene was all too reminiscent of her own near end. The cry escaped her lips before she could bite it back. She wrestled her fear into place and was steady by the time Roland spun around to check on her.

"It took me by surprise," she explained. "I am fine. But I hope you understand if I do not come any closer."

"I would prefer it if you left this horrible scene behind entirely, but it is too late for that now." Roland bade Ravenscroft to help him. "Check the desk drawers to see if you can find anything we know for certain was written by Sinclair."

In the meantime, Roland studied Sinclair's unnaturally still form. His gaze narrowed as he moved around to view from different angles.

For her part, Grace allowed her gaze to roam around the rest of the room. It was furnished with a mix of pieces from the previous century. The covers of the mahogany bed showed no wrinkles. The matching tray-top commodes on either side bore simple oil lamps and nothing else. The room was smaller than the one occupied by Lady Waddington, appropriate to his status as the lowest-ranking guest. There were no signs that anything was amiss, if one excluded the writing desk and man slumped in the wooden chair.

"What are you thinking?" Grace asked when she could bear it no longer.

"Our first instincts were wrong. Look carefully at how Sinclair is sitting in the chair. His feet are angled strangely."

Ravenscroft crossed the room holding a diary in his hand. "The handwriting does not match. The styles are completely different. Whoever did this was not even trying to approximate his stilted penmanship."

"It was a rushed job," Grace breathed.

"And a recent one," Roland added after daring to touch the dead man's skin. "He is still warm to the touch."

Grace pictured their suspects in her head. Ravenscroft must have been with Roland at the time of Sinclair's death. Grace had cleared the others of the attack on Lord Danforth and Sir Julian. There was no one left.

No one except...

"Roland, we got this wrong. No one struck Lord Danforth. It is the only possible solution to this mess of a crime."

"What?" Roland cocked his head to the side. "Are you suggesting Lord Danforth faked the incident?"

In lieu of a reply, Grace spun around and rushed to the room where Lord Danforth was staying. She threw open the door just as Roland caught up to her. Inside, there was chaos. Clothing had been tossed about with little care for its value. A stack of half-burned papers still lay in the smouldering hearth. There was no sign of Lord Danforth.

"Search the grounds!" Roland ordered.

The ever-dutiful Sergeant Briggs had accompanied them. At Roland's words, he leapt into action, throwing open the window to send a rousing call to arms to his fellow guards.

"He could be hiding inside," Ravenscroft shouted, having caught up with the group.

Roland stalked across the room and threw open the door to the connecting dressing room. Danforth's valet sat on a small cot with his hands, feet, and mouth bound. The poor man mumbled incomprehensible pleas. Roland grabbed the letter opener from the nearby desk and sliced through the silk cravat that was tied around the man's mouth.

The man spluttered and coughed before finally managing a few words. "It was my lord. He has gone mad!"

Roland knelt at the man's side and worked to free his hands. "Where has he gone? How long ago did he leave?"

The valet rubbed at the red marks on his wrists. "Ten minutes? Maybe fifteen?"

"A lifetime," Roland groaned. He motioned for Lord Ravenscroft to take his place. "See what else you can learn."

Ravenscroft gave a nod of understanding and stood aside to allow Roland to take his leave with Grace and the sergeant accompanying him.

Roland headed toward the staircase to the ground floor. "If he was hiding inside, he must surely have heard the commotion and know the game is up. Come, we must focus our search on the grounds."

At the bottom of the staircase, Sergeant Briggs turned toward the front of the house. Roland led Grace in the opposite direction, running through the pavilion library at full pelt and out into the glassed conservatory. He burst through the rear door to the gardens, shouting calls for anyone near to come his way.

"Lord Danforth is our killer. We must find him," he instructed the guards as they caught up. "Is there a back entrance to the pavilion grounds?"

"This way," a heavy-set guard replied. Despite his bulk, he moved as fast as Roland, huffing and puffing as he ran.

A sharp pain tore at Grace's side. She no longer had the stamina of her childhood days, and her nights avoiding the ballroom floor had also taken a toll. Yet she dug deep, ignoring the painful stitch in her midsection and the pebbles dancing in her summer slippers.

"Hoi! Ross!" the guard called out to the guard who must have been posted ahead. No one answered.

The guard shouted again and again got no response. Grace's misgivings grew. How many people was Danforth willing to kill to escape their clutches?

The path came to an abrupt end with no sign of Lord Danforth. Had Grace not been searching so intently, she never would have spotted the fallen guard lying still in the shadows.

<h1 style="text-align:center">20</h1>

There was no question about it. Danforth had made good on his escape. His trail went cold at the pavilion's back path exit—a sturdy wrought-iron gate across the narrow gravel passage lined with hedges and ornamental trees. The guard who had been minding it had been clouted in the back of the head and knocked insensible, but he was coming around.

As he waited for the guardsman to collect himself, Roland sent someone back to the pavilion. There was no time to dally. The contingent of the Royal Army needed to move out to head off Danforth's easiest escape routes at the roads and docks.

The back path guard was a little woozy, but it seemed he possessed a hard enough head that there would be no permanent damage. "I am sorry to press you while you are still collecting your wits," he told the guard, "but I hope you can understand the need for haste."

"Yeh. Beggin' yer pardon, Lord Percy, but I saw yer man coming, I did." The man agreed in a thick cockney accent as he straightened himself. He must have been one of the guards who had accompanied Prinny from London. "I remembers movin' to stop 'im. But afore I could get to 'im…" the guard's voice trailed off, lifting his hands in frustration. "Someone must've banged me in the nob from behind."

"Danforth had a man outside," cursed Roland softly. "He was not working alone as we had hoped."

"Sorry, my lord, I didn't see nuffin' more. It was fast, and I never saw 'im coming. Wish I could be more 'elp."

"You did what you could. Thank you," Roland told the man gravely, turning on his heel to find Grace close behind him.

"What do we do now?" she asked.

"We must ensure there is a swift response," he told her briefly, taking her by the arm and leading her back to the pavilion at a somewhat faster trot than she was used to walking with her shorter legs. He was sorry for that, and he tried not to rush her too much, but time was of the essence.

Already, the inside of the pavilion was a scene of organised chaos, with guardsmen and soldiers rushing to and fro, but they were pointed in the direction of the King's Apartments. There, the Prince Regent was closeted with an intimidating array of faces, including the leader of the household guards, the commander of the local army garrison, the chief constable, and a senior naval officer. Grace felt somewhat cowed to be the only woman in such a setting, but she straightened her backbone and made every effort to appear as though she belonged.

"We have taken the Brighton docks, Your Highness, and are in the process of signalling the few patrol ships in the area," said Rear Admiral Cavendish. "I have sent a message by semaphore to the ones I could. It is a vast area to cover for only a few ships, however. Most of the fleet is deployed," he indicated apologetically. "A few points are working in our favour—all the local fishers are still out at sea or only just about to return for the evening, and the tide is unfavourable for anything larger to dock nearby. We are keeping an eye out for smaller craft leaving the area."

The Prince Regent grunted acknowledgement. "So our rat is likely still trapped nearby?"

The Rear Admiral nodded. "High tide will be in the wee hours of the morning. So Danforth would most likely lie low until the cover of darkness in any case—either to catch a boat large enough to sail for France, or to take a smaller craft to another area to meet one."

There was a pause as Prinny turned towards the new arrivals. "Thank you for your timely message about the back gate this time, Lord Percy and Lady Grace," the prince formally acknowledged Roland and Grace, salting his greeting with the reminder of past failure. "You flushed the pheasant, and we have hope of being able to apprehend the traitor before he is able to abscond with Sapphire."

"Was the garrison already mobilised, then?" Roland asked, turning to Colonel Pembroke, the army's commander.

"Yes. I sent out several riders along each path headed back inland and along the coast," Pembroke explained. "We were blessed with a clear day today, and with so little vegetation in the area, the riders can see far. I doubt Danforth would be fool enough to try to strike directly for Shoreham or Newhaven while there is light to see him by. But the riders will inform the local constables and harbour masters to keep an eye out."

From there, conversation swiftly turned to arguments about strategy, including whether it was better to hold the majority of their men in reserve in Brighton, or to send them in advance to the most likely routes of escape. Grace and Roland were quite forgotten by the others, but since no one was dismissed, they waited and listened quietly, side by side, as time passed.

Before the assembly came to an agreement, a rapid knock at the door admitted a windblown despatch rider, his cheeks nearly as red as his coat. "We found a ship he booked passage on in Shoreham," the man conveyed his message, gulping a breath. "The boat has been secured awaiting your orders."

Roland let out a breath in relief. Had they finally received a lucky turn of events?

"We should arrest the captain and question him," said Cavendish gruffly.

"Wait. Your Highness," Roland interrupted, shooting the Rear Admiral an apologetic glance. "We should bait a trap. If we make it look like we have not detained the ship... Danforth may walk right onboard into our arms."

Cavendish ruffled his moustache briefly in irritation, but he inclined his head towards the regent, indicating that Roland's plan was not without merit. "I can send the naval patrols in that direction to sit out of easy view in that case, Your Highness."

"Lord Danforth did not strike me as foolish," Lady Grace murmured, with only the slightest quaver of uncertainty in her voice before she strengthened her nerves. "If we leave his ship in plain view and act as though we know nothing, he will suspect the trap."

The constable finally spoke up. "If Danforth's got any ties with the locals, 'e might be 'idin' out in one of their safe houses." The man's Sussex accent was lighter than some, but it still swallowed his H and R sounds, "Best we start checkin' the usual places straightaway."

"It might be wise to use some of our ground forces," suggested Roland. "We station some of the garrison in Shoreham where they can keep a roving eye on the docks and the roads from Brighton. If we start sending searchers house to house from the north and east ends of Brighton, perhaps we either catch him before he is able to move, or at least drive our quarry in the direction we want him to go."

"Make it so," Prinny said to the others, settling himself more heavily in his chair. "Lord Percy, my mother would not let the burden of being queen deter her from boxing my ears like a disobedient young savage if I allowed harm to befall Grace again. Your part in this is finished. Take the young lady home and secure her and her family until we have Danforth in hand."

Knowing how she would feel about this dismissal, Roland touched her arm to keep her from arguing, and he could see Grace's throat bob as she swallowed her words. "I shall remain ready to lend a hand, if you decide you have need of me, Your Highness. Or my man Thorne, if you need another able-bodied man in the search."

Prinny narrowed his eyes briefly in consideration, almost as if he did not recall the dramatic introduction of the man as Roland's half-brother, and jerked his chin in acceptance.

Roland grazed her elbow with his fingertips to subtly guide her out of the King's Apartments, and Grace kept looking between him and her feet, confused. "Surely our part in this is not really done?" she asked plaintively, once they were on their way out of the pavilion and he offered her his arm again. "We have not caught him!"

He understood her sentiments, and it made the corner of his mouth twist a little wryly. "It does feel anticlimactic," he acknowledged, putting his free hand over hers again. "Still, I will force myself to be content knowing you have not been placed in such desperate danger again." His heart sped up even thinking about how near a thing it had been, and it made him want to lock her up in a distant estate in Northumberland.

But he could not seriously consider such a thing. He was convinced Grace would be unhappy about being stuck on a backwater country estate for any length of time.

As he stroked her hand briefly, she grew limp with fatigue beside him. "I do suppose we have other things to worry about," she confessed. "I can hardly believe it was just this morning that your grandfather marched into the pavilion to argue with the regent and..."

When her voice trailed off, he understood where her thoughts went. "It has been an eventful day. I am sorry for the incident about Thorne."

"No, you do not need to apologise. I should not have been so angry with you," she said distantly, looking out towards the sea. Then she let out a little sniff of amusement. "I did not tell you in all the fuss—I ran into him when I stormed out of the pavilion. Or, rather, he kept a horse from running into me."

Shocked, Roland stopped and turned to face her fully. "A horse? What happened?"

Grace made a small gesture of dismissal. "I was paying more attention to my feelings than my surroundings and was fortunate that he was there to pull me out of the way of a carriage. And... he disabused me of some of my churlish thoughts. It seems rash acts of heroism run in the family," she gave him a sidelong look as she began walking again.

"Heroism—" Blinking, Roland digested that statement, blood heating in his face. "Not from the Percy line, it does not. I give full credit for actions to my days in the military, where I had the chance to learn about true courage and decency. But enough of that. If you ran into Thorne... does that mean you have not eaten anything all day?"

"As you said, it has been eventful."

"You must be starving by now," he said as they approached his grandfather's property.

"Famished," she agreed, tugging him to a stop before he could turn up the walk. "But... if you do not mind, I think there is someplace else I would rather dine with you, if you think it is possible."

His brows drew down. "Left to me, I will find a way to make most anything possible. But... where did you have in mind?"

"Do you suppose we could eat dinner with your brother and the Sprouts? I should like an evening... where I see what it feels like to be a family."

Her voice was both hesitant and hopeful, and Roland's breath was squeezed from his chest by the force of emotion. "You know it would raise eyebrows to go out, so the only place we could do so would be if we ate at the cottage."

"I would not mind that—but I would not want Mr and Mrs Archer to be upset about my presence."

"Well... they will think it is irregular in the extreme. But I daresay I have already set something of a precedent for being odd. I must warn you, however, if we drop in on them, the food might be a little plainer than you are used to."

She wrinkled her nose in amusement. "But the company shall make it a feast. Speaking of family... Do you suppose there is a way we would not have to endure your grandfather and my mother seated together at the same table for our wedding breakfast?"

Roland chuckled at that. "No. But at least that will be a horror we only have to endure once."

21

They stopped first at Grace's home to get permission for her to accompany Roland to dinner. Lady Tilbury seemed ill-inclined to agree—until Roland explained he wanted to introduce Grace to his household as the future Duchess of Northumberland. Those words worked like a magical spell, turning Lady Tilbury's no into a fervent yes.

Once on their way, Grace and Roland did not speak, both thinking over the day's events. It seemed impossible that they had identified the murderer, only to have him escape their clutches mere minutes before. But for once, Grace did not intend to put the blame on herself. If Prinny's guests had been honest with them from the start, they likely would have uncovered Lord Danforth's treachery sooner.

The army and the watch could have the joy of locating the betrayer now. She and Roland were free to move on with their original plans for the summer—to discuss plans for their future and set a date for their wedding. Tonight, she would get a small taste of her new life.

Suddenly, the evening took on even more significance, for it would be her first chance to set the tone for how she would treat the servants... and how they would treat her. A small quiver of uncertainty arose in the pit of her belly. The Archers would disapprove of her eating with the lower class. But it was not their approval she was seeking tonight. In the end... it was Thorne's.

She glanced at Roland from under her lashes, noting how the setting sun cast shadows on his handsome profile. He was higher born than she, yet here he was, happily going on to dinner at the small cottage he had rented for his household.

No matter what the Breaker might threaten, nor what her own mother would advise, Grace realised she did not want her presence to drive a wedge between Roland and his brother. She did not want to be the one who forced them to dance around their true relationship. It would be tricky to navigate, but she was willing to adopt a strange, more egalitarian way of thinking.

Now if only she could keep from creating a muddle of it.

The cottage Roland had rented was on the outskirts of town. It was a charming, single-story structure with a thatched roof that gently sloped down over the whitewashed stone walls. He led the way to a small wooden door painted in a soft blue hue and used the brass knocker in the shape of a lion's head to announce their arrival. The curtains hanging in the two mullioned windows on either side of the door swished and the matching faces of the Sprouts peered out at them.

Lavender and rosemary bushes filled the air with their fragrant scents, bringing Grace a deep sense of tranquillity. That peace held even after Thorne answered the door.

Surprised, Thorne rocked back at finding the pair on his doorstep. "Is aught amiss?" he asked in a fraught tone.

"No. Relax, Thorne. Things are well. The problem of Sir Julian's killer is now out of our hands, and we thought we might come over for another reason. Assuming, that is, that Mrs

Archer does not toss us out on our ears," Roland added with a grin.

Before Thorne could ask what Roland meant, the children elbowed their way into the discussion.

"You brought the lady here!" Wes gasped. The scrawny lad had filled out even more, and his cheeks bloomed a healthy pink underneath the line of freckles on his nose. Beside him, his sister was busy studying Grace's gown. She reached out a finger to trace the swirl of flowers embroidered on the skirt.

Grace moved closer to let Willa touch the delicate fabric, completely unconcerned that she might leave messy fingerprints on the muslin. "Hello, Sprouts. What would you two say to us having dinner together?"

"Where?" Wes's excitement dimmed and his brow creased. "We ain't got to wash, do we?"

"'We do not have to wash, do we?'" Grace corrected him, feeling awkward. She raised her gaze to meet Thorne's eyes. "Roland and I thought it would be nice to join you and the children here, if it is not too much of an imposition on Mrs Archer?"

Thorne paused in surprise and darted a look at Roland. Roland inclined his head to show his agreement with the request. Then Thorne glanced down at the children, still busy sizing Grace up. "I, err, I am sure it will be fine. Mrs Archer always makes extra."

"I will explain things to her," Roland said, setting a hand on Thorne's shoulder, and making his way to the kitchen.

Thorne and Grace stared at one another for a moment, and then he lifted one eyebrow in query. Grace smiled a little, to explain everything was fine. But beyond that, her thoughts failed her, and she did not know how to put into words what she wanted out of this whole endeavour. She was not comfortable speaking freely yet... especially in front of the children.

In the end, Thorne regained his footing by adopting the formality she hoped to avoid, showing her to a simple parlour off to the left and inviting her to sit. Grace sighed and took in the sense of the room. Unlike in the grander houses, the watercolour paintings of the seashore hanging on the walls and the seating had been chosen for comfort over style. That was a concept entirely foreign to her, but it seemed so sensible, she wondered why the upper class did the opposite.

Footsteps heralded the arrival of the twins, along with Mr and Mrs Archer. The older couple seemed even less at ease than Thorne. There was nothing to it but for Grace to start as she meant to go on, and she strode forward and offered Mrs Archer a hand. "It is a pleasure to make your acquaintance, Mrs Archer. I have heard much about your skill in the kitchen and in keeping the rest of the house in order. I hope we are not causing too much of a disturbance."

Mrs Archer took Grace's hand in hers and squeezed it tight. "No, his lordship has explained it to us. If I might be bold just this once, my lady..."

"Of course, Mrs Archer. You may speak your mind."

"I—I am of two minds about saying anything at all. It is... I know it is very improper, but... I know it is also a kindness you are doing for Lord Percy. My husband and I will look the other way and say nothing, but I would beg one favour of you."

Grace saw how ill at ease Mrs Archer was, and she could nearly guess what the favour was. "You have my permission to be frank. What I wanted tonight was the foundation to find our way forward from here, and I cannot imagine how that can happen without honesty."

Mrs Archer gave her a stern look that softened when she saw the truth on Grace's face. "Then I will be both honest and bold once. As a duchess, you cannot forget the boundaries entirely—and you cannot allow Lord Percy to either. Those two love one another in the same way those scamps Willa and Wes do. They are as good as a pair born together. Mr Thorne remembers his station when he must, but Lord Percy... he forgets. He grew rather wild and has never embraced the notion that given his title, he must hold himself apart from the lower class."

A lump formed in Grace's throat as she experienced the sting of those words herself, but she forced herself to smile serenely at Mrs. Archer. It was not her fault, after all, if the truth reminded Grace that only so very recently had she begun to see Elsie and the other servants she had taken for granted as more. "I will remember what you say and take those words to heart. But only... only if we can find some opportunities when it is safe for the two of them to be brothers."

Mrs Archer bobbed her head. "Fairly said, my lady, and I accept that bargain. You are both as kind and thoughtful as Lord Percy and Mr Thorne have said. I am pleased to serve such a mistress of the household—but I hope you will not be offended if my husband and I do not join you for dinner." She smiled a trifle wryly at that. "You should know that Lord Percy has had aspirations to make us unbend, but we are too old and set in our ways, and at any rate, it would not be a situation that could last."

So dinner began as a somewhat stilted affair after all. Thorne was still being carefully formal in front of her, which bemused and irked Roland. Grace, for her part, was distracted by the echoes of Mrs Archer's words and the deep divide between Thaddius's two sons. Mrs Archer was right; being gathered at the table would be an increasingly rare event once they returned to London. When more servants joined the staff, nights like this would be impossible.

The whole situation was like a puzzle. Grace was certain there was a solution... but for the moment, she could not see it.

The Sprouts, however, were in fine form, and it was their

own antics that finally brought a touch of normalcy to the table. Wes chattered away about all they had seen and done since arriving at the seaside, and when he refused to allow Willa to get a word in edge-wise, she launched a spoonful of peas in his direction. Both Roland and Thorne stiffened in shock, darting their eyes towards Grace to see how she would respond, but Grace's peals of laughter assured everyone else that she was far from horrified.

At the end of the meal, Grace thanked Mrs Archer profusely for the fine supper and complimented her on the summer berry crumble. She promised to send Elsie over soon and then told Roland it was time for her to go home. "Not that I am in any rush," she added. "But my mama will call for the watchmen if I fail to arrive soon."

Roland glanced out the window and noted the star-filled sky overhead. "We tarried long. Perhaps we should call for a carriage."

"Nonsense." Grace had no intention of rushing the wonderful night toward a conclusion. "I am happy to walk. If you are concerned, perhaps Mr Thorne would accompany us."

"Can we come, too?" Wes asked, with Willa nodding her agreement. "If anybody comes for you, I'll throw rocks at 'em til they run off. I've been practising with my slingshot."

Grace looked to Roland, giving him the final decision. He shrugged his shoulders and gave in. "Fine, but you two have to stick close to us. No running into the middle of the road, either!"

Wes and Willa hurried to find their shoes and jackets and they all left the cottage in fine spirits.

The Sprouts pestered Roland with questions about how his horse Arion was doing, and whether he could arrange for them to go on a boat. Grace slowed her steps and allowed him and the children to pull ahead. Thorne, ever the protector, stayed back with her.

"Thank you," he said after a while. "Though no one said it to me, I feel I am somehow part of the reason you chose to dine with us tonight. I hope you will not be offended if I say you are an exceptional woman, Lady Grace. It is good to finally see Roland so truly... happy."

"I confess I have only done the barest minimum of what you deserve, Mr Thorne," she replied. "I would do more if I could. Circumstances will force us to play other parts, but I want to privately acknowledge what others will not let us do so in public. When Roland and I marry, I would be happy to think of you as my brother-in-law, and I would like us to act as family. So please, let there be no walls between us, nor any uncertainty. You and Roland long ago abandoned any pretence at home of being lord and servant. I only... I wish you would not have to play the part of his valet to maintain a presence in our household."

Thorne covered his mouth with his hand and coughed to cover for his emotional response to her generous words. When he could speak, he said, "I would play any role required. Please do not do anything which might damage your standing in society, my lady. Your private thoughts on the score are more than sufficient."

Grace did not spoil things by telling him Mrs Archer had more or less warned her of the very same thing. And at any rate, Roland turned back then to see what was taking them so long. The children raced back and forth between the groups until Grace and Thorne had caught back up.

The streets of Brighton were unusually quiet that evening, the usual hum of activity replaced by an eerie silence. Word must have got out of the royal edict to search for a criminal on the loose. The group's footsteps echoed off the cobblestones as they approached the dense streets of the town centre. A shiver raced along Grace's spine and, on instinct, she inched closer to Roland.

From behind, the heavy clip of horses' hooves, at first faint, grew louder. The group hugged closer to the buildings, wanting to be well clear of the carriage. A flicker of motion drew Grace's attention. A short way ahead, a man stepped into the lamplight. Though he wore a dark cloak, there was something vaguely familiar about his movements. The cloaked man turned their way, allowing the light to highlight his features.

Roland drew up short and shouted to get the man's attention. "Danforth!"

The bang and clap of the speeding carriage grew louder and louder. Danforth stepped forward with his arm raised, intent on flagging down his ride. Roland pulled free from Grace and took off, determined to prevent the man from getting away.

The carriage driver must have sensed the danger, for he did not stop for his passenger. The horse-drawn contraption blew past, sending a gust of wind to ruffle Grace's hair. She raced after Roland, not wanting to let him go off without her. Thorne's rough shout fell on deaf ears.

Danforth spun around and dashed between two buildings, with Roland hot on his heels. Grace was only a few paces behind them, her breath heaving as she pushed her feet to go faster. She did not slow until she turned into the gap between the buildings.

The narrow alley was cloaked in darkness, the faint glow of distant gas lamps barely reaching its confines. The air was thick with the damp, salty scent of the nearby sea, mingling with the musty odour of decaying refuse. Rough cobblestones underfoot made each step precarious, while strangely shaped objects lined the walls of the building on either side. As Grace's eyes adjusted, the shadows resolved into piles of rubbish and stacks of wooden crates.

"Stop there," Roland called to Lord Danforth. Danforth kept going until he reached a small pool of light from a lantern hanging above an unmarked door. He halted there and hunched his shoulders up. The man's eyes darted nervously around. Grace noted the sweat glistening on his brow despite the cool night air. His hands trembled uncontrollably, clutching his coat tightly around him as if it were his only protection.

Roland stopped a safe distance away. "Give yourself up, Danforth. If you beg, mayhap Prinny will show you mercy."

Danforth shook his head feverishly. Thorne crept closer until Grace sensed his hulking form looming over her shoulder. As soon as Thorne ceased moving, Danforth's demeanour shifted. His desperate, quivering upper lip transformed into a predatory grin.

A sudden, sharp scraping noise came from Grace's left. Heavy, ominous creaks were the only warning they had before a thunderous clatter as the crates stacked by the wall began to tip.

As the crates toppled, Grace's eyes widened in alarm, and she dropped to a crouch on instinct. Roland swiftly wrapped his arms around her, shielding her with his body. But Thorne also leaped forward, positioning himself in a way that protected them both. The crates crashed down with a deafening noise, with Thorne enduring the impact. A sickening crack followed by a yelp of pain left Grace fearing one of the two men had suffered a serious injury in the process.

22

Roland arched sideways in pain as the corner of a falling crate jabbed into his shoulder, but he did not loosen his hold on Grace. Together, they stumbled clear of the worst of it. Thick dust filled the air, causing them to choke and blocking their view.

The bold cries of the children only added to the confusion. Roland wiped his face along his sleeve to clear his eyes. There was no sign of Lord Danforth, but Thorne was hunched over, his arm hanging at a terrible angle. Swifter than the rest of them, the children had leapt into action, taking on their attacker. Wes wrapped himself around the henchman's legs, hindering his escape, while Willa harried him from the side. Furious, the henchman made the mistake of grabbing a hold of her, and quick as a snake, she twisted and sank her teeth into his arm.

Unable to help himself, Roland raked a glance over at Grace, who was dirt smeared but otherwise unharmed. Then, at her urging, Roland rushed to aid the children... though truth be told, they were fast gaining the upper hand. He grabbed a wooden board from one of the broken crates on the ground and swung it like a club, catching the henchman on the side of the head. The thug swayed, and the children leapt clear, giving Roland space to swing again. This time the man crumpled, senseless.

Still, Roland was not taking any chances. He called for the Sprouts to sit on the downed man while he went to check on Thorne.

"I am fine," Thorne assured him through gritted teeth, his face white with pain.

Roland glanced down and saw blood dripping from Thorne's injured arm and the unnatural protrusion of bone. "Do not be foolish. You are far from fine. You need to get that seen to."

"I shall. Later."

"Now," Roland countered. "You have done enough, my friend. I must keep Danforth from getting away, but we cannot leave you to faint in the street. I fear even taking your coat off to check on it. Grace... can you bind him somewhat so he can move? Sprouts!" Wes and Willa glanced up at Roland, where he stood over them. "I need your help to accompany Thorne to my grandfather's house. It is not far from here. More importantly, a doctor will come more quickly at his call than at mine."

"What of you? Of him?" Thorne growled, glaring at the downed man.

"I will question him as soon as he rouses to see where Danforth is hiding. With that information in hand, the watchmen can do the rest."

Thorne seemed keen to continue his arguments, but Grace's manipulations of his arm while she fashioned a crude sling from her shawl made his pallor change from white to grey.

"Please, Thorne. Neither Roland nor I could live with ourselves if something worse happened to you. You saved me from injury twice today. Let us take care of you," she told him, laying a hand on his shoulder while he panted through a wave of dizziness.

Thorne gave a small nod, sending a fresh wave of pain coursing along his arm. He gritted his teeth and allowed the Sprouts to escort him away.

With them gone, Roland set to work dealing with Danforth's henchman. He half carried, half dragged the stunned brute deeper into the alley. He was regaining his senses, and Roland had to disable the man or shortly, they would have another fight on their hands. But they also needed answers.

Thrusting the ruffian to the ground behind a pile of crates that held rotting vegetables, if the smell was any indication, Roland hastily stripped his cravat with one hand and pressed his knee into the man's back to keep him there. Then, swiftly, he began to bind his arms.

"Get... off..." the man panted groggily, beginning to thrash a bit, and Roland leaned harder on him.

Jerking his head around, he looked for Grace and found her looking back at him. "Dash it, Grace. You should not be watching this violence."

She pursed her lips repressively. "I daresay I have survived worse. I am not going to swoon."

Thorne's broken arm would pale in comparison to what might follow if she didn't turn around again. Roland knew something of how ugly questioning a hostile enemy might get. He didn't want to subject any woman to that harsh reality, much less the woman who was going to be his wife. He did not want her to know he was capable of this, even though he would do far worse to keep her safe.

"That is not the point," he growled, pressing the hooligan's greasy head against the pavers to keep him from bucking. "Protecting your safety and your sensibilities is my concern, and this is no place for you." Not only could he not afford her to have sympathy for this villain, the man was far from broken and cooperative. The ruffian would have no qualms about taking advantage of any laxity.

Grace crossed her arms, standing her ground. "And leaving you to deal with this alone is supposed to keep me safe?"

Roland suppressed a sigh, recognising the look in her eyes. "I need you to be out of harm's way. And I do not want you to watch me do this," he snarled. "Please."

Whatever she saw in his face, she concluded there would be no give. Reluctantly, she turned around. "I'll stay nearby and watch to make sure that no one happens upon you. But if you think I'm going to flag a hansom and return home without you, you are sorely mistaken, Roland."

With the man's arms adequately secured, Roland took some of his weight off the brute's upper back and pinned him at the hips instead. He could thrash his head all he liked; all it would get him was a headache from cracking his skull against the bricks.

"Are you in league with Danforth?" Roland asked him, taking the dangling tails of his cravat in hand. When the man spat and told him to go to hell, Roland pushed the man's bound arms up his back slightly, twisting his arms in a manner that would hurt.

Finally, the man grunted a pained noise. "And what if I am?"

Roland let the tension slacken on the man's arms when he talked—a reward for good behaviour, so to speak. "Why would you ally yourself with a traitor?"

"Traitor? I know nothing of that, and I don't care. What does it matter if I take a coin from a toff to do what I'd do anyway to earn my daily bread?" The man laughed at them. "You rich tossers have no idea how the rest of us live."

"Fine. Then tell me now: where is he bound?"

"Sod off with you, kind sir," the man laughed again, finding this whole situation suspiciously amusing, and Roland's patience snapped. He wrenched harder on the man's arms, causing him to yelp.

From the corner of his eye, he saw Grace startle slightly. Roland hated this man at this very moment for putting them both in this position, but he stayed the course.

"Leave off, leave off!" the man nearly shouted in agony. "Let me go, and I'll tell you. The toff only paid me off to watch his back until he made his getaway, and I did my part, right? I don't give a fig about whatever else you are about."

Roland cursed at that. Of course, the man was only slowing them down so Danforth could make his escape. All the more important that they learn where he was headed, then, so they had a prayer of catching up.

When his shoulders were able to relax into a more normal position, the man spilled his guts. "I ran into your man tonight at an establishment that caters to, shall we say, procurers of goods that are difficult to obtain and most unfairly taxed."

"Smugglers."

"Aye, my lord. I drink there from time to time. The ale's cheap. Anyhow, overheard him negotiating with a friendly lot for passage on a black sail. They've a skiff on the water out front of The Lamb & Stag, and that's where your 'friend' is bound. I reckon he won't mind me telling, since you'll be too late to catch up with his lordship now."

"Faugh." Roland grunted with disgust, dropping the man entirely and getting to his feet, dancing to one side when the man rolled to trip him. He set his hand to the small of Grace's back, urging her quickly out of the back alleyway. If no one had seen him roughing up the tough, no one would see this, and he did not want to say anything to her where Danforth's henchman would overhear.

"Do you know where it is?" Grace asked him softly.

He nodded. "Perhaps—if we hurry—we might catch him before he finds his compatriots after all. He will not want to run and attract attention."

"You left your cravat," Grace hissed at him in concern as they turned the corner of a building and returned to the public streets. She also reluctantly took his offending hand from her back, laying her hand upon it instead.

Without his cravat, his shirt yawned open at the neck and he touched the bare skin of his throat, which felt curiously naked when exposed to the cool night air. This was worse than having his appearance dishevelled and people would stare. But he could hardly go home for another.

"It cannot be helped. Hopefully, no one will look closely enough to comment on my indecency. The streets are more guards and soldiers than anyone else anyhow," he told her in a low tone, waving his free hand to catch the attention of a roving soldier and raising his voice. "We were attacked by a man back in that alley! He's in league with the traitor!" He pointed in the right direction.

That would catch the infantryman's attention, and indeed, the man came at a run. Not waiting to see how that would play out, Roland lengthened his stride, tugging Grace along again at something just short of a run.

When he realised she was struggling to keep up, he slowed himself. Grace frowned at him and disengaged her arm from his. "Do not slow down," she told him, sounding only faintly winded. "It was only difficult to keep pace with you tugging me off balance. Go faster. I will be only a step behind you, I promise."

Blessedly, she had proved true to her words, and she fell

back only a short distance. And they did not have to concern themselves with being seen running, for as they headed in the direction of the pub, the little foot traffic that Brighton enjoyed at this hour all but vanished.

Ahead, barely outlined against the darkness by occasional lamps, they could see a familiar shape of a man walking towards the sea.

Roland experienced a surge of elation at their success in finding Danforth for only the briefest moment. On its heels came a growing sense of foreboding. Surely the man had heard them—

"Roland!" Grace shrieked behind him, and he spun so quickly that he nearly lost his footing. She was arched backwards, the mass of her hair caught in the left hand of another muscular reprobate, this one even larger than the one who had accosted Thorne.

Before he could comprehend anything beyond that she was caught, the man stepped out of the shadows. He neatly clouted Roland with his free hand across the face. The blow was so swift and hard, it was as if he had been hit with a brick. Unbalanced, he toppled like a sack of grain, the darkness sparkling behind his lids. He maintained just enough sense to struggle to flip from his back to his knees, attempting to protect his gut while recovering his equilibrium.

"You two just cannot help meddling," a man's voice spat, and a foot landed deep in Roland's side, causing him to lose his breath. He collapsed again, this time facedown on the stone, gasping as his lungs struggled to obey a demand to inhale.

Grace cried out again at that. "Please, Lord Danforth, do not hurt him."

"Give her to me," Danforth ordered the man, and Roland heard the swish of her skirts as she passed by. "You, bring him. Drag him if you wish."

Fury gave him the strength to regain his wits and his breath as the henchman holding him began to drag him along by the collar and waist. He would not again let Grace be held hostage. "Let her go!" he cracked, struggling to get the leverage he needed to free himself.

Danforth's boots turned and there was the distinctive sound of a click before cold metal rested against the back of his head. "My pistol will attract unnecessary attention, and a few more people may die, but I will use it if I must. I have a timetable to keep, Lord Percy. You can die here on your bellies like dogs being put down, or you can both be quiet and live for a few minutes longer. I leave the choice of it up to you. What will you choose?"

Roland closed his eyes briefly, feeling the sting of failure commingling with rage. "Living."

He was under no illusions that Danforth planned to let them live any longer than it would take to ferry them out to sea far enough that there was no hope of swimming to safety. But perhaps they would find an opportunity to overpower them or escape.

"Excellent choice. Up with you, then. Let us all enjoy a walk this very fine evening."

23

Grace kept her gaze looking straight ahead, despite everything in her body calling her to turn around and check on Roland. But that was why she dared not do it. She was terrified, and rightfully so. If Roland caught a glimpse of that on her face, he would throw his all into saving her, no matter what the cost to himself.

She sought whatever inner fortitude she had gained over the last few months and determined not to show any signs of fear or weakness to Lord Danforth. Let him think her docile. Let Roland find patience through her calm. Freedom would only come if they picked the right moment in time to fight for it, and that moment was most certainly not now.

Lord Danforth led the march along the moonlit beach of Brighton, their footsteps sinking into the wet, compact sand. The rhythmic crash of the waves provided a haunting soundtrack to their forced march. The salty breeze whipped the loose strands of Grace's chestnut hair against her face and into her mouth.

As they neared the water's edge, the low tide revealed a small skiff tied to a weather-beaten wooden post, its hull rocking gently with the ebbing waves. The villain pushed them forward into the water. Icy water soaked Grace's slippers and kept rising, lapping at her ankles as they waded through the shallows. She lifted her skirt higher and higher still until a cresting wave finally caught the hem and dragged it down. The material wrapped around her legs and pushed her off balance just enough that the receding tug pulled her feet out from underneath her.

Bitter cold stole her breath as the water grabbed hold of her gown. A pair of strong hands caught her under the arms and tugged her free of the sea's tow, bringing Grace face to face with Roland.

His dark eyes were lost in the shadow of his brow, and his face carved of granite. He clutched her tight against him, with his arms wrapped around her, as though they could offer any protection against their current difficulties. Grace longed to remain there, but Danforth gave them no time for solace.

"Get in the boat."

Roland clenched her even tighter. Grace knew that if she did not speak up, he would do something utterly foolish out of desperation to keep her safe.

"I am fine so long as you are with me," she whispered. With that, she laid her hands flat against his chest and pushed him back, so that she could stand on her own. She stared deep into the black holes of his eyes and silently pleaded with him to go along with Danforth's orders.

The henchman untied the skiff with practised efficiency, and Lord Danforth guided Grace and Roland towards it at gunpoint.

"Help her into the boat," Danforth ordered again. The henchman climbed on board first and took the middle bench so that he could row. Danforth instructed Roland and Grace to sit together at the narrow bow of the small skiff.

The henchman grimaced at them both, with a wooden oar raised in readiness to swing if they tried anything. Danforth was the last to board. He claimed the stern of the skiff and remained standing, once again training his gun on the pair.

The hired hand struck a match and lit a candle inside a small lantern. Black slats shielded most of the light from view. Grace did not understand the point of it until they set off. Danforth swapped his gun for the lantern long enough to raise it into the air. He opened and shut one of the black slats three times, sending three long flashes of light. He peered into the distance, squinting at the horizon. Curiosity drove Grace to glance over her shoulder. Far off, she saw a faint light flash three times in return.

At that signal, the henchman set off. His muscles bulged as he set a steady cadence with the oars. His huge hands gripped the wooden handles as he pulled them through the water with steady, powerful strokes. The skiff glided further out into the choppy sea.

Grace huddled closer to Roland, absorbing the heat from his body through her thin summer dress. Brighton shrank with every stroke of the oars until it was little more than a faint silhouette on the horizon. So too grew smaller the chances of anyone coming to their aid.

Any hope of surviving the night lay with the two of them. Unfortunately, she had no idea how to get them free. Already, they were too far from shore to chance swimming back. One dip in the frigid water had been enough to convince her of the futility of that plan.

The answer, therefore, had to lie on the boat for which they were bound. She refused to consider the alternative.

She heard the gruff voices of the sailors before she saw the boat. In another few strokes, it loomed overhead, casting the skiff and the surrounding water in full shadow.

"Toss us the ladder," Danforth hollered up at the faces looming over the side. A pair of ropes slithered down the side. The sailors shook them until they revealed themselves to be a rough rope ladder. Danforth waved his gun at Grace. "Ladies first."

The ride in the chilly night air had cleared Grace's thoughts, but also frozen her limbs. Her whole body ached when she forced herself to climb to her feet. The skiff bumped against the side of the boat and made her sway, but Roland shot out a hand to steady her.

"I will be right behind you," he promised.

Grace was thankful for the gloves on her hands, even if they had not been designed for such a task. They kept her hands from feeling the worst of the burn of the ladder as she climbed higher. When she neared the top, the ladder suddenly jerked. She glanced down and found that Roland had joined her. He was not taking any risk of them being separated.

Finally, she reached the top. A pair of sailors grabbed hold and pulled her over the railing before dropping her unceremoniously onto the deck. While she waited for Roland and the others to catch up, she got her first good look at the ship. It was a two-masted schooner, around twenty-five metres in length. Sleek and dark-painted to blend in with the sea at night. It was no wonder she had not seen it. The main and fore sails had been furled tightly to avoid detection, but men stood ready to deploy them quickly if a swift escape was needed.

Grace counted seven men arranged around the deck, busying themselves with various tasks. Too many for Roland to take on, especially if at least one had a gun. Roland's head rose above the railing as he reached the end of the ladder. He shrugged off the sailor's offers of help and threw first one leg and then the other over. He stalked to where Grace sat and pulled her to her feet. With a protective arm thrown around her shoulders, his menacing glare threatened retribution should anyone think about approaching her.

Danforth came last, wearing a feral grin. He motioned for the sailors to pull up the ladder and asked where was the captain.

"I'm o'er here," a gruff voice replied. A grizzled old man strode into view. His silver threaded hair hinted at his age, but the weathered state of his skin meant he could be anywhere from his forties to his sixties. There was no bend to his shoulders as he adopted the practised stance of a man who had spent many years at sea. "What's the meaning of this? You paid for one trip, not three."

"These two are stowaways. As soon as we get a little further from the coast, you are welcome to toss them overboard."

Grace bit her lip to keep from gasping in surprise at Danforth's casual disregard for their lives. The ship's captain seemed equally uncomfortable.

"Now see here," he growled, stepping closer to Danforth. "Just because the sea is fond of claiming lives, don't mean I plan to feed it."

Danforth shrugged his shoulders. "Then take them back with you and set them free. When they tell everyone of your tendency to skirt the law, you will have no one to blame but yourselves."

Annoyance flashed across the captain's face, and his men grumbled.

"Will it make you feel better if I shoot them before we toss them over the side? Their blood can be on my hands alone."

The captain sighed heavily at Danforth's offer and then threw his hands in the air. "So long as their ghosts haunt you, then I will hold my tongue about the rest. Take 'em below. We've spent enough time wagging our chins, as it is. Men, hoist the anchor while the tide is still with us."

The stiff sea breeze and their wet clothes robbed the heat of Grace's body quickly. She did not particularly want to descend into the bowels of the schooner, but Danforth waved the gun her way to force her to comply. Roland's cheek muscle thumped with impotent fury while he reluctantly obeyed.

At least the both of them would be locked down there together. It drove Grace wild with panic to imagine that they might be separated—to imagine Roland being sent to a watery grave, her never knowing what became of him before she was sent to her own. She did not want to even think about what the character of these men might be.

A sailor flipped the hatch on the deck to reveal the stairwell into the hold. It was as dark as pitch.

"I do not suppose you have a candle," she said to the sailor holding the hatch door. The slightest tremor to her voice vexed her. But so be it.

The sailor scoffed, but Danforth laughed aloud. "Sources of open flame on ships are dangerous enough without putting them in the hands of unwilling prisoners. Women are bad luck even when they come willingly. No sailor worth his salt would pair those two."

Of course, it would be too much to hope for a light. So she stepped down as carefully as she could, not wanting to fall down the slippery wood steps and break her neck. At least Danforth did not seem to care how slowly she went, so long as she did.

"Did you find the floor, my lady?" Danforth called down. "Back off so your man can find his way down to join you."

She scooted back with her arms outstretched to keep from bumping into anything. Roland leapt down the final two steps and hurried again to her side. She shivered uncontrollably, unsure how much of it from cold versus fear. She had been held with a knife to her throat only weeks before, and still bore the scar. Yet, somehow, that seemed less terror-inducing than the dark, dank hold.

Danforth came down the stairs next, but stopped before he reached halfway down. He swung a lantern in front of him, illuminating the stairs in a pale orange glow. His mouth twisted into a sadistic grin when he took in the sight of the pair.

"Why, Danforth?" Roland asked. "Prinny trusts you. Depends upon you. Why betray him and your country?"

Danforth shook his head at Roland's naivety. "Prinny betrayed me. He betrays you, her, your families. I am amazed that word has not got out of his secret doings."

Roland scoffed. "The only secret activities Prinny has are his adventures into the slums to gamble."

"If only that were the end of it, I would not have been forced to act." Danforth shook his head and displayed something approaching genuine remorse. "Prinny is far too susceptible to pleas for help. One has only to provide some sob story and he twists himself into a knot to accommodate them. Those documents he had me reviewing marked a new low. He is planning to betray the upper class by secretly supporting the abolitionist movement, aligning himself with radicals who seek to dismantle our very way of life. His dalliance with these reformists threatens our wealth, our power, and the traditions that uphold society. He will be the ruin of me... of all of us."

"But then, why not out him for this instead? Why steal the Sapphire codes? And why would you deliver them into the hands of England's enemies?"

"In the grand scheme of our war with France, giving them Sapphire will not make much difference. As you know, codes can be replaced. In the meantime, Prinny and the government will have to devote their time and resources into security matters, where they should! Prinny will learn the importance of stability, and pull away from any changes, like abolishing the slave trade."

"What of you?" Grace asked in a firm tone. She gritted her teeth against another chill until it passed. "Do you expect him to welcome you back after this?"

Danforth rolled his eyes. "I am not so foolish, Lady Grace. The French will compensate me well for this, and I have my estates in the West Indies where I may ride out the storm. It is a sacrifice, but I make it for the greater good. The same with the two of you. Your deaths will ensure the financial security of so many of England's families. Take heart in that while you sink to your grave."

24

Roland watched Danforth disappear through the open hold door. In the darkness, he barely made out the outline of the sky—a small square of the deepest indigo speckled with stars, bracketed by the purest darkness— and shadows standing near the bottom edge.

In the receding light, Roland stepped backwards, tripping over something. There was the screech of wood on wood as he landed with his back against a barrel. A sailor snarled at him from the deck above. "Mind our water and cargo, guv."

The urge to snap back at the man was strong, but Roland held his tongue. The steps descending into the hold groaned softly as the shadows grew deeper.

With no warning, the sailor threw the hold door shut. With even the little light from the night sky gone, it plunged them into a blackness so absolute that Grace gasped in terror.

"Shhh, I am here," he said, and he reached out to find her, his fingers finding soaked muslin and skin like ice. "Come close," he demanded, pulling her carefully to him. His legs were as wet as hers, but at least he was dry from the waist up. Mostly. She was so cold.

Wrapping one arm around her, he pulled her deeper into the hold, using his left hand to guide the way and steady him against the rocking of the ship. Surely there must be something on board this ship that might prove useful.

His fingers glanced over piles of burlap sacks, but they were filled with small, rock-hard objects. Inhaling softly through his nose, he caught the earthy mineral smell of damp coal. Perhaps he would find an empty sack he could use to dry her off. It would be dirty, but being filthy was better than catching her death from a chill.

Assuming they survived long enough to worry about such things, that was.

As abruptly as the thought occurred to him, however, the pile sloped away. Taking another step forward, Roland encountered another pile—this one containing soft but firm rows of lines. It had the impression of bolts of cloth. "Here," he said, gingerly lowering them both to the floor beside the stack.

Grace was sitting in a sodden heap on the floor where he left her, leaning against the piles, but he heard her teeth chattering. As swiftly as he could, he pulled the nearest soft-ish sack to himself and fumbled with the thong tying it shut. Once he got a finger beneath it, he snapped it with a quick wrench.

His guess was correct: these were sacks of cloth. It was hard to be entirely certain when exploring with water-rumpled fingertips, but it felt like cotton. Something with a light weave. Wool would have been too much to hope for, but at least he could dry her off somewhat.

Reaching out again in the dark, he found her hands and pulled her back into his lap, opening his coat to share what little warmth he had. She was no longer shivering, and her soaked skirts must have weighed fifty pounds, but he didn't dare strip her of anything besides her wet gloves on a ship full of men.

The only blessing of being kept in this dark hold was the

protection from the wind it offered, but it was far from warm. Though Grace was not at risk of freezing to death, she was most certainly miserable. The front of his shirt was wet from her dress, and it wicked his body heat between them. So be it, as long as it took it towards her.

"Talk to me. Please. Are you all right?" he asked her, his mouth against her temple as he unwound the cotton bolt and began to dry her with it.

"I am cold," she complained, her jaw moving near his collarbone. "Wet, cold, and furious."

"I know," he told her, stroking her damp hair away from her face. "But you are being brave."

"Am I?" Her breath hitching. "I am scared, Roland. I keep thinking about how this hold is as dark as a grave. I think we are in trouble this time."

"Bravery is not the absence of fear. It is what you do despite it." His protective instincts surged to the front, stifling his wounded indignation at their predicament. "Let yourself be angry. It is better than being scared. We are here together. You can touch me and hear me. There is air. It may be as dark as a grave, but do not let yourself make it easy for Danforth by conceding the battle before it is over and putting us in one before our time."

Grace shivered again, but the rise and fall of her chest grew steadier. "You are right. Did you come across anything here we can use as a weapon? I have the most curious urge to live long enough now to flog Danforth myself."

"Grace!" Roland scolded, barely covering a scandalised laugh and gasping as the sudden movement jarred his bruised ribs. "Unfortunately... I am unsure how sacks of cloth and coal will save us against a crew of at least seven, not to mention Danforth himself. Unless, that is, you have some use for whatever I seem to be sitting on. My guess is a used fishing net, judging by the smell of it."

Grace let an amused sound escape her lips, but then she shifted away from the heat of his chest, leaving a cold sensation that went deeper than skin. At least she did not go far. She rummaged around, patting her hands against wood and burlap as she explored their surroundings. "I would have thought smugglers would carry more nefarious items to France," she muttered. "Why could we not have found a shipment of gunpowder or swords?"

Roland shrugged, even though she would not see it. "Most smugglers are otherwise law-abiding men in search of a means of providing some security for their future. As fishermen, a poor catch would mean hunger for their families. The warships and blockade disturbing the waters do not help. Transporting goods to and from France due to the war that are scarce, and not weapons—things they can sell to the toffs, as they say—they likely view smuggling as a victimless crime."

She stiffened. "And us? Murder?"

"The captain did not sound too pleased about that part, did he?" Those were all the only hopeful words he was able to muster, however. Smuggling wine and cloth might be a victimless crime, but that didn't mean there wouldn't be a severe penalty if they were caught. Regardless of the cost, the captain would let Danforth push them overboard or shoot them, if only to protect his men.

His attempts to give her some hope were fruitless, because there was a silence after his words, and it stirred his pulse with worry. "Come back to me. You are still too cold."

She did, and for a while, they sat in silence, nothing filling the space but the creaking of the ship and the few words from the sailors filtering down below. It wasn't an overlong journey across the channel—perhaps some half a day—but he was sure

Danforth did not intend to even let them see the dawning hours, much less the opposite shore. A few hours of sailing was all that was necessary to drop them far enough from shore to condemn their bodies to a watery grave. Would anyone learn what happened to them?

Roland cast around again and again for a solution to their predicament, but the seconds and minutes ticked past with no inspiration, and as they grew colder, the anger and determination that had been buoying their spirits trickled away.

There was something about the utter bleakness of this wooden oubliette that felt nearly like a confessional, and the passing of their final moments hung heavy around his neck. "In case we cannot find a way out of this muddle…"

Grace twisted around. Although he could not see an inch of her, her breath warmed his cheek. He did not need any light to imagine her expression.

"What?"

"If these are our last hours, there are but two regrets I will take with me. I regret not finishing my ambition for Thorne. So many years I spent scrimping… I never told him I was planning to use the money in my small investments saved up these last years to set him up with a business venture. Or something. Whatever he wanted. At least I was possessed of enough sense to leave him a bequest in my will before we went to war." Roland sighed into her hair, holding her closer. "I hope it is enough for him to build a life for himself—one where he can find happiness. If not, I pray my grandfather is… somehow moved to be generous."

Although, knowing his grandfather, the most generosity he should expect of the Breaker would be to stop short of persecuting Thaddius's illegitimate son for Roland's disappearance. Thorne would look for them. That much he had faith in. It wouldn't be his fault that a search would be in vain.

Maybe he truly had been luckier than he thought in life. His father was no great prize... but he was glad Thaddius's womanising had given him his brother. The Archers, he had no fear about them doing well wherever they ended up. And certainly, between them and his brother, the Sprouts would thrive.

"The other," he finally continued, "is that I regret not protecting you better. A gentleman should keep you safe from all harm, and here we are. I could not have failed worse had I tried, and that is why I am sorry."

"Did I ask you to protect me?" Her voice slipped up a notch as she arched away from him, but she took his hand and put it to the side of her scarred neck. "You need to forgive yourself. You are not to blame for Sir David's actions, and certainly not Danforth's. I know you are hurt, even though you pretend otherwise. How long will you wear the sackcloth and ashes?"

His lips compressed into a hard line. "Certainly longer, I would reckon, than the time we may have left. I should have sent you with Thorne."

Her voice raised higher. "No, you should not have. We walked into this together, and together is where I want to spend whatever time we have left. How do you think I would feel to not be here? How could you possibly want me to be cosseted behind walls while you go into danger, grieving, wondering if you will ever return home?"

Roland opened his mouth, but words failed him. Instead, he wrapped her in his arms, pressing his forehead to hers. "I cannot help it. Soldiers are expected to lay down their lives for the realm and others—and when it comes to you, I would do that unstintingly."

"You are so blind to your own worth. You have people who care for you now, and you are important to us for reasons beyond the protection you can offer," she whispered. "Perhaps not your father or grandfather. But the rest of us do. Besides, if there is to be blame, I am the one who should be sorry," she said eventually, sounding a little more like herself, but she burrowed against his neck again instead of pulling farther away. "You would not be involved in any of this if it were not for me."

He blinked, surprised, his eyes wide open despite the darkness. "Is it your turn for my sackcloth?" he teased her gently, not wanting her to be so upset. "How is it possibly your fault that we are here?"

"I would have to be a fool to not recognise my role in the choices you have made. I went to London with no plan at all to marry—at least not this year. I just wanted to see more than one small corner of the world before it was decided I must become a wife and a mother."

He shook his head, not seeing the connection.

"I did very much want to find and protect Charity, but there was also a part of me that saw the chance for... a grander adventure. The same again when we stumbled across the murdered guard in the palace. I leapt into the opportunity to continue my adventures, and time and time again, you were compelled to aid me. I was... selfish."

Was that all? "It is not selfish to want a chance to look and grow beyond yourself."

She scowled against his chest. "But there are safer ways to go about that than pursuing a kidnapping or murder investigation. If it were not for my... my constant meddling, as Lord Danforth put it, I would not have a scar upon my neck, you would not be blaming yourself for the danger I put myself in, and we would not be headed across the channel to be drowned. My mother was right. My headstrong nature will, after all, be the death of me."

An abrupt laugh escaped his throat. "Imagine her standing on the deck of this ship shouting 'I told you so!'"

Grace made a small noise that might have nearly been a laugh of her own, but then she struck him lightly on his chest, mindful of his tender spots. "That is not funny."

"It is, a little." He cupped her head, trying to warm her with his own skin and the cotton as much as he could. "Your headstrong nature is not one I wish you would regret. Because... in the end, that is what brought the two of us together. Well—as long as you do not throw me out for any protective tendencies."

There was an indistinct sound of frustration. "I cannot be angry with you for that, even, because I have the same tendencies towards you. I am selfishly glad you are here with me, even though there is another part of me that wishes you also were far away. Safe." Grace's voice trailed off as emotion tightened her throat. She snuggled closer against him, tucking her head under his chin. "Speaking of regrets, there is one I will not add for leaving it unsaid. I... I love you, Roland," she finally said. "And I should have told you sooner. I should have said it somewhere nice, some place romantic, when you were smiling at me—"

Roland could not help himself. His hand curled around the back of her head, and he tilted her lips towards him so that he could crush her mouth to his. His other arm cupped her legs, and he pulled her closer to him. She hesitated in shock for only a heartbeat, and then she melted willingly into his touch, throwing both arms around his neck.

That gentled him, and he stopped, easing the clutch of his fingers in her hair and behind her knees, not wanting to hurt her. He had no right to kiss her at all, and yet...

She nipped at his chin and pulled him back to her. Her fingers threaded through his hair, wiping away all thought. This time, she met his kiss head on.

He couldn't force himself to back away, but after a long stretch, he lifted his mouth just enough to allow them to catch their breath, still close enough that the evening shadow of his growing whiskers rubbed against her cheek. Her pulse thundered beneath his fingers on her neck.

"I, too, realised there was one other thing I would regret not doing," he whispered in apology against the corner of her mouth, letting his lips barely touch her skin so that he could trace the curve of her smile, just as he meant her to.

Before he had the chance to say anything else—before he could admit that he never expected to be so lucky that he would find love, find her—the hold door was thrown open with a crash, and a lantern shone down into the darkness.

It was the same man who had caught Grace by the hair, and he peered suspiciously in their direction. "Time's up," he grunted, jerking a thumb in the direction of the sea.

25

Grace wanted nothing more than to cling to Roland, even if it meant remaining there in the dark, damp depths of the ship. Perhaps that was why she was so slow to move. For his part, Roland made no effort toward loosening his hold on her.

Eventually, Roland helped her to her feet and then rose to stand behind her. He leaned forward and whispered in her ear, "I will go first, and then you follow. I do not want to risk you being trapped up there without me. Wherever we go, we go together. And Grace," he added, "we should not go silently. Agreed?"

Grace gave a single nod and then stepped aside to allow him to pass. She shrugged off the bolt of cotton fabric he had wrapped around her shoulders and left it in a puddle on the floor. Her heart pounded in her chest as the henchman descended into the hold, his presence a menacing reminder of their precarious situation.

She glanced at Roland, his handsome face a canvas of bruises and cuts, yet his eyes burned with defiance. The henchman motioned for them to ascend the stairs, shoving Roland forward when he failed to move fast enough. Then, he grabbed Grace around the waist and pushed her upwards to the deck, following closely behind.

Roland did not wait. As soon as they got topside, he sprang forward, driven by a surge of desperate courage. She barely leapt to one side as he collided with the henchman, fists flying, and for a moment, Grace's hope soared.

But the henchman recovered quickly, brandishing a wicked gutting knife, the blade glinting ominously in the moonlight. There was a shout from someone closer to the bow, and Grace gasped, her heart lurching with fear as the two men grappled violently. Roland fought with every ounce of his strength, but he was hindered by his bruised ribs and the henchman was formidable, his movements swift and deadly.

Just as the blade arced towards Roland, several men rushed in, yanking the henchman back and prying the knife from his grasp. The deck erupted in chaos, but Grace saw that Roland was unharmed, albeit shaken. Relief washed over her, mingling with the ever-present fear of what might come next, and the brisk, salty wind nearly stole her breath as she hurried to him.

Into this melee, the ship captain strode, his movements effortless across the rolling surface of the ship. Shoving the brawling members of his crew apart from the brute, he turned and spat upon the deck, looking at Lord Danforth where he stood at the forecastle. "Your man shows no honour in fisticuffs, m'lord!"

The ruffian sneered, and Danforth crossed his arms over his chest." Take that one," the captain told his sailors, pointing at Danforth's henchman with his chin, "below. An' tie up the other so we don't have no more fightin'."

The ship rocked from side to side, adding to her sense of

unquiet, but the sailors left Grace alone to deal with Roland. Once his arms were bound behind his back, one sailor stepped forward to lead them to the bow of the schooner. Once there, nothing stretched before them except for black, roiling water as far as the eye could see.

The sailor left them with Danforth, and based on the gleeful expression on Danforth's wicked face, Grace did not rate highly their chances of seeing the next five minutes, much less the sunrise.

She shifted her attention back to the captain, not wanting to let the traitor's face be the last she saw. His expression, at least, was grim—but he wouldn't meet Grace's pleading gaze. "Their bodies won't wash up on shore at this distance, m'lord. If yer still set upon this foul course, that is."

"There is no other course. Not unless you fancy a rope necklace," Danforth replied before Grace got a word out.

The grizzled old shipping captain grunted and turned his back to walk away. Angry, Grace called for him to stop. "If you are man enough to sign off on our deaths, you should be man enough to witness them!"

The captain's shoulders dropped a half inch, and he halted in place. He did not, however, turn around.

Grace tried again. This time, she allowed the terror gripping her spine to bleed through into her tone. Her pitch went up and her voice trembled. "This is not right. Letting this happen will leave a mark upon your soul."

"It ain't my concern," he replied over his shoulder in a gruff tone.

"Tell that to your wife. To your children," Roland added. "Or will you find it just as hard to look into their eyes as you are looking into ours?"

"Enough jabbering," Danforth growled as he pulled the gun

from his pocket and cocked it, the audible click causing Grace to flinch. "Which one of you will be first? Him, I think. Say goodbye to your betrothed, Lady Grace."

Grace covered her mouth in horror, unable to let out a squeak as Danforth pointed the muzzle of his flintlock at Roland's head. Roland held her gaze, his eyes speaking volumes.

Wherever we go, we go together.

"No!" shouted Grace, her throat cording with the force of her cry. She tried to throw herself in the way, but the captain caught her around the waist as she made to launch herself at Danforth.

The metal click and scrape of the flint striking the frizzen didn't end with the distinctive bang of a discharge. For a moment, everyone blinked, confused. The captain let Grace's waist leave his hands in surprise, and then one of the sailors behind Grace let out a mighty hoot of laughter. "Ha! Look at that, the fancy gent's flintlock's gone and misfired! Guess you should've kept yer powder dry, milord!"

Danforth snarled a curse and tried to fire again, but the sailor was right; the gunpowder had got damp. In frustration, he hurled his weapon over the side, causing it to land in the water with a splash. "I do not need a gun to end the both of you. I only have to push you over the side. Between her gown and his bound hands, they will both sink like stones."

He stepped closer to Roland and Grace grabbed onto the traitor's arm before he could do something foolish. "If you push him, I will do my level best to pull you over with us, you reprobate," she snarled in his face. "I have nothing to lose for trying!"

Danforth truly was an utter coward, because rather than shake her off disdainfully, his face grew tinged with a very real concern. "Remove your hands from me, you brazen hussy!" he demanded, looking to the captain for aid. "Roberts, get her off of me."

The captain, however, was disinclined to acquiesce. "I'm not the sort to harm a woman, an' you're the one who wants her dead. If you're unable to handle a young lady yourself, yer a bigger milksop than I thought."

The loss of his gun removed not only their most immediate risk, but also fundamentally changed the nature of the game. If they wanted Grace and Roland gone now, they would have to toss them over and listen to their screams. Clearly, the more time that passed, the less the captain felt it possible to deny any culpability. And even Danforth's bluster seemed to pale at the thought of having to murder them directly with his bare hands.

The longer Grace studied the ship's crew, the more they struck her as honest men. Or, at minimum, God-fearing. They had objected to their unexpected presence, saved Roland from being gutted by Danforth's henchman, and refused to have a hand in killing Grace and Roland.

She had seen the contents of the hold. Where there should have been fish lay bolts of cloth and other smuggled goods. But as she and Roland had noted, not munitions or the materials to make weapons.

These men had a code of honour. Though it differed from her own in some key ways with respect for the law, underneath, there was more common ground than not.

That was information she could use.

She cleared her throat and spoke up. "Captain, what is your name? Roberts?"

"What does it matter to a dead woman, eh?" he asked. When she didn't answer, the man shrugged in indifference. "Aye. It is Roberts."

"Pleased to meet you, Captain Roberts. I am Lady Grace Tilbury and this is Lord Percy."

"Egads, does the girl think we are at a tea party?" Danforth grumbled, but he quieted at a fiery glare from Roland. Grace ignored him.

"Captain, I would beg a favour from you. Lord Danforth is caught between the necessity and distaste of condemning us to the deep, while others look on and judge him. I expect that desperation will win out soon enough."

"I hate to disappoint a lady, but I'll tell ye the same as I told the toff. He paid money for passage. We didn't sign up for murder, kidnapping, or brawlin'. Passage for him and the lout. No more an' no less. Anything else goin' on is between God, you, and him."

"That is all right, Captain Roberts. I am not asking you to intercede between us and Danforth; I have another request. You know our names now. If you consider yourself a man of honour, I would be grateful if, one day, you would send an unsigned letter to our families to tell them our fates. I would not ask you to give yourself up... only to let them know so they can give up hope. As sailors, I am certain you can understand that the only thing worse than hearing of a loved one's death is spending the remainder of your days wondering if they will ever return."

Danforth blustered, grabbing the collar of Grace's dress and tearing the fabric that hid her neck loose. "Of course he will do no such—"

Roland shoved himself at Danforth in a blind rage, prepared to crack Danforth in the face with his own skull if need be, and the man had to drop Grace to hold him off.

"You. Shut it," Captain Roberts told Danforth. "You don't speak for me an' mine." He eyed Grace with a newfound respect. "'Tis a reasonable request, my lady. I will try to see it granted. Perhaps not soon, but someday."

"Thank you, Captain," Grace continued with all the dignity she could muster, despite her pounding heart. She could feel

Danforth's ire rising. The furious tremor of his hand. Soon his patience would snap, she was certain. Death felt close enough to breathe upon her neck.

And then, when things seemed darkest, she was possessed of an idea so desperate it might work—if she could keep Danforth at an impasse.

"Captain, you fear Lord Percy and I might reveal your names to the authorities and out you as smugglers, correct? What if I offered an alternative solution?"

The other sailors, apparently finished with hogtying Danforth's oaf and putting him below, moved closer to stand behind their captain.

"Promises don't fill our bellies, Lady Grace."

"Then it is lucky that is not what I had in mind. You seem like honest, hardworking folk. Why would you dabble in something as dangerous as this?"

"Why do we?" Roberts glanced back at his men and uttered a dark laugh. "Lady, I don't expect someone like you to understand, but since you asked, I'll tell ye. My foremost responsibility is to my men, and through them, to our families. Times are hard enough as it is. War brings high taxes, high prices, and little new work. Add in the blockades and we nearly lost all our ways of earning an honest living."

The sailors shouted in agreement.

"Look at the two of you, dressed in your finery," he continued disparagingly. "Even wet and torn as it is, it's worth more than most of us will see in a season of fishin'. If we can help feed people by thumbin' our noses at the spoiled rich folk— bringing in the wine they can't get and ferry cloth and other goods back across to get it—so be it."

"So, then you are not doing it because you support Napoleon's position in the war?" Grace asked, sliding herself between Roland and Danforth as Captain Roberts and his men drew closer to listen to what she had to say. Edging backwards, she pushed Roland inches farther from the traitor.

She was gambling quite a lot on the hope that the sailors would cow Danforth into inaction. And Roland was most certainly staring daggers at the back of her head for putting herself between them.

The men laughed. "We would never," said Roberts coldly. "We're loyal patriots to a man, and we help the little folk—even if the toffs misunderstand what it means to be loyal to the people of England."

At that moment, Danforth realised exactly what Grace meant to do, and he leapt for her. Grace threw herself away from the railing with all her strength. Towards Roberts. Towards the other men. She tumbled, but that was fine. Her momentum aided her in slipping through his fingers.

Grace raised her voice to be heard over the shouting men. "Captain Roberts! How will your families fare when the prince discovers you aided a traitor?"

The sailors went quiet.

Snarling, Danforth grabbed for Grace's ankles, yelping as she kicked him. Roland tried to help her, but without the aid of his hands, he was unbalanced by the rocking of the ship, and he fell.

"You didn't know, did you?" she continued shouting. "But it is too late for that now. The traitorous blackguard has already brought ruin to your doorstep. You are now abetting the most dire enemy of the crown!"

"Eh?" Captain Roberts raised a hand to hush his crew. "What do you mean?"

Roland struggled to his knees. "If you want to learn why, you have only to check his coat pockets."

Danforth clasped the front of his coat shut—the most foolish thing he could have possibly done. Captain Roberts decided there was enough cause to stride across the deck with a pair of his burliest sailors in tow, circling around to grab Danforth by the arms. Though the man struggled, Roberts ripped his coat open, sending buttons flying, and rifled through the inner pockets. His hand emerged clutching a thick rolled document.

"That pack of bound papers is worth more than your ship, more even than the lives of everyone on it, us included." Roland frowned at Danforth. "If that makes it to the French, they will have the means to translate our military communiques. Think about the impact of that on the British soldiers manning the front lines. The deaths that will happen because the French know what the Sixth Coalition are doing."

Roberts eyed the document with a healthy level of fear. He pulled his arm back to toss it over the side, but Grace shouted for him to stop. "You throw that away and you will have no hope of redemption. People know we are missing. They were with us shortly before Danforth and his man caught us and dragged us here. How long will it take the authorities to learn your identities? How much of a reward will it take for someone on the shore to offer up your names?"

Roberts lowered his arm and tucked the papers inside his own coat. "All right, Lady Grace. We're listening. Tell us what this proposal of yours is, then."

Though Grace had hardly dared hope for this chance, now that it was here, her words failed to rise. Fear of getting this wrong had closed her throat tight.

Roland shuffled closer, bumping her with his shoulder. "Tell them. I believe in you, and will support what you say."

"How can I promise so much on behalf of the prince?" she whispered.

"Have faith. To recapture the cipher and Danforth, I daresay Prinny would give up more than you would believe."

His support lent her the confidence she needed to make her

last gambit. She coughed to clear her throat of the last of her terror. In a firm voice, she made her offer. "How would you like to be heroes, Captain Roberts? Well-compensated heroes, I add. For I am certain, the Prince Regent will offer a vast reward to anyone who can deliver his former confidante-turned-traitor into the arms of the crown."

26

The morning sunlight glinting off the waters was so blinding it was fit to make his battered head split, but fortunately, the two sailors guiding the Black Hawk's skiff from the front and back benches took a slightly southwesterly tack back to the shore so it was more behind them.

Roland and Grace had taken the middle bench to be out of the way. After their long hours at sea, Grace was mostly dry—and in no small part because of the stiff winds that had turned her hair into a charming disaster—but she still huddled on the seat beside him. He tried to shelter her somewhat, putting his arm around her, but she stiffened when he did.

"What are you thinking?" he asked her softly, although it was hard to have any private conversation on a small boat. Sound carried on the water with nothing to baffle it, but the two sailors pointedly ignored their discussions to give them what privacy they could.

"So many things. My head is a muddle," she confessed. "I am glad we stopped Danforth. That we are alive. But... Now I cannot help but think about how things will be very awkward when we find our families," she said obliquely, her voice sounding a little despondent.

She was as ruined as Charity had been. It did not matter that he did not care. His grandfather most certainly would. Even Grace's father would be within his rights to demand satisfaction.

"That is just your fatigue talking." He tightened his arm around her waist, drawing her closer. "You managed to talk us out of a near certain death. Do not worry about the rest."

"I am exhausted," she admitted. "But we will have a long time before we can put our heads to a pillow."

The skiff drew close enough to the beaches at Brighton that they started making out the figures of a few people on the shore. Not many—it was quite early by the standards of the nobility— but there were some. And they had been spotted, to judge by the pointing and activity.

Many minutes passed as the sailors fought the retreating tide to bring them inexorably closer, but slowly they grew larger, and finally Grace sat up taller, frowning as she studied the cluster. "Oh my. Is that Thorne there?"

Whipping his head around, Roland did indeed spot a suspiciously familiar dark head standing on the beach, one arm in a white sling, among a cluster of red-coated guardsmen. Beside him were two smaller bodies that must have been the Sprouts. "Yes, that does look like a dunderhead we know! Good God."

The two sailors rowing them were most visibly nervous now that they could see the red coat of the guard. "I promise, I will insist on amnesty for the both of you when we speak with the Prince Regent," Roland told them. "You and the rest of the crew of the Black Hawk. We left you Danforth as part of that good faith agreement, and His Highness will definitely want to acquire him."

As the skiff pulled into the shallow waters, Roland held up a hand to stave off Prinny's approaching soldiers. One of the sailors hopped out into the waist-deep waters and helped guide the craft to the edge of the water. "Hold this, Grace," Roland told her, giving her the stripped Sapphire codebook. Then he, too, hopped out of the craft, helping the sailor beach it. His clothes were already ruined, after all. What was a little more water on his breeches?

The captain had wanted to hold either Danforth or the codebook as surety that the crown would not act against them for their part in the traitor's schemes. Roland doubted the prince would have been happy if they had left the book behind. Grace gripped it in her slightly uplifted hands, not wanting it to get wet, and wavered a bit as she stood. Then Roland scooped her up, wincing as his bruised ribs howled. But that did not stop him from carrying her to dry land and planting her directly in front of Thorne and the kids.

"Lord Percy! Lady Grace," Thorne said, his voice cracking. "You're alive."

"Yes, brother," Roland said, achy exasperation creeping into his tone as he took in Thorne's pain-lined face and the dark circles beneath his reddened eyes. Thorne looked half-broken, but Roland could not comfort him as he wanted to. "Why are you walking around at this hour with a freshly broken arm? Have you completely lost your senses?"

The expression on Thorne's face wavered between relief, joy, and apprehension as Roland named him as family in front of the guardsmen, and cleared his throat to cover a rougher emotion. "Perhaps, Lord Percy. It is difficult... it is difficult to keep them when someone has scared you out of your wits." Then Thorne's voice grew abruptly firmer. "And if I lost mine, it would be a direct result of you not having any sense at all. At least someone seems to have spared me the trouble of blackening your eye, so I was not obligated to throw a punch left-handed."

Roland grinned, feeling the urge to hug his brother, although he refrained from doing so. Not so much because he gave a damn any longer about how improper it would be. Because he knew it would hurt. He was willing to risk his ribs, but Thorne was doing enough to risk the healing of his arm already.

"Mr Thorne wouldn't take no laudanum, sir," Willa volunteered, so upset she was slipping back into her old mannerisms. "He let the doc set his arm but then he joined the searchers, hopin' you hadn't been taken out to sea like that big tosser in the alley said. But Wes an' me, we hung round the beaches. We figured you might swim to shore or somethin'. Then Wes saw the skiff, and we got 'im."

Grace stepped forward and staggered a little, unused to the stillness of the land after they had spent the hours of the return trip standing on the rolling deck of the Black Hawk, but Willa steadied her. "That was very clever of both of you. But Mr Thorne should still be resting." Her arched eyebrow conveyed clearly her agreement with Roland on that score.

"Willa, can you go to the Tilbury residence and find Elsie?" Roland asked her. "We must go to the pavilion and deal with... a hundred things, but Grace at least needs a change of clothes. Can you have Elsie bring it there? I expect we will be His Highness's guests awhile yet. And Wes—" he added, dividing a cross look between Thorne and the boy, "get this idiot home and safely into bed, would you?"

"As you wish, sir!" Wes laughed and nudged Thorne away towards Brighton's streets, even though Thorne clearly did not want to go. Willa patted at Grace's hand to ask her if she wanted any message passed along, but she resisted long enough to face Roland. He could only imagine what she was thinking right now, as her face, too, was commingled with a riot of conflicting emotions. Amusement. Resignation. Fear. But also... love. He let himself gaze back at her with all that he could not express in words in front of the rest of these men. Have faith, my lady. I will not let you down.

It took him some minutes to explain to the soldiers standing by that the two sailors were to be taken to the pavilion as guests —not prisoners. The red-clad soldiers split into three groups, some to escort them directly to an audience with the Prince Regent, the others to inform both the Tilbury residence and His Grace, the Duke of Northumberland, that their relations were no longer missing.

At the pavilion, Walker met them, his eyes stretching to see their bedraggled and battered condition. "Lord Percy! Lady Grace! I—I... Let me order you baths and clothes. His Highness will surely want you to have a chance to clean up..."

"After, Walker," Roland told the man, although not unkindly. "There are some things that simply cannot wait."

Startled and uncertain, the man glanced between Roland and Grace when Roland offered Grace his arm. Out of the corner of his eye, he could see flags upon her cheeks, but otherwise she took a pose as if she was finely gowned and coiffed instead of garbed in wrinkled muslin, her hair looking like a nest of snakes.

Inwardly, he smiled, glad she understood the need for this embarrassment. He wanted to confront Prinny with the direct evidence of how she—how both of them suffered. He suspected he would need that leverage to drive this next bargain with the prince.

Prinny received them in the King's Apartments, the selfsame place he had conducted his strategy meeting. However, this time, the room was devoid of members of the military and all but one unfamiliar face.

To his credit, the Prince Regent made a paltry attempt not to notice their dishabille, but the glances he stole at Grace's hair and Roland's lack of cravat spoke volumes. The other man didn't even manage Prinny's level of discretion—his eyes bulged at the both of them.

"Lord Percy and Lady Grace," the regent said slowly and clearly as he opened his hand in the direction of the other man. "May I present Viscount Sidmouth, the Home Secretary? His expertise and authority are invaluable in addressing the matter of the... traitor."

Grace remembered then what she had clasped in her other hand, and she offered it forward. "We were successful in recovering Sapphire from Lord Danforth."

The viscount took the stripped book from her hands, opening it and flipping through to confirm that there were no other missing pages. "So it appears, and it is intact except for the cover. Your Highness, given the evidence, I would recommend stripping the title and the seizure of Danforth's assets."

Prinny's jaw tightened beneath his jowls. "Agreed. The court may have their final say in his punishment, but Danforth is a lord no longer. Well, Lord Percy. It seems I owe the two of you a boon after all. I must assume the state you presented yourselves in is part of your haste to collect. However, I do not see the traitor himself here."

Forgetting himself, Roland nodded slightly, jarring his sore head. "Yes, Your Highness. I am in haste to seek your aid—but not for myself. The crew of the Black Hawk, the ship that returned us safe, is holding Danforth and waiting word that you will not seek retribution against them for what Danforth has done, nor for the... minor crimes of smuggling they were conducting. I am asking you for amnesty for all of them, including their captain, Roberts."

"Minor crimes!" the Home Secretary squawked.

"These sailors are not traitors to Britain," Roland insisted. "They are fishermen, with families. Yes, they have padded the income of fishing with smuggling, but they have a code of honour. Wine. Cotton cloth. Coal. Nothing that could be used to aid in the war—only to feed, warm, and clothe people hurt by the fighting with France. Once they learned Danforth was a true traitor, they took down him and his man, and they aided us willingly. This—it was our idea. Roberts was prepared to make an exchange of himself to beg clemency for the rest, but I left him Danforth as comfort that I would do my best to plead their case to you."

Eyebrows drawing low, the regent drummed his fingers on the arm of his chair. "I am minded to grant it as long as they will return Danforth, so I can throttle him myself."

"If someone can send one of the patrols to greet them with an assurance, I asked them to allow themselves to be escorted to the docks at Shoreham. They will forfeit their cargo if you will let them return to their homes."

"Fine. Done. Is that all?"

Grace inhaled to speak, but Roland nudged her arm, begging her to wait, and she held her tongue. "No, Your Highness, that is not all. There is the matter of Lady Grace. My haste in seeking your audience was not just for the crew of the Black Hawk. It is for her. I knew if she was escorted home, it would be..." He swallowed and reordered his thoughts. "Your Highness, if she went home, her father would either be standing on my doorstep to demand satisfaction, or she would be in the first possible carriage to the countryside, never to be heard from again. Worse, and most assuredly, my grandfather, the duke, will actively oppose our marriage.

"She has suffered so much this season because of her loyalty to you and your mother, the queen. She has served the crown with as much dignity and devotion as one might hope for from the military. I know she does not need my protection to do well in this world," Roland said softly as he spun towards Grace, who stared at the floor and looked like she was fighting tears. Reaching out with his free hand, he tugged her other arm, turning her slightly in his direction. "Still, what kind of gentleman would I be to stand by and watch such a brave, clever woman be called ruined for her service, especially when she saved our lives?"

Then he faced the prince again. "I cannot imagine spending a single day without her, but even that happiness I would sacrifice if it meant she would not suffer for Danforth's actions. Help me salvage her reputation and smooth the way with the duke so I can offer her the protection of my name—and hopefully my love to go with it."

Prinny glanced at Grace, who seemed overcome, but she nodded furiously. Then he got a wicked gleam in his eye. "I believe a bonus for heroic service to the crown will supplement her dowry nicely and appease your grandfather. Shall we say— five thousand pounds? And perhaps I shall boast too about my intrepid little couple so that the Breaker will be seen as a miserly old cad if he attempts to affect the distribution of your wealth or unentailed assets. You did not ask, but I also suppose I could throw my privileges around a little and dictate the location of your wedding, Roland. I am certain the queen would love to host. Your grandfather will have a hard time arguing with that."

Swallowing again, Roland smiled and nodded, happy that the Prince Regent saw fit to give them what they needed to protect Grace.

"Easily done. You two are the easiest of vowels to manage. You would not believe what that ingrate Lord Sebastian Vaughan wanted—"

"Wait, Your Highness!" Grace interrupted with an

apologetic glance at the assembled men. "You have been exceedingly generous and kind to us. I know Roland would not ask you this for fear of abusing your generosity, but there was one other person involved in the pursuit and capture of Danforth, and if not for him, I believe Danforth would have succeeded in escaping—possibly even in killing Lord Percy and me."

Roland stood ramrod straight in surprise, and Prinny sat forward, intrigued. "Where is this third champion you speak of, Lady Grace?"

"He cannot stand before you now because he was badly injured protecting us," Grace said in apology. "But I speak of Mr Thorne, Thaddius Percy's illegitimate son and Roland's valet. I believe His Grace, er, dropped a word about his existence in the audience."

"Yes, I recall," Prinny drawled, his mouth curling in amusement.

"Danforth's man accosted us in an alleyway, and Mr Thorne threw himself between us and Danforth's trap, shielding us from the weight of falling crates. We are hoping he will not lose the use of his arm, but of course, you understand the prognosis will be uncertain for a while yet." She paused and twiddled her fingertips a bit, a slight, nervous gesture. "Mr Thorne knows how highly both of us regard him, and, of course, we will make sure he is always taken care of. But..."

"But the crown should show Mr Thorne recognition as well, especially since he has also sacrificed and suffered," Prinny finished her sentence with a slow smile, showing her he did not take her request for disrespect. "Not to mention protecting Thaddius's bastard from the wrath of the same bad tempered duke. Tell me, Lady Grace... what do you have in mind?"

27

L ittle more than a week after their dramatic rescue, Grace and Roland walked arm-in-arm into Brighton's Assembly Rooms. They were not there for an evening of dancing, but instead to see a display of justice.

Faced with insurmountable evidence of his guilt, Lord Danforth wisely chose to avoid putting his family through the display of a lengthy public trial in favour of a private confession and sentencing. Prinny used his royal sway to demand the court judge travel to Brighton and conduct the final hearing in a venue convenient to him.

The Assembly Room proved to be the only suitable venue in town. Grace and Roland entered the spacious room to find it set up for the proceedings. At the far end, a raised platform had been installed for the judge's bench. The high-back chair sitting behind the wooden table was empty, ready and waiting for the judge to enter.

Grace noted the padded, upholstered chair and small table arranged to the judge's right. Prinny's guests sat in a row of chairs behind his royal seat. Baron Langley and Lord

Ravenscroft nodded in recognition of Grace and Roland. Lord Blackwood and Lady Waddington were nowhere to be seen.

A guard showed Grace and Roland to a seating area directly across from the judge and behind the chief prosecutor's desk, and bade them to take a seat. High-ranking officials and military officers filled in the remaining spaces. The Breaker had declined to join Grace and Roland in their carriage and had said he would make his own way to the event. He was still smarting over Prinny's foiling any future efforts to stand in the way of his grandson's happiness. The old man entered through the far side doors, leaning on his cane, and took a seat next to Baron Langley.

Soon, only the judge's seat and the makeshift throne stood empty. The court usher strode to the front of the room and called for order. "All rise for the entrance of the Prince Regent."

As one, the collective attendees rose from their seats. Prinny entered the room, standing tall, but with a decidedly sombre expression marring his face. He remained standing once he arrived at his chair.

The usher called for attention again. "Remain standing. The Court is now in session, the Honourable Judge Smythe presiding."

A distinguished older gentleman strode in, wearing a red robe and a white powdered wig. Here, in this room, he was the man in charge. His decision could not be challenged by anyone, not even by the Prince Regent himself. He stepped onto the raised platform and laid claim to his chair and desk. The usher motioned for everyone to sit.

The judge arranged a few pieces of paper on top of the desk and then addressed the room. "I hereby call this sentencing court to order. Please, bring in the accused."

A pair of guards escorted Lord Danforth, the confessed traitor, into the room and led him to a wooden dock beside the judge's table. He looked defeated and resigned, standing before the assembly. Shackled and dressed plainly, he was a stark contrast to his former status.

"Please read the charges for the court."

The chief prosecutor cleared his throat and then faced the judge. "Mr John Danforth, formerly Lord Danforth, has confessed to the crimes of high treason, theft of a military code book, and conspiracy to undermine the security of the realm. I will now read his confession in full."

Grace shifted closer to Roland and laid her hand atop his as the prosecutor detailed Danforth's misdeeds. She had no need to listen to the details of his actions, motives, and the extent of his betrayal. She had witnessed firsthand how far the man was willing to go to betray the crown and his country. Roland closed her hand in his and gave it a gentle squeeze, reminding her they had won in the end.

Around the room, women gasped and men grumbled as the prosecutor carried on. A man sitting behind Grace grumbled that death would be too good for the villain. For his part, Danforth never raised his gaze from the ground. He did not have the strength to face his accusers.

Only one group appeared to be distraught. Grace tilted her head close to Roland and motioned their way. "Who are they?" she whispered.

"Danforth's wife and two sons."

The woman wore all black and cried into a handkerchief. The boys, near grown, seemed stunned. They stared at their father with matching heartsick expressions on their faces.

"What will become of them?" Grace asked.

"I am not sure. Perhaps her family will take them in. Danforth's treachery ruined multiple lives."

Finally, the prosecutor uttered the last words and declared the confession at an end. The judge motioned for him to retake his seat. He glanced again at his papers, and then at Prinny. Prinny gave him a nod of respect.

"John Danforth, in light of the serious nature of your crimes, you are hereby sentenced to death by hanging. You may have two days to say your goodbyes to your family and any other loved ones. The court's decision is final. May God have mercy on your soul."

With that said, the judge rapped a gavel on his desk, stood up, and left the room without a backward glance. The guards bundled a sobbing Danforth away, with his family following behind. The Prince Regent left next, with his guests and The Breaker walking out behind him.

Soon, it was time for Grace and Roland to go. She took one last glance around the room, thinking again how strange a setting it proved for such a serious event. Yet, it was also somehow a fitting end for a crime that began in the royal halls and ended with a terror-filled sail on board the Black Hawk. No matter how high a man stood in the social order, he was not immune to the vengeance of the crown.

Roland rested a hand on Grace's back. "We should get moving. We are due at the Royal Pavilion in an hour."

That reminder brought a smile to Grace's face. "I trust you will see that our guest of honour is suitably attired?"

"After all the times he has trussed me up, I will do so with great pleasure."

"Do you remember how you laughed at me when you helped me dress for the dance at Carlton House?" Roland asked his brother, barely containing himself.

Thorne scowled at Roland. "Yes. Are you suggesting I look like a peacock?"

"Since these were my clothes, given to you for this purpose, I am suggesting that the phrase 'do unto others' has never before seemed more appropriate, and the divine has seen fit to give me a moment of retributive justice."

They were lucky, in fact, that the two of them were so near in size, for the speed at which the regent had organised a special ceremony to recognise Thorne nearly outpaced the tailor's capacities. It took very little effort to alter the navy blue waistcoat and the silk breeches to suit his narrower waist. But the tailor had manufactured a very elegant, lined sling in silk to match the coat.

Poor Thorne looked distinctly uncomfortable to have their roles reversed for the first time in his service, but Roland had a sneaking suspicion that—even were he not hindered by a broken arm—Thorne would be at a loss tying a cravat upon his own person anyhow. The thought of it made the corners of Roland's mouth turn up even as he wound the fine cloth around his brother's neck.

"You're laughing at me," Thorne said sternly, and Roland met his brother's blue eyes.

"I am not! Well... perhaps a little. But you must admit you deserve a little turnabout for all the years of hell you have given me."

"I never gave you more than you deserved," Thorne said, finally smiling slightly.

"Well. Then I suppose it is high time you are getting what you deserve. There," Roland said, making final adjustments to the waterfall of Thorne's cravat and setting his hand reassuringly on his brother's good left shoulder. "You are almost fit for polite society. Let us help you put on your coat, and we can be off."

Putting on the waistcoat over his broken arm was a feat that took both Roland's and Albert's assistance, and Thorne was a little pale by the time his arm was put securely back in its sling. But the physician had assured them it was mending well, and while Thorne would need to work to regain its strength, he had every expectation of regaining full use of his dominant arm.

While it wasn't a far jaunt, Roland insisted Thorne do nothing to risk his healing. Albert had offered to drive the carriage for them, but Roland had opted for a hire instead, and it was waiting outside by the time Thorne recovered his colour.

Settling against the seat, Thorne fretted. "Tell me, again, why am I being summoned before the regent? I do not understand the need to thank me so publicly."

"You should be honoured, you know. Prinny has a tendency to forget that he owes people." Roland couldn't help but tease him a little, seeing the worry furrows on his brother's brow.

"I am honoured, but..." Thorne's mouth opened and closed again. "I am not a fancy sort. A nice letter would have been plenty gracious."

They arrived at the Pavilion in a trice, and Roland stepped down first to offer his brother aid. An obsequious official hurried up to them both. "Welcome, Lord Percy, Mr Thorne. Mr Thorne, would you please follow me to the main hall where the ceremony will take place?"

Thorne's face leeched of colour again. "Ceremony?"

Roland's smile grew wide. "Yes. Ceremony. I will see you inside." And then he entered the pavilion, leaving his brother with the official.

"I, er," Thorne said, running a shaky hand over the back of his neck.

"At your pace, Mr Thorne," the man offered, holding out a hand to invite him through the doors, where Thorne found... a tremendous number of well-garbed nobility turning to face him.

"Ladies and gentlemen," a herald boomed, nearly startling him. "Today, we gather to honour Nathaniel Thorne for his extraordinary service to the Crown. Mr Thorne showed bravery and fortitude despite injury to himself as he safeguarded the lives of Lord Percy and Lady Grace. As a direct result of Mr Thorne's sacrifice, Lord Percy and Lady Grace were able to apprehend the traitor, John Danforth, ensuring the safety and security of our nation."

Awed and a little humbled, Thorne walked up the centre aisle to where the regent stood waiting for him.

"Nathaniel Thorne," the Prince Regent's voice rose, even as a delighted glimmer shone in his eyes, "your courage and dedication have not only thwarted a great threat to our kingdom but have also set a shining example of valour and loyalty. The Crown recognises and deeply appreciates your service. Kneel before me."

Bewildered, Thorne knelt carefully in front of the regent.

"In recognition of your gallant deeds, I dub thee Sir Nathaniel Thorne." The Prince Regent lay his sword gently upon both of Thorne's shoulders. "Arise, Sir Nathaniel."

Thorne felt as though he could hardly breathe, but he somehow rose to his feet again.

"Furthermore, the Crown is pleased to grant you the grace-and-favour usage of the London townhouse formerly owned by Lord Danforth. In addition, you are also awarded some of Lord Danforth's lands, ensuring a stable income for you and your descendants. Let us all applaud Sir Nathaniel Thorne for his exemplary service and dedication to the Crown."

The applause was thunderous, and the ringing in his ears went on beyond the herald inviting everyone to the gardens for the reception.

"Are you quite all right?" Lady Grace swam into focus before him. She had taken his hand, and he clung to it to keep his balance.

"I am... absolutely flummoxed, Lady Grace," Thorne

answered honestly, turning to Roland. "I don't understand why I would get these accolades instead of the two of you. My part in things was so small."

"Nevermind that. Prinny granted us each a boon for our own efforts, and we saw them put to good use," Grace said pertly. "Besides, you belittle your assistance. You have been of the greatest help this season—not just with Danforth, but with Charity and Sir David too."

"You wasted a favour from the regent on me?" Thorne gave his brother a disbelieving look.

"Actually, it was not mine," Roland confessed. "You may put the blame and thanks for this one squarely on Lady Grace. It was her idea to see you rewarded. But I have to say... I wholeheartedly approve."

Thorne paused, thinking hard, and he frowned at Roland and Grace both. "You are still protecting me from the duke."

"My father's and grandfather's sins are their own," Roland said dismissively. "But I was recently reminded about the nature of regret and how quickly fortunes can change. I will always want to protect the ones I love, and this way I can be certain that my younger brother will be taken care of no matter what happens to me. No matter what my grandfather thinks." He hesitated, softening. "Your mother was right, you know, to name you Nathaniel. Having you, and these last ten years, have truly been a gift to me."

"And everyone else who has been fortunate enough to get to know you," Grace added.

Thorne swallowed hard, his eyes growing a little shiny. "Sir Barbarian, you are growing ever more polished and poetic in your elder years."

Roland barked a laugh. "You have been a bad influence, I admit. But now that you bring it up... I think it is high time you have a nickname of your own."

Grace covered her mouth with both hands, her eyes dancing.

Thorne's eyebrows slammed down. "Oh no. No. You cannot mean it."

"No? But Sir Bastard has such a nice ring to it," Roland said, barely able to get the words out before dissolving into mirth, and Thorne's answering laugh rang through the pavilion's main hall.

"Brothers," Grace said both fondly and repressively, looking on at the two of them.

28

Grace turned from the window to survey her Mayfair bedroom for one last time. During the days of her forced confinement while she had healed from the cut on her throat, she had vowed to spend as little time as possible there in the future. But now that the time had come for her to marry and move into Roland's townhouse, she found herself strangely nostalgic for the space.

Goodness knew there was little enough left in the room to offer any reminder of her first season, as most of her things had been sent ahead. But the memories of her early days whispering secrets with Charity, the nights she had spent worrying over their futures, and the hours passed watching Roland walk past her window remained. She thought back to her first days in London, and to her pledge to search out adventure instead of a husband. How ironic then that she had found both.

Grace's heart overflowed with so much emotion that tears blurred her vision. Before she dashed them away, Elsie rapped on the door and strode into the room. "My lady, is aught amiss?"

Grace wiped her eyes and smiled at her lady's maid. "All is well. I simply find myself ill-prepared for my own wedding day.

How can one event be both beyond your wildest dreams and yet also bittersweet?"

Elsie motioned for Grace to sit at her dressing table so that she could style her hair. "My mam says all of life's big changes should carry a hint of sadness."

"Really?" Grace settled on the stool and met Elsie's gaze in the mirror. "Did she say why?"

Elsie bobbed her head. "Because it means you have had a good life. If things were terrible, you would not be sorry to see them end."

The simple truth struck Grace as imminently wise. She would have to ask Elsie what other guidance her mother had to offer. But not today, for the sun was rising higher in the sky and she would soon have to be on her way. Arriving late to her wedding would be bad enough, but with Queen Charlotte herself acting as host, it was unthinkable.

Lady Tilbury delayed her appearance until it was time for Grace to slip on her wedding dress. She arrived in a whirlwind of perfume and lace, her hands fluttering as she rattled off instructions. "Where are the diamond clips I loaned you? Surely you do not intend to leave your hair down?"

"They are here, Mama," Grace answered, holding up the items in question. "Elsie said we should wait until after I put on my gown so that they don't catch on the fabric."

Lady Tilbury waved for them to get moving. Grace held her arms out while Elsie tightened her corset and shifted again so the maid could slip the gown over her head. She did not dare glance in the mirror until Elsie put the finishing touches on her gown and hair.

Finally, she rose from her stool and turned to give her mama a full view. Lady Tilbury mashed her lips together while fishing a cotton handkerchief from her pocket. She raised it to her nose and shook her head. Her silence stretched so long that Grace feared the worst.

"Darling girl, look at you," Lady Tilbury cried, sniffling into her handkerchief. "I fear I have done you a great disservice."

Grace goggled at her mother. "I cannot imagine how."

"Seeing you now, so elegant and poised, I realise what a mistake I made in not setting our sights high from the start. You are truly and forever will be a diamond in my eyes."

Grace felt the scratch of tears at the back of her throat again and promptly forbade herself from crying. Instead, she took her mother's hands and squeezed them tight. "Thank you, Mama, for doing exactly as you did. You allowed me the space to find my own way forward."

"You always were far too headstrong, but I suppose being the third child required you to work harder to gain our attention. Rest assured, you have it now. Come, dear, and take a look at the woman you have become." Lady Tilbury guided Grace over to the full-length mirror and then stepped back so that Grace could look her fill.

For a moment, Grace hardly recognised the woman staring back at her. In her frock of striped gauze over a white satin slip, with a deep flounce of Brussels lace, she was impossibly elegant. A band of white roses encircled her neck, hiding away the fading scar. The longer Grace stared at herself, the more uncomfortable she became. Though she was the very picture of a blushing bride, she had the impression of being a child playing dress up in someone else's clothing.

Without a word, she reached up and untied the ribbon from around her neck. She pulled it free and handed it to Elsie. "Find somewhere else to attach these. Perhaps underneath the bodice."

"But your scar," Lady Tilbury gasped, again fluttering her hands.

"Mama, please. Roland loves me for who I am, not what I wear or how much dowry I bring to the marriage. I wish to stand beside him, and pledge my heart just as I am. Scars and all."

If he was annoyed at the necessity of having to take a coach to his own wedding instead of ride astride, at least Roland had to own that the coach that the queen had sent to take them to Kew Palace was a startlingly luxurious vehicle with deep burgundy lacquer and polished brass fittings. Lest even a Philistine like him miss the mark of favour being bestowed, it was being drawn by four perfectly matched Windsor Greys with elegantly braided manes and tails.

After being assisted up by the footman, Thorne settled with a sigh against the thickly padded seat, wincing as he caught the tails of his coat awkwardly behind himself. Roland reordered his thoughts, grateful for the queen's thoughtfulness on his brother's behalf. Thorne's arm was healing, but Roland knew it still ached with a fury at times. He certainly could not ride.

Thorne caught his brother studying his sling and furrowed his brows. "The physician says it will be at least another few weeks. Perhaps a while longer than that. But you shouldn't be spending your thoughts right now on me, given today is your wedding day."

"I am the least of my own worries," Roland informed him. "But I was thinking you make the loveliest popinjay now that you have been forced to upgrade your wardrobe and use my tailor."

Thorne scowled at him, and Roland grinned wickedly. "All this time you spent teasing me about being uncouth, Sir Bastard, only to see you hoist with your own petard. Admit it. At heart, you are a bit of a barbarian yourself."

"In that, I do but follow in the mile-wide swath of bad influence cleared by my elder brother."

A light knocking on the carriage wall sounded just before Albert's gruff voice filtered through from where he rode on the back of the carriage. "Behave, children."

Both of them grinned at that, and Thorne leaned backwards some, letting the weight of his arm be supported by his chest. "See? You have even begun corrupting poor Albert," Thorne told him. "He never would have said something like that to you a month ago."

"He has stepped up rather admirably and kindly into the hole left by your absence. Albert did an exceptional job of dressing you, but I should think we need to hire a few more hands around the house to help him. And you."

Thorne fretted a bit. "Wes helped him dress me. But... If you think that is necessary."

Roland gave his brother a softer smile this time, understanding exactly where his head was at. "Broken arm or not, your days as my valet are done, Sir Nathaniel. I will need to find another. And you will need one too—not to mention the other staff to help you manage your new affairs."

The man took a swift, pained breath at that. "I know. I know you always wanted better for me than the lowly roles I deemed appropriate, but... I was happy to do it because we were together. There is, I confess, a part of me that wants to give everything up to stay. I find the idea of us being apart... of going my own way without you hurts so much more than I expected."

"You are not going your own way—not now. We are just taking a brief leave of one another on short journeys. You will always be welcome in my house. Once your mother and your affairs are sorted, we expect you to show up for Christmas."

"You have a journey," Thorne said tightly, to conceal his

distress. "My journey is going to consist of managing sheep farms and tenants paying rent."

"Truly, I doubt that," Roland said with a chuckle. "Now that you are a proper member of society, I am certain someone will decide you would be wasted on the sheep. And if it makes you feel any better, my next 'journey' is taking Lady Grace on a honeymoon tour of parts of England and Scotland before we return to Northumberland and my grandfather's estate for the winter. I know my lady would like to travel, but I think between the war and what happened with Danforth, she's less interested in finding ways to imperil herself."

"You hope she is, at any rate."

He laughed and nodded. "A winter with my grandfather while we learn the ins and outs of managing the estate will probably have her itching to strike for India in the spring."

Thorne could well imagine. His elevation and Prinny's insistence on this being a royal wedding had pacified the Breaker, but any such lull was likely only a temporary affair. "It shames me to admit it, but there is a part of me that is jealous she usurps my place at your side. And yet, I cannot resent it either, because for what seems like the first time since we struck out together, you are happy. I am glad that you did not marry Lady Charity. Grace has healed that restless, broken part of you. I just wish this was not going to be the end of things."

Roland leaned forward, clasping Thorne's good left forearm. "Do not think of these changes in our life as an end, my brother. After all, if things had stayed the same, I would not have been able to have you with me at my own wedding. However strange it seems right now, you stand at the start of a new adventure. This will not be a goodbye. It is only 'until we meet again.'"

29

Grace shifted the curtain from the window as the family carriage slowed. Outside, the view of Kew Palace, a charming red-brick mansion, greeted her. It was modest in size compared to the grander royal residences she had previously visited, yet exuded an inviting elegance. Nestled within the expansive and meticulously maintained Kew Gardens, the palace stood out with its distinctive Dutch gables and large sash windows that allowed sunlight to illuminate its simple yet graceful façade.

On either side of the drive, vibrant gardens beckoned visitors to meander along their pebbled pathways, where they wove between the summer blooms and lush greenery. Grace breathed in the tranquil atmosphere like a balm to soothe her frazzled nerves. Lady Tilbury had used the ride from London to Richmond to remind Grace of her new duties as the wife of the heir to a dukedom. After an hour of listening to the litany of obligations and expectations, Grace allowed her mind to wander elsewhere, namely toward her upcoming honeymoon with Roland. Though her mama meant well, and likely spoke only the truth, there would be time enough to face the realities of her new station after the fun was done. For today, none of that mattered.

A pair of matching footmen hurried forward to open the carriage door and help the women down. The royal butler met them at the entrance and invited them inside. "Lady Tilbury, if you will follow young William, he will escort you to the other guests. The queen would like a private word with Lady Grace."

"What of Lord Percy?" Grace asked.

"He is outside with the others. All are ready for the ceremony to begin. But first, the queen."

Lady Tilbury gave Grace a reassuring pat on the arm before heading off with the footman. Grace followed the butler up the stairs. He knocked on a closed wooden door. A woman's voice, faint but still audible, gave him permission to enter.

"Lady Grace Tilbury for you, Your Majesty." The butler bowed and then backed from the room, leaving Grace to stand alone.

She was surprised to find herself in a bedroom, decorated with the floral flounces and lace of a younger woman's tastes. Queen Charlotte was impeccably dressed in a pale purple gown threaded with silver and embroidered butterflies. There were no lady's maids or footmen accompanying her.

"This is my daughter's room," the queen explained, after telling Grace to rise from her curtsey. She surveyed Grace from head to toe, her face inscrutable smooth. When Grace's nerves reached their breaking point, the queen dared to flash a hint of a smile. "I still stand by my initial impression of you, Lady Grace, but you have proven that, in some exceptional moments, thumbing your nose at convention is beneficial. My son was correct to demand we host your wedding ceremony. We have kept the invitee list small. There is one guest who, for reasons that will soon become obvious, cannot attend. But she very much wanted to wish you well. You may have ten minutes."

Her piece said, the queen swished her skirts and left through a side door, leaving it open behind her. A breath later, a gorgeous woman with blonde hair and a bright smile walked into the room.

"Charity!" Grace gasped, hardly daring to believe her eyes. Even more than the surprise of finding her dearest friend there was the fact that Charity was dressed in the deepest shades of black. "Oh, Charity," Grace moaned as the significance set in.

Charity waved off Grace's words and hurried to wrap her friend in a hug. "Do not worry about me, Grace. I went into the wedding with full knowledge of just how short the relationship would last. The duke was a kind man, and I do mourn him, but I am not overwrought."

Grace pulled back and smoothed her gown of any wrinkles. "I am so sorry. I should have—"

"What? Allowed me to marry a man in love with you? To take away your chance at happiness? Please, do not insult us both by apologising for any of that. I do not begrudge you even a second of joy in your life, and despite my current appearance, I promise I am not suffering in the least."

Grace searched Charity's face for any hint of a lie, but found only the shining truth. "Thank you."

"Consider us even, if such a thing can ever be said. Now, let us be done with all talk of the matter. I brought something to show you." Charity pulled a folded paper from her pocket and opened it with care. She angled it so that Grace saw the bold pen strokes marked on the page. "Do you remember the night that I made this list?"

Grace wrinkled her nose as the memory swam to the surface. They had been in Charity's bedroom, past bedtime, early in the season. Charity had diligently updated her list of potential suitors while Grace had imagined future adventures.

"I had Lord Percy at the top of my list, as well I should, for he is by far the most eligible of the season. I asked you what you planned, and you replied—"

"That I might consider becoming a widow. For the freedom it would provide." Grace blushed at her naivety.

Charity folded the paper and passed it to Grace. "I want you to keep this as a reminder that we never know where life will take us. We were both so determined in our path, and neither of us saw the possibility we might go another way. Yet, look at us now, happy, free, and soon to be more powerful than either of us ever dared to imagine."

Grace forgot about her gown, about propriety, about everything, and threw her arms around Charity. "You are the dearest, greatest friend a girl could ever want. I must go, lest I turn into a weeping mess and risk the wrath of the queen, but please, tell me when I can see you again. Surely you will not have to spend a full year in deep mourning."

"I will show my respects to my departed husband, but not for any longer than the queen deems necessary. When I return to London, I expect you to be the first visitor to pay me a call."

"Count on it." Grace loosened her hold on Charity. "I wish you would come down with me. Will you at least watch from an upper floor window?"

"Queen Charlotte ordered a chair set aside for my use. I had some input into the planning. I am certain you will approve of the bold, red roses decorating the canopy and petals lining the walkway. As for the reception, there is a whole plate of iced cakes set aside just for you." Charity latched arms with Grace and escorted her to the door. "Above all, enjoy this day, for it is the first of your new life with a man you adore—the only man whom I trust to love you as much as you deserve."

Roland stood under the rose festooned canopy and surveyed the faces staring back at him. Despite the short notice, the royal staff had organised an elaborate setting for a summer garden ceremony.

Elegant wooden chairs with cushioned seats formed a semi-circle around him. The Breaker sat alone off to Roland's left, and standing behind him,Thorne graciously was struggling to keep the excited Sprouts in check. Roland bit back a smile when he noted Thorne giving each of them a harsh glare. Not that it did much to quell either of them.

Lord and Lady Barbour had accepted their invite and made the journey up from Brighton. They beamed at Roland and chose chairs near Roland's grandfather.

At the other end of the semi-circle, Lady Tilbury sat beside Lady Anwen. The dowager duchess of Sussex gained an invite by sheer happenstance of her stay with the queen. The wise old woman was likely committing all to memory so that she could recount the details to whomever she met next. To Lady Tilbury's right, Felix tugged at the neck of his cravat. Roland wondered whether he was over warm or simply feeling the pressure of being the last unmarried child. He was fortunate that Grace's older sister had been unable to attend.

Queen Charlotte and Prinny entered together and sat in the middle, as was their due. The strains of the violin signalled the start of the ceremony.

At long last, a vision in white stepped onto the stone path. Roland's throat grew tight as he drank in Grace's glowing figure. Her chestnut hair shone in the sunlight while she walked in on her father's arm. He cared little for her gown, though it must have been fine, nor for the jewels adorning her hair, ears, and wrists. What captivated him most were her sparkling hazel eyes, the scattering of freckles, and the infectious grin on her face.

With a brief stab of embarrassment, he recalled their earliest meeting. How he had thought she possessed none of the beauty of the diamond. How wrong he had been. The way she looked at him with such love made her sparkle brighter than the crown jewels themselves.

Together, they stood before an ornate table covered in a fine lace cloth. Under the eyes of their family and friends, before the representative of the church, they pledged to honour and love one another for the rest of their days. It was the easiest promise Roland had ever made.

Lady Anwen earned her invitation thrice over as she used her wiles to keep the Breaker placid. Time and time again, Roland saw her and the queen manage the old man whenever he glanced in their direction. It was apparently Lady Anwen's turn.

"Let me take this moment again to thank you both personally for your heroic services rendered to us this season," Queen Charlotte told them, her son by her side.

"Your Majesties, it was our privilege," Grace said demurely, but the queen was looking Roland in the eye.

Roland inclined his head to her, uncertain why she was pinning him with such a steady look, but the queen finally stepped back with a small smile. "I must say, Lord Percy. It looked doubtful for a while, but in the end... very well done."

"Thank you, Your Majesty." He bowed in gratitude to the ageing queen, and then to the regent, who just gave him a knowing smirk.

Lord Barbour and his lady then approached the couple. "I am sorry we did not find the opportunity to have you for dinner!" Lady Barbour told Grace, but her face took on a mischievous look. "However, given the circumstances, I do suppose this was just as entertaining, Lady Percy."

Grace laughed lightly at that. "I love the sound of my new name, but I confess it is still going to take me time to get used to it."

"Do not worry, it will happen more quickly than you expect," she said, giving Grace a knowing smile and drawing her away from the men. "My dears, I must borrow this blushing bride for a few moments. We will leave you boys to discuss your boring things so we can gossip as married women."

Taking Grace to one corner of the room, away from listening ears, Lady Barbour glanced around and whispered. "Though I am not your mother, and it is truly not my place to instruct you on anything that happens between a man and his wife. I remember the things my own mama told me about my wedding night. What neither of our mamas could have told us—but which I can tell you now—is how much more wonderful it is when love is part of the equation. I wanted you to know, so you can go forward tonight with the lightest of hearts when you take your leave."

Grace reached forward and took both of Lady Barbour's hands. "That knowledge eases my nerves considerably. It is a most generous wedding gift, Lady Barbour."

"I hope you will still find time to come to dinner the next time we are in proximity to one another. You will have to let me know if Lord Percy has read you any poetry."

Both laughed aloud at the idea of Roland reading stuffy prose.

"What do you suppose they are discussing with one another over there?" Roland asked Barbour suspiciously.

"Women's secrets," Barbour said with a wink. "Never you mind."

"I have the most curious sense I am being laughed at," he remarked.

"Indirectly, perhaps. It is far more likely they are discussing how to spend the money I worked so hard to earn this season—but they are out of luck! I have my own plans."

"Worked? Earned?" Roland blinked at Barbour, wondering what on earth the man was talking about.

Barbour smiled lazily over the edge of his wineglass. "Yes, with the hundred pounds I won as a result of my bet I placed on you earlier this season. Remember? It was a near thing, Percy! I nearly thought I was going to be out a small fortune when the queen announced your engagement to the diamond, despite you and Grace so clearly pining for one another. Given how you so heartlessly toyed with my expectations, I am sure you will understand why I shall not bet on you again."

"And yet, if you won a hundred pounds, I cannot imagine you are too sorry you took the gamble," Roland said with an eyebrow raised.

"True. But you see now why I called it work, yes? I shall use this to fund a trip to Amsterdam."

"Amsterdam?" Roland exclaimed. "What is in Amsterdam?"

"Among other things, a pleasant journey, lad! But I was also minded that I might reach out to a few old connections while I am there to see if I might catch any word of Lady Fitzroy. Mind you, I hope I do not, actually, cross paths with her trail. Still... I am reminded that the royal family can be generous when someone does them a favour." Barbour saluted Roland with his glass and went to offer his arm to his wife, who appeared to be finished with her conversation with Grace.

Before Roland could approach Grace, he saw the Sprouts pelt in her direction, Thorne following at a more dignified pace. So he tarried, letting them have their moment together. Despite their conversation in the carriage on the way to Kew Palace, Thorne was clearly trying to put a good face on things, using the kids as a convenient distraction.

But while he gathered wool, Lady Anwen slipped in beside him. "You have done a wonderful thing for that young man, and you have done it without needing the assistance of the duke. I think that is what irks your grandfather more than anything. He shows it in the poorest of fashions, but for whatever it may be worth, in his way, your grandfather has tried to do some right by you. He wanted you away from Thaddius. It was by his own hand you ended up in the cavalry, far from the more dangerous fronts, and I do not believe he would have let you go to war if you had not been bringing Sir Nathaniel at all."

He hadn't known that, and it eased his heart more than he had expected to, but he still was prickly about the subject. "And yet he offered my brother up as a sacrifice in my stead, and he was set against my marriage to Lady Grace."

"I know," the lady said, taking his arm and patting it lightly. "The old man is thorny and jealously protective of what he considers his. That title sits more heavily on his shoulders because he is keenly aware of how very new it is, and how easily it could slip away. So he has the most terrible temper—especially when it comes to what he perceives as duty."

"I believe I see your point, Lady Anwen." And he did. He only hoped that the Breaker would not continue to be vindictive against his brother or lady wife. Perhaps he wouldn't. The attention and lavish favours of the royal family had done much to mollify the old man.

That Roland did not not anticipate needing to—or even wishing to—continue investigating anything on behalf of the crown probably also softened him. Not that there were many members of society in Northumberland to interrogate for any reason.

Lady Anwen prodded him with her elbow, calling his attention back to the present, and she lifted her chin, pointing to Grace, who now stood alone. As their eyes met across the room, he caught his breath at the loveliest sight he had ever seen. His lady wife, her cheeks flushed with high emotion, and her eyes only for him, as if no other person was in the room.

He did not even bother saying goodbye to the old dowager. Seeing his chance, he strode away to recapture his bride's undivided attention.

"Are you ready to make our escape? If we go now, they might not notice," he asked her teasingly, seeing her flush deeper. The queen had been generous enough to give them a small, private cottage on the palace grounds for their wedding night, and he planned to make the most of it.

Before they could sneak away, everyone noticed them whispering together, and with great shouts, the Sprouts and adults chased them out of the room with rice and flower petals—and some colourful last-minute advice. Grace shrieked in delight, ducking, holding hard onto Roland's arm with one hand for balance so she could lift the hems of her gown with the other. She was such a clumsy, charming mess that in the end, Roland swept her off her feet, train and all, so that he could run away from their well-armed well wishers.

His wife laughed at him. "I know there is a tradition of carrying the bride across the threshold, but I do not think you are required to carry me the whole distance there."

"If you think I plan to let you leave my arms tonight, you are sorely mistaken," he scolded her, but he was unable to keep from smiling tenderly as he said it. "Besides, it keeps you at a convenient height."

He captured her mouth with his, showing her in great detail what he meant, until both of them needed to part to breathe. He had stopped on the lawn to give his full attention to the task, but lifting his eyes, he noticed that someone had, most conveniently, left the door of the cottage open so he could keep his promise.

He rearranged her tenderly in his arms, pressing his forehead to hers. "Are you afraid of what will happen next?" he asked her, because even though she had thrown one arm around his neck, he could see the other clenched against her chest, trembling.

"Nervous. Excited, I think," she whispered into the small space between him. "But no—I am not afraid. I know you will keep me safe, and Lady Barbour... she told me love changes everything."

"I suspect the Barbours would know better than most," he said, his lips curling as he pressed another kiss to her temple. "But I have learned the truth of it for myself. I cannot even begin to explain all the ways you have changed me. Loving you has remade my entire world."

"Well, then... perhaps you should show me... how the rest of this love thing goes?" she asked, her cheeks flaming, but in the sweetest way.

And like the barbarian he was, he swept her across the threshold, kicking the door shut behind them to enjoy this next conquest.

Roland and Grace will be back again in THE EMERALD THREADS.

Northumberland, 1813: Lord Roland and Lady Grace arrive in Northumberland, expecting to celebrate the Christmas season. Instead, they are drawn into a frantic search for a group of local children who have disappeared overnight.

Roland's grandfather urges them to leave the matter to the townspeople, but when they learn this is just the latest in a string of so-called runaways, they suspect something far more sinister is afoot.

With determination and compassion, Roland and Grace work to weave together the fragile threads of trust between them and the community. As they delve deeper into the mystery, they uncover a disturbing pattern that hints at a web of deception.

Just when they believe they are close to unmasking the culprit, someone they hold dear is taken in the dead of night.

Roland and Grace are forced to decide—how much they are willing to risk to bring the criminal to justice?

Find out in THE EMERALD THREADS. You can order it now on Amazon.

Looking for something to read right away? Skip forward to the 1920s in Lynn's other historical mystery series.

When a bright young man teams up with a glamorous femme fatale, the identity of a murderer won't be the only secret they'll unmask.

From ballrooms to back alleys, follow Dora and Rex as they solve crimes in 1920s London.

You can find the series on Amazon.

Want to keep updated on our newest books? Subscribe to Lynn's newsletter for book news, sales, special offers, and great reading recommendations. You can sign up here: LINK

Historical Notes

When we chose the Brighton Pavilion as the setting for this book, I must confess I pictured a grandiose mansion with turrets and Eastern influences. Instead, I discovered that Prinny's massive building project took place a few years later. During the summer of 1813, the Royal Pavilion was known instead as the Marine Pavilion. It boasted more stables for horses than rooms for guests, but that worked in our favour. Instead of having to worry about a long suspect list, we found a ready excuse to keep it short.

The Royal Collection Trust website provided us with drawings of the Marine Pavilion as it looked at the time, including floor plans and layouts of the grounds. We took some small liberties with the placement of the guest rooms, but otherwise stuck true to what would have been there. We hope you will forgive us these changes in the interest of crafting a good story. If you would like to learn more about the Pavilion as it looked in the early part of the 19th century, you can find more here: https://www.rct.uk/collection/918957/marine-pavilion-brighton-july-1801

Another interesting tidbit we uncovered was the awarding

of the Longitude Prize. In the 18th century, tracking position as you sailed east and west was impossible once out of sight of land. Sailors could determine their position relative to the equator based on the position of the sun or the length of the day. The British government sought to solve this problem by offering an incredible cash prize to anyone who could invent a way to track their longitudinal position. This became known as the Longitude Prize.

A man named John Harrison stepped up to the task. He was a carpenter by trade, and had no formal training in clockmaking. He spent fifty years on the task, producing four iterations of his longitudinal clock, and in the process, revolutionising maritime safety.

The Longitude Prize exists still, funded by the UK to tackle the greatest challenges known to science. You can learn more about the history of this prize and which initiatives it is tackling now at the Longitude Prize website: https://amr.longitudeprize. org/the-history/.

As to Lord Ravenscroft—as soon as he walked onto the page, we were certain of his amorous intentions. The only question on our minds was whether Prinny would overlook his illegal relationship with his valet. In researching the matter, we found that Prinny had a number of unwed bachelors in his set. While it is possible that those men never found reason to wed, given the time period, it does strike one as odd. Think for a moment about Beau Brummell, his elaborate cravats, and passion for fashion. So yes, we decided Prinny would not hold Ravenscroft's preferences against him, particularly if the man was willing to spy on his behalf.

Keen eyes may have noted the brief appearance of Viscount Sidmouth. Henry Addington, 1st Viscount Sidmouth, served as Prime Minister from 1801 to 1804, and later took on the role of Home Secretary.

Acknowledgments

Thanks to Melody Simmons for creating another fantastic cover for us.

Thanks to Brenda Chapman, Ken Morrison, and Lois King for pitching in again as beta readers. We are grateful for their willingness to deal with typos and provide feedback on the story.

The Emerald Threads
A Crown Jewels Regency Mystery

Can they stitch together fragile trust and unravel a sinister tapestry in time to save the Christmas season?

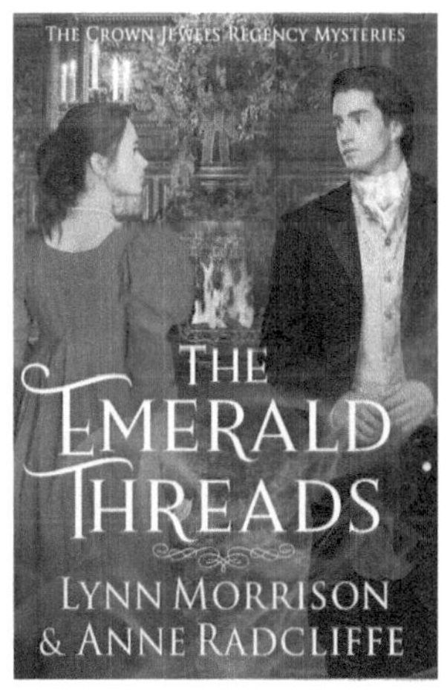

Northumberland, 1813: Lord Roland and Lady Grace arrive in Northumberland expecting to celebrate the Christmas season. Instead, they are drawn into a frantic search for a group of local children who have disappeared overnight.

Roland's grandfather urges them to leave the matter to the townspeople, but when they learn this is just the latest in a string of so-called runaways, they suspect something far more sinister is afoot.

With determination and compassion, Roland and Grace work to weave together the fragile threads of trust between them and the community. As they delve deeper into the mystery, they uncover a disturbing pattern that hints at a web of deception.

Just when they believe they are close to unmasking the culprit, someone they hold dear is taken in the dead of night.

Roland and Grace are forced to decide—how much they are willing to risk to bring the criminal to justice?

Find out in THE EMERALD THREADS. You can order it now on Amazon.

About Anne Radcliffe

As an American Expat living in Ontario with a husband and teen son, Anne Radcliffe spends a lot of time editing or writing in order to avoid having to become a Maple Leafs fan. Anne loves a great story no matter the genre or medium - books, graphic novels, TV, movies or video games. You can find out more about Anne on her website at AnneRadcliffe.com.

BB bookbub.com/authors/anne-radcliffe

g goodreads.com/anneradcliffe

a amazon.com/stores/author/B0D1VMVDZ1

About Lynn Morrison

Lynn Morrison lives in Oxford, England along with her husband, two daughters and two cats. Born and raised in Mississippi, her wanderlust attitude has led her to live in California, Italy, France, the UK, and the Netherlands. Despite having rubbed shoulders with presidential candidates and members of parliament, night-clubbed in Geneva and Prague, explored Japanese temples and scrambled through Roman ruins, Lynn's real life adventures can't compete with the stories in her mind.

She is as passionate about reading as she is writing, and can almost always be found with a book in hand. You can find out more about her on her website LynnMorrisonWriter.com.

You can chat with her directly in her Facebook group - Lynn Morrison's Not a Book Club - where she talks about books, life and anything else that crosses her mind.

facebook.com/nomadmomdiary

instagram.com/nomadmomdiary

bookbub.com/authors/lynn-morrison

goodreads.com/nomadmomdiary

amazon.com/Lynn-Morrison/e/B00IKC1LVW

Also by Lynn Morrison

<u>The Crown Jewel Regency Mysteries</u>
The Missing Diamond
The Ruby Dagger
The Sapphire Intrigue

<u>Dora and Rex 1920s Mysteries</u>
Murder at the Front
Murder, I Spy
The Missing Agent
Death Undercover
Double Cross Dead
The Roman Riddle
The Cryptic Cold Case

<u>The Oxford Key Mysteries</u>
Murder at St Margaret
Burglary at Barnard
Arson at the Ashmolean
Sabotage at Somerset
The Eternal Investigator
Post Mortem at Padua
Homicide at Holly Manor

<u>Stakes & Spells Mysteries</u>

Stakes & Spells

Spells & Fangs

Fangs & Cauldrons

<u>Midlife in Raven PWF</u>

Raven's Influence

Raven's Joy

Raven's Matriarch

Raven's Storm

<u>Wandering Witch Urban Fantasy</u>

A Queen Only Lives Twice

www.ingramcontent.com/pod-product-compliance
Lightning Source LLC
Chambersburg PA
CBHW061544210726
48287CB00006B/2072